No Resting Place

Delta Books by William Humphrey:

Home from the Hill
The Ordways
Hostages to Fortune
Open Season: Sporting Adventures
No Resting Place

No Resting Place

WILLIAM HUMPHREY

Delta/Seymour Lawrence

A Delta/Seymour Lawrence Book
Published by
Dell Publishing
a division of
Bantam Doubleday Dell Publishing Group, Inc.
666 Fifth Avenue
New York, New York 10103

The trademark Delta® is registered in the U.S. Patent and
Trademark Office.

ISBN 0-385-30079-4

Reprinted by arrangement with Delacorte Press/Seymour Lawrence
Printed in the United States of America
Published Simultaneously in Canada

June 1990

10 9 8 7 6 5 4 3 2 1

To the memory of Mr. Jack Boss,
who shaped my life

Part One

"Victory is certain! Trust in God and fear not! And remember the Alamo! Remember the Alamo!"

The youngster playing the part of Sam Houston was going through the change of voice. Even in so short a speech his broke repeatedly. To the spectators this sounded like uncontrollable fervor and, rather than impairing the illusion, made that familiar exhortation to the troops all the more rousing. They had learned their Texas history in grammar school, had taken part as eighth-graders themselves in the San Jacinto Day pageant, had seen their sons and grandsons stage it like this annually, and had come insensibly to equate the state's childhood with their own and to think of its founders, Sam Houston, Davy Crockett, Jim Bowie, as boys—as, indeed, they were: overgrown boys, bad boys, runaway boys, "G.T.T."— "Gone to Texas"—often just one step ahead of the law. Like the painted lead soldiers we played with as children, these diminutive figures in their small numbers fighting their miniature, make-believe battle seemed the linear equivalent of time long past. Their small size lent perspective into which those distant events, those early people had receded. History is heavily edited for schoolchildren and, for most of us, commencement puts an end to study. Thus we go through life with notions of our past which, for depth, complexity, subtlety of shading, rank with comic books. Texas history particularly lends itself to this: it is so farfetched that only a child could believe it. About to be reenacted now was the most improbable of the world's decisive battles. It had been the kid with nothing but his slingshot and God on his side against the giant Philistine. Nothing was ever more *un*certain than victory on that twenty-first day of April, 1836. And yet it had been won so easily it seemed now like child's play.

"Remember the Alamo!" the Texans shouted, and one among them completed the battle cry, known to every member of the audience so early in life it might have been an ingredient of their mothers' milk: "Remember Goliad!"

They were mustered on the fifty-yard line of the junior high school playing field, in front of the grandstand. No two of them were costumed alike. Among them were buckskin breeches, high boots, woolen vests, coonskin caps, battered old felt hats too big for them, belonging to their fathers. Galluses held up their breeches, belts their bowie knives. Some had trouble keeping false mustaches in place. They brandished a variety of muskets and pistols. They puffed on corncob pipes, spat manfully.

Meanwhile, the uniformed Mexicans, secure in their superior numbers, smug from their recent victories and scorning to believe that their upstart foe would have the audacity to disturb them, were taking their siesta in the western end zone. They lay sprawled on the ground, slumped against the goalpost, seated with their backs supporting each other like bookends without books. They were the Texas stereotype of Mexican sloth, Mexican *mañana*. With such an image as this of our enemy, no wonder we grew up thinking that a handful of Texas boys had won us our independence! The boys' hair was longer now—a touch of authenticity that had been lacking in their grandfathers' time; otherwise it was all just as it had been when I took part in it. 1936, that was: the year of Texas's centennial of independence, and that San Jacinto Day pageant was the town's first. I was an eighth-grader then. Now on this, my first visit home since moving away, upon the death of my father, shortly after that, I found people who still remembered me for my part in that first pageant.

Sam Houston flourished his silvered wooden saber and spurred his Shetland pony. The fife and drum corps struck up that most unmartial of marching songs—the only tune the musicians that earlier day had known how to play together: "Won't you come to the bower I have shaded for you?" The Texas artillery, the two little mortars known as the Twin Sisters, brought up the rear as the Texans went on the attack.

The Alamo and Goliad were recent memories on that twenty-first of April, 1836, and going into battle with them, while meant as an incitement to vengeance, would have made it impossible not to fear. For although it would not be until years afterward that some orator would say, "Thermopylae had its messenger of defeat—the Alamo had none," it was understood by every member of that ragtag-and-bobtail little band of Texas volunteers at San Jacinto that should they lose the battle their fate at the hands of the heartless Mexican tyrant Santa Anna would be that of the 190 defenders of the Alamo, the 330 who had surrendered at Goliad: death to a man. Outnumbered, inexperienced, ill-equipped, they were also far from united in trust behind their commander—later authors of school textbooks to the contrary notwithstanding. This they never taught us in school, but many of the soldiers had gone home in disgust, the remainder had nearly mutinied against Houston's long Fabian retreat from the enemy, and in their ranks had rearisen all the doubts, all the innuendoes about him. He had proved himself brave in battle, but that was long ago; more recently he had fled from wagging tongues, unwilling or unable to defend his name against slander so gross it would have brought another man to the field of honor. He had resigned his governorship of Tennessee in disgrace, had renounced his American citizenship, and had gone off to the wilderness to sulk—to lead, some said, a life of squalor and debauchery. Which of his two violently contradictory sides to believe in? Was he the great man he had once seemed to be, or was he, as was whispered after the fiasco of his marriage, no man at all? Which was he, the friend and protégé of the President of the United States, once clearly destined for that highest of offices himself, or was he that riverboat gambler and drunken tavern brawler, ashamed of his comedown in the world and traveling under an assumed name? Man of vision and breadth of spirit, champion of the oppressed, or a scheming, ambitious, unscrupulous would-be dictator of a country of outcasts, fugitives and adventurers like himself? Most basic question of all: was he a white man or was he a red savage? On that he himself seemed undecided. Half hero, half ham: that he certainly was, and a boy with an immature voice seemed perfectly cast to play him, an army of a dozen adolescents seemed perfectly to represent the following that such a discredited man would be able to recruit for the foolhardy campaign now coming to its issue.

The field artillery opened fire with satisfactory puffs of smoke and on this signal the infantry fell with vengeful glee upon their drowsy foe. From out of the grove of pecan trees bordering the playing field on the east, the Texas cavalry— seven horsemen strong today, originally just over fifty—came galloping to the fray. In that first, that centennial-year San Jacinto Day pageant, I was to have played the commander of the cavalry. However, I never got to—when the time came I no longer wanted to.

The Mexicans were routed, and comical in their flight, especially one caught with his pants down and trying to heist them as he fled, and another, a cowardly officer trying to disguise his rank and responsibility by pulling on a private's uniform over his own gaudy one with its absurdly broad epaulets. All over the field they were falling in exaggerated poses of well-deserved death. Cries of "Me no Alamo! Me no Goliad!" came from those who, on their knees and with supplicating hands, pleaded with their captors to spare their worthless lives.

Wounded in the leg, General Sam Houston was helped from his horse and propped against a goalpost. From there, oblivious to his pain, he directed the battle to its conclusion. As on that original twenty-first of April, it was all over in little more than a quarter of an hour. The Texans' losses were negligible, their victory decisive. The world had a new nation, wrested from tyranny, and it was a nonesuch: big, brash and boisterous, made of men each worth two of all lesser breeds. The ease with which its birth had been accomplished would fill it with lasting self-wonder—would be the origin of its tiresome self-assertiveness. To their successors its founders would seem men ten feet tall, even when impersonated by boys half that size.

The prisoners were rounded up and marched triumphantly to the post of command. The last straggler was flushed from hiding and brought in at gunpoint. Seeing him, the other prisoners all fell on their knees, removed their hats and exclaimed in awe, *"El Presidente!"* His shirt was torn open and, lo, there was that officer in disguise, none other than the loathsome Santa Anna himself, betrayed by his own imperiousness and by the sheepish simplicity of his subjects. As it did annually, the crowd roared with derision and delight.

That was the part I had finally taken in my hometown's first San Jacinto Day pageant: the part of Santa Anna, the archvillain of my state. The boy who had drawn it by lot positively refused to play it, and the teachers could not force him against his will to play so odious a part. All were grateful to me for solving the problem, and commended my patriotism and my self-sacrifice, when I volunteered for it. My teachers mistook my motive. A piece of intelligence about that old battle had just recently reached me. The way I felt now, I would have reversed its outcome if I could!

"Hang the rascal!" the Texans clamored, and one of them

threw a rope with a noose over the goalpost arm. But canny old Sam Houston quieted them. He knew that Santa Anna was worth nothing to them dead. Alive, he would be hostage for the freedom they had just won for themselves.

The dead Mexicans all came to life and dusted themselves off and both armies marched to center field to accept the applause of the crowd. Then all together stood and, to the tune of "I've been working on the railroad," sang that odd, disquieting, oppressive, even vaguely menacing song that nine out of ten Texans think is their state anthem but is not:

> The eyes of Texas are upon you
> All the livelong day.
> The eyes of Texas are upon you—
> You cannot get away.
>
> Do not think you can escape them,
> From night till early in the morn':
> The eyes of Texas are upon you
> Till Gabriel blows his horn.

In my native state patriotism flourishes as does the prickly pear: evergreen and everywhere, however poor the soil, and just as thorny. The cactus may be made edible for the Texas cattle by singeing it with a flamethrower, but not even one of those things could smooth a Texan when, rubbed the wrong way, his patriotism bristles.

Born a Texan, one remains a Texan, no matter where life takes one; however, it is not necessary to be born there to be one. Texans may, like cuckoo birds, hatch in strange nests, then when fledged find their way to their own kind. Texas is not a state but a state of mind, and Texans existed before Texas did. They came to it at first, and they have come to it ever since, like Jews to the Promised Land. As Sam Houston said of himself, he was a Texan as soon as he had crossed Red River.

It was during that centennial year of 1936 that the chronic Texas patriotism turned acute and reached fever pitch. Indeed, one year was not time enough for it to run its course, be contained and subside. Both Dallas's Centennial Exposition and Fort Worth's rival Frontier Days were held over through 1937 by popular demand. I was taken with my class to both. We were reminded that ours was the only one of the states that had been an independent country all its own, and that before we were defeated southerners we had been victorious Texans.

For us schoolchildren that year it was hard to believe that Texas had begun in 1836; to us it seemed more as though it had stopped then, for the study of that annus mirabilis all but preempted the curriculum and turned back the clock. With school out, on Saturdays, in vacant lots all over town, the Battle of the Alamo was refought weekly, and the following day, in Sunday school, there was a deliberate confounding of that exodus led by Moses of Egypt with the one of Moses Austin, and of Sam Houston at San Jacinto with Joshua at Jericho. In every home, whatnot shelves accumulated commemorative plates and miniature plaster busts of Texas revolutionary heroes. The winds of bombast, seldom still, blew over the land as incessantly as the dust storms.

To this epidemic of patriotism my father was immune and from all the hoopla he stood aloof, Texan born and bred though he was, with roots reaching back to the state's, or rather the republic's, beginnings. This was not a newfound streak of contrariness in him; Father always stood aloof from anything civic-minded, public-spirited, communal. He was an outsider—indeed, it is not too much to say that he was an out*law*. Texas, as we were reminded everywhere we looked that year, had lived under six flags; grandson of a Confederate veteran, and thoroughly unreconstructed, my ornery father would have sworn allegiance to any of those six flags indifferently, not caring what its regulations were, because he interposed the right to abide only by those that did not inconvenience him. As most regulations did inconvenience my father, he was what has since come to be known as an internal emigré, living in a country all his own, where he was a law unto himself. Which may be another way of saying that he was your true Texan, your Ur-Texan, a throwback to those rambunctious firstcomers whom we schoolchildren that year were studying about—in much expurgated accounts.

As part of the celebrations, our town, like most others throughout the state, planned its first San Jacinto Day pageant. Soldiers for the two sides would be levied from the boys of the junior high school. Our mothers would tailor and sew our uniforms, if we were to be Mexicans, or more motley costumes for us Texas irregulars.

Without a trace of real interest in my answer, my father asked me which I was going to be, a Texan or a Mexican.

As none of us boys wanted to be a Mexican, yet some of us—indeed, most of us, in order to reflect the original odds—had to be, we had drawn lots. I had been the second luckiest in the draw, after only the Sam Houston himself. I was not only to be one of the vastly outnumbered Texans, I was to be one of the two heroes of the battle, the man with the most resonant name in the annals of the state, none other than Mirabeau (My-ra-bo in the Texan pronunciation) Buonaparte Lamar. A lowly private only the day before the battle, Lamar had so distinguished himself in that day's inconclusive skirmish with the enemy that Houston elevated him on the spot to the rank of colonel and put him in command of the cavalry, the first rise in that meteoric career which in just three more years would make him the second President of the Republic, succeeding Houston himself.

"That sorry rascal!" my father exploded. "Like hell you are!"

It was not the blasphemy against one of our state's great men that made this so astonishing to me. What was astonishing was that my father should have an opinion of Mirabeau Buonaparte Lamar, that he had ever even heard of him, beyond, perhaps, knowing that the county adjoining ours to the west was named after him. My father's knowledge of history was that of a man taken out of school after only four grades and put to work on the family farm. When I say "history" I mean Texas history, for that was the kind we were taught in school—two solid years of it, to one year, later on, for the remainder of the union; but we did not begin the study of it until the fifth grade, the level my father never reached. What he knew of history he had picked up from me as I brought it home piecemeal from school, and in that he had shown no more than a fatherly interest. In fact, of all my subjects history was the one that interested him the least. Not from me had he gotten his unaccountable prejudice against Mirabeau Buonaparte Lamar.

"No son of mine is going to play-act that devil!"

And thereupon my father, who lacked book learning but who had history in his blood, told me of an episode from out of the earliest years of our state not known to my teachers, and which if they had known, they would have found unsuitable, especially in that glorious centennial year, for transmission to us schoolchildren.

Whether or not to tell me this old story after all had lately been causing my father perplexity. This indecision of his was something new. He had meant to tell it to me all my life, for he felt himself singled out and charged with a duty to keep alive in us this memory of the dead, and I was his only child. It was such a terrible story, he had been waiting until I was old enough for it, or at least until I was as old as he was when he was told it. With this, my thirteenth year, that time had come. Meanwhile, my father had begun to think not only of how old I was, but of how old he was.

With this year had also come our state's centennial celebrations. All those parades, all that pomp and pageantry, all that oratory, all that Lone-Star-flag-waving roused to even louder indignation and cries for redress the throng of ghosts that haunted my father and piqued him to speak out, to enlighten, which was to say to disillusion me, with their story, of which he was the custodian. The glowing account of the Battle of San Jacinto that I brought home from school omitted any mention of the contribution that was decisive in the Texans' victory, and of the ingratitude, the perfidy and the persecution with which that contribution was repaid. All accounts omitted it, suppressed it. My father was one of a bare handful of Texans, the others being a few college professors of history, who knew about it. The impulse for him to tell me was strong. What deterred my father was my wholehearted participation in those centennial observances. Texas molds its sons early. Had he waited until too late to tell me?

Having once hesitated, my father faltered in his purpose and temporized with his ghosts. Theirs was an old, old story, and nothing that anybody could do now, certainly nothing that a thirteen-year-old schoolboy might do, could atone for the injustice they had suffered, for history's neglect of them. By criticizing the textbook version of events, held gospel by all, I would only get myself in trouble with my teachers and my schoolmates.

My father began to wonder whether his child might not be happier not knowing about some of the things that had happened on his native soil. Evidence was everywhere that ignorance was bliss and that those who got ahead in life were not the mavericks like him but those of the herd, all bearing the same brand. In inheriting the suspicions and ancient hatreds of my color and class I would have a sufficiency without the addition of one all my own. Perhaps he ought to take that old story and that tribe of troubled spirits with him into the grave. Let my heart not be a battlefield for the strains of blood that coursed through it. Let the roses that bloomed wild in the spring have no more thorns for me than for others; let them be for me, too, pretty to look at, fragrant and above all mute—not fraught for me alone with bitter memories.

The roses were much on my father's mind just then. In fact, for the past several days they had allowed him no rest. They disturbed him waking and sleeping, mentally and physically: a steady prick to his conscience, a steady throb in his right forefinger from an infection following a prick by one of their thorns.

He had gone hunting in Red River Bottom. That was the roses' territory; however, this was not their season. They would not bloom for yet another month. But it was impossible for my father ever to find himself in those woods at any time of year and not think of the roses, of the story of which they were so much a part, of which they were the sole surviving reminder, and it was this, of course, this old association in his mind, that made him imagine now that he smelled them. As real as real the scent was—and just as bitter. Such a sweet smell to everybody else—of all roses, one of the most fragrant; to him all the more bitter for their seeming sweetness. He had gone there to get away from all that saddened and disgusted him in the town: the preparations for the San Jacinto Day ceremonies—the bunting and the buncombe: all the more reason to imagine now that he smelled their bittersweet, their accusatory smell.

It was not solitude and silence that my father went to those woods in search of. To him they were populous, with a presence behind every tree trunk, and murmurous with a multitude of voices speaking in a Babel of tongues. The wind sighing in the tall pines: that was not the wind, that was the concerted, ceaseless sigh of a people persecuted, dispossessed, pursued, all but exterminated, forgotten. Quiet as a graveyard now, the woods had once echoed with a steady stream of humanity, most, but not all, of them on a one-way journey. The history books taught that the first American immigrants to Texas came in 1821. These were those Missourians, victims of the Panic of 1819, in search of a fresh start, for whom permission to found a colony had been won from the newly independent Mexican government by a former St. Louis banker, Moses Austin, who, however, died soon thereafter, bequeathing the completion of his mission to his son, Stephen F. But the Austin colonists were not pioneers, not the first immigrants. They entered and rode south through Texas over a well-traveled road, one that began where Texan began, on Red River—not a game trail but a man-made road, surely the first one in all the New World to be landscaped, beautified, a road bordered with roses that bloomed white streaked with red and by their fragrance fulfilled the colonists' dream of entering a new Eden.

Everybody now thought they were wild roses. My father was one of the few people who knew they were not wild, not even native to Texas, but descendants of imported roses carefully, lovingly set along the margins of the state's first highway, the one over which had come those founders, heroes and martyrs whom his son was being taught about in school, and, as that son was not being taught, over which had fled those who traced and blazed and cleared and decorated it—the ones who survived their massacre, that is. The roses had been in bloom then, and if the scent of them was bitter to my father now, when it was not even real but only in his mind, a product of the power of association, he could imagine how it must have seemed during that week when they were hounded out, hunted like wild animals the length of their own road, to those who had set them there.

The road lay so near to where my father stood that he could have sworn he smelled the roses although they could not possibly be in bloom yet. Lured by the promise of a new life in a new country, people had ridden over it coming from the states, from England, France, Germany, Scandinavia, people of every station and stripe, political refugees, utopians, cultists, speculators, failures, felons, soldiers of fortune, bankers and bankrupts, plain farmers, riffraff—the ordinary, the less than ordinary and the extraordinary. That very tree, that towering red oak now leafing out for yet another spring, had stood there when Davy Crockett, seeking a new life, had passed through here on his way to death at the Alamo, and Sam Houston, not yet two days ride from the wife he had left—the second one, the red one—having crossed his red Rubicon to found a red empire, and founding instead a redneck republic.

Again that scent assailed my father, so heady this time he could hardly believe that he only imagined it, unlikely as the alternative was. Never in all his many springs had he known one that forward. And yet as he crept nearer the old roadbed, drawn there by the chatter of a squirrel, it seemed to him that the scent hung still heavier on the air.

A bushy tail twitched high in the crotch of a tree. My father raised his rifle, took aim, drew a deep breath—then lowered his rifle and walked directly to the roadway, and found the roses in full, furious bloom.

It was unheard-of for them to bloom so early. Their doing so in this centennial year could only seem to my father a message sent to him, who alone could interpret it. It was as though the roses had been expressly forced so as to be out on this San Jacinto Day, reminders of a sordid betrayal connected with, yet forgotten amid, all the festivities, and an admonition to him to keep their meaning alive in me. Almost stifled by that scent, my father stood listening to the silence which for him was peopled by a host of spirits attending upon his decision to do his duty. But what was that? To whom did he owe it?

To disregard the roses' prompting would be for my father to renege upon a lifelong pledge. It would be to forsake an entire people. It would be to disinherit me from my birthright. Yet which was preferable for getting through life, knowledge of the truth or peace of mind? My father could not decide that question for himself; who was he to decide it for somebody else? He knew that once peace of mind was lost there was no recovering it. I might begrudge his taking mine from me, and all for the sake of events that had happened a hundred years before my time.

And then maybe it might not disturb me, not even touch me. This was a possibility that struck my father now for the first time. Suppose he told me the story, to him so unforgettable, so unforgivable, and I was insensitive to it, indifferent to it? Suppose I said glibly, "Yes, it's all very sad, but it was all a long, long time ago"? It was an old story even when he was told it; to me it might seem ancient history, far too remote from me for the people in it to be real.

Enough that he had had to know the story from my age on. Its poignancy undiminished by time, it would affect me the same as it had him. He could recall as though it were only yesterday his terror as he listened to it, his outrage, his indignation, above all, his feeling of helplessness. It had disaffected him from his country and his community, had given him a lasting disrespect for its laws, its leaders, and the dismay he had felt as a child on learning what lies history told, thereby calling into question every accepted truth, had colored his entire life, had kept him even into his old age a rebellious boy. Ought he not to spare his son that? As a southerner, I already had a separate history from that of most of my fellow countrymen—a history sad enough; did I need yet another one to alienate me even from my fellow aliens?

Thus did my father reach his decision to renounce his ghosts. To the injustice and neglect they had endured, he hardened himself to add this one: to bury them in lasting silence rather than spoil my simple joy, divide my loyalties and set me apart for life from those around me. Not even the prick that the roses inflicted upon him when he plucked one of them for a keepsake, not even the sight of his blood it drew, not even the reminder of that steady throb in his finger could undo his resolve.

Then came my announcement that in our town's first San Jacinto Day pageant I was to play the part of Mirabeau Buonaparte Lamar, and this was too much for my father.

It was first of all the story of a story. Of how, on another day, long ago, another boy, one just about my age, and another old man, one much older than my father, an old, old man, had made the trip he and I were now making. Over this same road they had ridden, only it was unpaved then, and they had traveled not by motorcar, there were few or none hereabouts in those times, but by horse and buggy. The boy held the reins, the old man told him where to turn. Told him that and little more. Where they were going and why, the boy did not know, little expected to be told, dared not ask. An independent and solitary old man, this grandfather of his was. "Peculiar," people said he was—a way of not saying that he cared nothing for the company of any of them. The same ones who said he was peculiar said the boy was peculiar too. In the old man's taciturnity and aloofness the boy saw an indifference to the common run of people and the triviality of most topics of conversation that accorded with his own.

That day the boy had done as he was told to do, had harnessed the horse and hitched the buggy, had packed a lunch—"dinner" he would have called it—and had driven the old man out this way on a pilgrimage of some sort, a sentimental, probably last, journey to some spot with distant memories for him, memories he was not likely to share with anybody, much less with a stripling of a boy. The fact was, the boy's age was an element in the old man's intentions. Had he been much older than he was that day the boy would not have been told anything, for the old man held the belief, one that the boy, when he got to be my father, would hold, too, that after the age of discretion the world's corruption soon set in and hardened the human heart, especially toward the trials and tribulations of people not your immediate own.

Endings are easily fixed upon but who can say when and where a story begins? The one I was about to be told: did it begin at Muscle Shoals, Alabama, on a day in 1794 with the massacre by Indians of one William Scott and his party of five men? Or was it when, just weeks after the marriage, the up-and-coming governor of Tennessee and his young bride separated without explanation? Was it at the battle of Horseshoe Bend, on March 27, 1814, when Junuluska, chief of the Cherokees, saved the life of Andrew Jackson, only later to regret not having killed him himself, given that golden opportunity? (And I thought I knew history while my father knew only what he had learned from me!) Or did it all start with the birth in far-off Genoa of Christopher Columbus? Be that as it might, one thing was certain: it had all ended here on this spot on the banks of Red River on a day in July, 1839.

I looked about me. The W.P.A. was being employed that centennial year to put up monuments all over the place—in many instances to memorialize fairly inconsequential happenings; however, nothing marked this spot, notwithstanding my father's contention that it was the scene of an event that changed the course of history. To me it seemed an unlikely-looking place for anything at all ever to have happened, much less back in the days when the country was only beginning to be settled. Out of the way now, it must have been even more of a solitude then: a barren stretch of river shoreline no different from any other except in being even lonelier, even more inaccessible. Instead of singling it out, time seemed to have detoured around it, leaving it to drowse undisturbed, undiscovered. Past it the sluggish water flowed no faster, no slower, no redder than elsewhere along its banks. To judge from the path we had taken to get there, or rather, the absence of any path, we were the first to make the trip in a long time. My father ventured that not since he was brought there as a boy had anybody come on purpose to visit the place, and this neglect of it seemed to confirm a feeling of his and to give him a sour sort of satisfaction.

On that day in 1839—July the thirtieth it was—the water had flowed redder here when four of a party of men trying to escape from Texas by swimming across to what was then called The Territory were shot and killed. Who were they? Their names were unknown even to their killers. They had been merely four of thousands like them; their distinction lay in their being the last of their kind: east Texas Indians. It was not even known which tribe, or tribes, these belonged to. The possibilities were many, for in Texas—Mexican Texas—the Indians had at last perceived where their hope for survival lay, had put aside their immemorial tribal enmities and formed a confederation, realizing the old forlorn hope of Pontiac, Joseph Brandt, Tecumseh, and for twenty years had lived in peace and brotherhood. A chapter in the history of not just Texas but of America had ended here on this unmarked spot where we stood. With the deaths of those four nameless and forgotten men had ended the long and terrible exodus of a people, as well as the dream of one ambitious man for an empire far vaster than the then United States.

My father had piqued my interest but he had also piqued my skepticism. Here was I, freshly crammed with Texas history, and here was he, on the eve of San Jacinto Day, about to launch into a tale known to him alone, which, before it was finished, was going to have to explain and defend this assertion of his, tossed off on our way out to this godforsaken place: that the battle had been won not by those 783 heroes of my textbooks but by over 1,800, led not by Sam Houston but by another man. Who was he? Somebody I had never heard of, nor any of my schoolteachers either. What had he done to win the battle? Nothing. He was, said my father, using a catchphrase going the rounds that year, the little man who wasn't there.

With a wild rose in my buttonhole that my father had plucked and put there, I sat myself down beside the water where he had sat to listen to the same tale when he was a boy like me. Only he had not known that he was about to be told a tale. His first thought had been that the old man was about to die, that he had had himself brought to die on this spot. If he had, the old man then replied, it would have been for the second time. On this very spot, long ago, when he was the boy's age, he had in the same instant both died and been reborn. Gazing across the red water to what even then was still not Oklahoma, still The Territory, the old man seemed to the boy to have quit this world and to belong already to the next one, to be silently in communication with it. When he broke the silence at last he seemed to be announcing in a tongue certainly not of this world his imminent departure from it, his imminent arrival on that other shore. To sounds—words, evidently—the like of which the boy had never heard before, the old man sang a hymn the tune to which the boy knew well. I knew it too. It was to the tune of "Amazing Grace" that, to my amazement, my father sang:

Unelanvhi Uwetsi
Igaguyvheyi
Hnaquotsosv Wiyulose
Igaguyvhonv

Asene Yiunetseyi
Iyuno Dulenv
Talinedv Tselutseli
Udvne Yunetsv

I forgot San Jacinto Day, forgot Mirabeau Buonaparte Lamar and why for some reason I was not allowed to impersonate him, forgot myself. Actually, as the telling would show, the story was about all three.

Part Two

Where were the Indians?

Here (in Georgia) he (the Reverend Malcolm Mackenzie) was, come all the way from Scotland to save the Indians, but where were they?

Some people, even some theologians, believed otherwise, but the Reverend Mackenzie believed that Indians had souls. To him had come the call to save them. Previous missionaries had had to flee for their lives, but saved the Indians were going to be, come hell or high water. Assigned the task was a man of determination. He was the wrong man for the job, he knew this, and, mistrustful of himself, he was on the watch for the first sign of any faintheartedness of his.

It was not the tomahawk, the scalping knife, torture and death at the stake that the Reverend Mackenzie feared. For a man on his mission to Georgia in 1837 there were many things to fear, but those barbarities did not figure among them. Nobody need fear those things anymore. They belonged to a past not so very remote in actual calendar time, yet so much had things changed that already they seemed antediluvian. That he might deny his God and lose his soul to save his skin, this the Reverend Mackenzie did fear, but not that he might do so in order to save himself from the fiery stake while naked and painted savages whooped and stomped around it.

God moves in a mysterious way His wonders to perform.

Of that truth no more puzzling example could be adduced than His choice of Malcolm Mackenzie to save the souls of His Cherokee children. A younger son, destined from birth for the church, he was newly ordained, newly married, newly settled into his comfortable living in his pleasant parish when he chanced to read a newspaper account of the progress made by the Cherokees in pacifying and civilizing themselves, and of their persecution by the white people of the state of Georgia. On reading that their tribal government, a model of its kind, had been abolished and that they were subject to the laws of the state while denied all rights of citizenship, that they were forbidden even to testify in court against whites, the Reverend Mackenzie said, "Shocking." This somewhere in the modern-day, English-speaking world! On reading that they were forbidden to dig for the gold on their own land, and that this land, theirs from time immemorial, was being taken from them and redistributed to white settlers while they were forced to leave their ancestral home and move to a far west, as wild to them as to white men, he said again, this time more vehemently, "Shocking!" Then when he read that their missionaries had been expelled and the converts among them, of whom there were many, denied the right of religious assembly, this in a state professedly Christian, the Reverend Mackenzie said, "Now see here! We can't have that!"

The Reverend Mackenzie read no further. Were it possible to unread something that one has read, he would have done so. Certainly, if he could have, he would have taken back those words of his. But he knew that they had been put into his mouth by a power who would not be gainsaid. He knew it was not by chance that he had read that account. He knew who the other party was to that "we" he had been made to pronounce.

What were the Cherokee Indians to him? he asked; and then he knew how Cain must have felt under God's withering gaze when he asked, "Am I my brother's keeper?" And as much if not more in need of spiritual guidance than the Indians were their white oppressors. But he hardly knew where Georgia was, he protested; and he was directed to go and find it on the map.

His case strained the Reverend Mackenzie's faith in God's infallibility. He respectfully suggested that a mistake had been made, that the call to this duty had been wrongly addressed. He was not made of the stuff of martyrs, and nobody knew this better than he. His letters from Georgia back home to Edinburgh during that summer of 1837 abound in expressions of his unfitness. He prayed for strength but his prayers went unanswered; he knew himself for the weakling he was. He prayed for resignation to whatever the fate that awaited him; he feared that, put to the test, he would turn tail and run, just as his predecessors—all but two of them—had done. It was the treatment of those two that daunted him. For refusing to swear their oaths not to minister to the Cherokees they were beaten, chained and forced to march thirty-five miles a day the one hundred miles from the site of their arrest to the jail, were tried, convicted and sentenced to four years hard labor, denied all privileges and any visitors. The stir this caused in more enlightened parts of the country carried their appeal to the United States Supreme Court. They were released after serving two years. They returned to their homes to find that they had been confiscated. The men were then run out of the state.

In Savannah, at the customshouse, the Reverend Mackenzie had sworn his oath of allegiance to the constitution of the state of Georgia, which oath was required of all white people wishing to reside in the Cherokee territory. He was one of many off his boat to swear their oaths, for that territory was a land of opportunity. The official who administered the oath drew the Reverend Mackenzie's particular attention to that provision of the constitution relating to which color of people might assemble for worship and which might not. His aim was to stay within the law by ministering the rites of the church to his red parishioners singly and in pairs, and meanwhile to convert his white congregation to a spirit of brotherly love for their red neighbors. His dread was that, in their determination to brutalize the Cherokees and to make their lives so wretched they would leave of their own accord, the authorities might tighten the law to forbid him to minister to them in any numbers at all.

Now here he was in this literally godforsaken place.

But where *were* the Indians?

Where were the wigwams and the tepees, the feathered headdresses, the colorful costumes? Where were the beaded moccasins, the bareback pinto ponies? Where were the queues of braided hair, the tattooed faces? *Where* were the Indians?

What he was seeing, the Reverend Mackenzie relates in the first of those letters home of his (to be published by a small Indian-oriented press, long after he had gone to his reward, under the title *The Missionary in Spite of Himself*), was a settlement different from the ones he had passed through in getting there only in being newer, recently prosperous, now all but deserted. There was a former church—the one he was to make his own—now a stable. There was a former school—now boarded up. There was a grocer, a dry-goods merchant, a chemist, even a printshop—the latter now shut down. Large white clapboard houses sat back from the streets on spacious lots. No grisly hanks of human hair hung drying on poles in the gardens of the houses. There were no naked dark-skinned children at play, rather there were fair little girls with golden curls in pinafores and buckle shoes, towheaded little boys more decently dressed than the urchins of the streets of Edinburgh. As for the townspeople, they were an outpost of Scotsmen like himself. Not Raindancer, nor Black Bear, not White-man-killer, but McIntosh, Dinsmore, Ferguson, Duncan, Ross, Stuart, Cameron were their names. *Where were the Indians?* Had he come just too late? Had they tired at last of their long, losing struggle, capitulated and gone west?

The Reverend Mackenzie's first pastoral duty in his new post, just days after taking it up, was the baptism of a child. Not a babe in arms but a boy of twelve or thereabouts. In part because this was the first person he had baptized in the New World, in part because of later developments, he would take a lasting interest in the boy—lasting at least for as long as events allowed. It is in his letter relating their meeting that my paternal great-grandfather, Amos, my namesake, the founder of our branch of Texas Smiths, makes his first appearance. However, at the time Smith was not his name—not even one of his several names.

He was a short, slender boy, a sandy-haired, fair-skinned, freckle-faced, blue-eyed boy (that was the sequence in which his features were revealed to Mrs. Mackenzie as she opened the upper half of the back door of the parsonage to him and he raised his head), and he was a painfully shy boy—"backward" was the word she resorted to. He had looked at her as if she were the first of her sex he had ever laid eyes on, and when she opened the lower half of the door to show him in (he had muttered that he was there to see the minister, please, ma'am; would she be so good as to ask him to step outside? That she would not, for the minister was prostrated by the infernal heat, but she *would* ask *him,* please, to be so good as to step *inside*) he had slipped past her as if afraid of contamination by her touch. (That, in fact, was exactly what he feared. For while it was over a week ago that he had been ritually scratched, and while he was now free to associate with women again, even to be touched by one, he was not yet used to this restored freedom. Besides, this one was an *Yvwunega* who would not have

known what it meant to be scratched if she were told.) Putting
the width of the kitchen between them, the boy said, "My
business with the minister is just between him and me, if you
don't mind, ma'am."

Yet such a different impression had he made upon her
husband, they might have been talking about not one but two
boys. (In fact, they were. Actually, three.) Rather a sobersided
little soul but perfectly polite, the Reverend Mackenzie found
their young caller. Welcomed him here, hoped they were settling in comfortably, wondered if there were anything he
might do to be of help. Then he stated his business. On his
own, without his parents, he had come to ask to be baptized.

Today? Now?

If it was convenient with His Reverence, the sooner the
better, for he was no longer a child but had reached the age of
discretion and was now accountable for his sins. And there
was no knowing when a body might die.

It was not cant. The boy seemed to have thought quite
seriously already about death and damnation.

Impressed, eager to get started doing God's work, the
Reverend Mackenzie readily agreed.

He knew a good place on the river for them to do it, the
boy said.

He must be from a family of Baptists. Now, the Reverend
Mackenzie had always thought of nonconformists as misguided at best, nitpickers and hairsplitters, and, at worst, as
outcasts for going against the kingdom's established church.
This boy brought home to him the fact that he was no longer
in that kingdom. On the contrary, he was in the only former
colony that had rebelled against the king, against an established church, and had won.

Surprised at the ease with which he did it, the Reverend
Mackenzie found himself thinking, well, better a Baptist than
a heathen—although he was quite certain that no Baptist
would have said the same for his own creed, and certain too

that he himself would not have said it so easily anywhere else but here. One must trim one's sails to the wind. His church had its tenets and its rites, and that these were the right tenets and the right rites he never questioned, yet here he was in this frontier outpost, the only Christian minister of any denomination—much like a general agent for several insurance companies, though the comparison was rather uncomfortably commercial. Sectarian differences seemed to lose here some of their importance. As a foreign embassy or a consulate sometimes handled affairs with the host country of nations with no representatives there of their own, so he now began to see his function. His bishop might not agree, but, yes, decidedly, better a Baptist than a heathen. The Reverend Mackenzie confesses that in that heat a cool dip while doing God's work seemed to him a jolly good idea. He confesses even to having followed the boy's example, stripping to the skin and enjoying a total immersion himself.

The spot was one at which two rivers met and joined to become one big river. Any one of the three would have fulfilled their requirements, but the boy insisted on being baptized in the big river. It symbolized something for him.

"I am like it," he said with a solemnity that, in one so young, would have been comical had it not instead been impressive. "Two in one." He did not volunteer to elaborate on this and the Reverend Mackenzie did not press him. It was himself the boy was talking to. He gave the impression of being a boy who talked to himself a lot. Plainly he found being "two in one" something of a burden. To his credit be it said that the Reverend Mackenzie did not find this precocious gravity commendable. "A child," he writes, "should be left in happy ignorance of weighty matters." A Scot, but not your dour Scot, is how the Reverend Mackenzie comes across in his letters.

But questions for the boy the Reverend Mackenzie did

have, in pursuance of his duty, and in the shade of a tree he catechized his young parishioner.

"What is your name?" he began. The response he got to this puzzled him. By what seemed the most elementary, the most innocuous question possible to put to a person—that is, a person with nothing to hide—the Reverend Mackenzie had unwittingly placed the boy in a dilemma. Plainly he had been dreading this moment. He visibly squirmed. He looked skyward as though seeking guidance.

His name? Which one of them?

He had at all times three names, and of these one was continually being changed—in fact, he was going to have need of a new one after the ceremony about to be performed. To most people he was Amos Ferguson. That had been his name at school, was his name to all the world outside the walls of his home. Inside those walls he was *Noquisi:* Bright Star. That name was not to be divulged to anybody but those of his own clan. An enemy who knew it had power over you, could conjure against you, and the world was full of enemies. You signed your X to any document, preferring to be thought illiterate, shameful as that had come to be in recent years, sooner than reveal your real name. That way too the real you had not signed the document. It was a part of the boy's dilemma now whether or not to reveal this name to the minister. If he did not, would he really be baptized? All of him? Would he not, in fact, be baptized under false pretenses and for this sin sent to hell?

But that was only a part of his dilemma. Inside these two names, one of them inside the other, like the meat of a walnut nestled within its outer and its inner shells, was yet a third name, the most personal, the most secret of all: his self's very kernel. This was the boy's name for himself, and only he called himself by it, even he never spoke it aloud; nobody else, not any of his friends, not his parents nor his grandparents knew this name. It was doubtful that even God knew it, so often, especially of late, was he obliged to change it in order to keep up with the changes in himself and in the world.

Once, long ago—three years at the least—when his mother, alluding to his restlessness, his tireless energy, called him her *walela*—her hummingbird—that had become his name for himself. Then all the world was in flower, with nectar to sip from every blossom. That name lasted him until his dream about turning into a bear, and then for a while he was *Yonva.* There were times when the name was not of his choosing, for instance, the phase when he was *Alsdisgi:* Troublemaker. Sometimes from the original to the translation it ran the opposite way, as when, reflecting conversations overheard at home about events rapidly overtaking them all, a time when it was dangerous to speak the old, mother tongue even to one's secretmost self, he was Worried One: *Uwelihisgi.* During one particularly troubled period just recently he was *Uhnalvhi:* Angry One. He had gone through two changes of name in this past week alone, such an eventful time this was for him. First he was *Awina:* Young Man.

He had been given the sign that the time had come for him to do two things. He had long ago run the four times around the house with the last of his milk teeth and then thrown it onto the roof with a prayer to *Dayi,* the Beaver, to put a new one its place; his voice had recently broken; he was expecting this latest and last sign. Its coming made him very proud of himself, yet a power for both good and evil was now his. His years of innocence were over. He would be prone from now on to a new and strong temptation, and he had arrived at the age of discretion and was accountable for his sins.

In olden times he would have gone naked from birth until given this sign. Boys did, back then. It was not thought good for boys to wear clothes. Clothes made the body soft when it should be getting hard for life as a man. Boys had nothing to conceal anyway. The coming of civilization, of Christianity, had long ago changed all that. But, pagan or Christian, boys had not changed. The change that boys underwent in ceasing to be boys had not changed.

When he was given the sign again the next day, sure of himself, *Awina* saddled his pony and, wearing his best moccasins, a turban and a sash, rode the five miles from town out to the farm to make his announcement.

"Agiduda. Grandfather," he said, "the time has come for me to be scratched."

"Osda, Sgilisi! That is good, my grandchild!" said his grandfather. "Let us go to water."

The rite was age-old. The man had undergone it, the boy's father had undergone it, now he. It had remained unchanged. But meanwhile in the span of those three living generations their world had changed and changed again and was now more than ever in the throes of change. It seemed destined to come full circle once more. Thus the ceremony's opening invocation, made meaningless in his father's time, an empty form, had now regained the force, the solemnity and the fearsomeness it had had for the boy's grandfather. It was a prayer to the Great Spirit to dispose this young brave toward war.

To the naked boy standing before him the old man said, "Noquisi, you are about to be made dreadful." *Usgasedi* was the word: dreadful, horrid, fierce. Qualities which, at the urging of the missionaries, their people had lain aside, qualities which, as their long, losing struggle neared an issue, they would have need of in their young men once again.

"What is your name?" the Reverend Mackenzie repeated.

For a moment longer the boy hesitated, then, "Amos Ferguson, sir," he declared. He had decided to leave it to God to decide which he was, whether red or white, and of the two which of them might be saved. He could not decide for himself, and he had been told so often that the red part was damned past redemption, he had about come to believe it. He reckoned it was only the white part of him that this God was interested in.

There was some little difficulty over the doctrine of the Holy Trinity but it was not the difficulty that the Reverend Mackenzie had foreseen. He dreaded having to explain the matter to a simple mind because the truth was he had never understood it himself. One God in Trinity and one in Unity. The Father uncreate, the Son uncreate, and the Holy Ghost uncreate. The Father incomprehensible, and so forth. The Father eternal, and so forth. And yet they are not three eternals nor three incomprehensibles nor three uncreate, but one eternal, and so forth. The Father almighty, the Son almighty and the Holy Ghost almighty, yet they are not three almighties but one almighty. And so forth and so forth. The arithmetic of this made the Reverend Mackenzie's head ache. The requirement of professing to believe it literally had very nearly kept him from taking his vows of ordination, and was a vexation to his spirit still.

Said the Reverend Mackenzie with an encouraging smile, "Don't let it bother you, my boy, if that is not quite clear to you."

Said the boy, "But it is, sir. Quite clear. Three in one, one in three."

They got through the Ten Commandments and the Lord's Prayer, the Sacraments and the Last Supper, then for the eighth time in as many days the boy stripped himself for immersion in the river. *Usgasedi* for a name had lasted him no longer than that. Busy days they were at his turning time of life!

"Great heavens, boy!" cried the Reverend Mackenzie. "What on earth has happened to you?"

He looked as though he had been mauled in barehanded combat with a bobcat. From top to toe, down his arms, down his legs, across his chest, across his back the scratches ran. Music paper was not more lined than was the boy's body by the claws of some wild beast. Recently inflicted, the wounds were still scabbed over.

The Reverend Mackenzie had found his first Indian.

He thought of those stories so common of white children taken captive and raised as Indians. But no.

"Jijalagiyai," said the boy—outlandish sounds, all the more outlandish issuing from the mouth of a freckle-faced, blue-eyed bairn. "I thought you knew. *Jijalagiyai.* That means, 'I am truly one of the Real People.' " That was said proudly, this bitterly, "If you don't believe me, that I am an Indian, just ask any of these true-blue white folks hereabouts, Your Reverence. They will set you straight right quick." Then this, though with a laugh, ruefully, "The other day I heard a man say—he was a man whose house was being taken from him because he was an Indian, 'Our Cherokee blood must be very strong blood. It takes so little of it to make one of us.' "

In the long-laid-aside rite that he and his grandfather were reviving, the boy had been scratched with a comb made from a wolf's bone. Just so had it been done in former times. The comb was cracked and yellowed with age. The wolf would have been killed by a wolf-killer, a professional, the office hereditary, the formula for deceiving the wolves into believing that the killing had been done by somebody from another settlement, and thereby deflecting their revenge for their brother's murder, handed down from father to son. The comb was sharp-toothed; his blood had flowed and the pain he endured without flinching filled him with pride of manhood. He washed away the blood by a plunge in the river. Afterwards, to toughen him, his grandfather bathed him in a solution made from the catgut plant. As always in former times whenever any new phase of a Cherokee's life was about to be entered upon, he purged himself with the black draught, an emetic and a laxative.

That week after being scratched and going to water, and before being baptized, he spent out at the farm, in sequestration, in a sort of male purdah. During that time he was not to be touched by nor eat with a woman, not even his grandmother. His days he spent sleeping, his nights he spent with his grandfather in the *asi,* the hothouse, his eyes washed with owl-feather-water to keep them open, listening to the stories of the Creation, of the early history of his people and of their recent period of glory, their present peril, the portents of their impending disaster. And although, to his grandfather's sorrow, theirs was only a makeshift *asi* (was, in fact, a deserted henhouse), nonetheless, with the ceremonial fire blazing on the stone in the center of the floor, hearing his grandfather begin, as such séances must, always had, with "When I was a boy like you, this is what the old men told me they had heard from the old men when they were boys," he felt that he had come into his own, that he was now truly one of The People, the Principal People, the Real People, with all the privileges and all the pressing present responsibilities of that membership.

Beginning at the beginning of the end, his grandfather went back to the beginning of things, then throughout those seven nights in the *asi* traced their course back to the end. Many were the gaps in the chronicle, for, alas, the Cherokees were a people like none other for shortness of memory, irreverent toward their past, disposed to chase after newness (the boy was even then lighting their ceremonial fire not with a coal brought from another fire in a *tusti* bowl, as had been the custom ever since fire was first fetched to the Chosen People by *Dayunisi,* the Water Beetle, but with one of the white man's newly introduced locofocos), but as best he could he would relate all that had been passed on to him. Once there were priests to remember everything, and when they gathered in the *asi* to recite the legends of how the world began, and life and death, and where The People originated and by what wanderings they were brought here, promising boys were admitted to attend the fire and listen and they grew up to be the priests of their time. But that was before Sequoyah invented the alphabet and nothing of it was written down and meanwhile the Cherokees had ceased to be Indians and now from their book many pages were missing.

The beginning of the end was when that old chief of the tribe heard, at a distance of thirteen moons, unfamiliar sounds coming through the forest from the direction of the coast, journeyed there and returned to report that strange men with fair hair and pale skin had come from out of the ocean. So rapid was their spread that within a generation the wise men of the tribe made a prophecy. This prophecy his grandfather did not need to recollect. With the light of the flickering fire glinting on his spectacles, he read from the Cherokee newspaper *The Phoenix,* since suppressed, its type seized. It was an article that had appeared there three years earlier. It was entitled "Remarkable Fulfillment of Indian Prophecy."

"Our elder brother" (meaning the white man), said the prophets, "has become our neighbor. He is now near to us, and already occupies our ancient habitations. But this is as our forefathers told us. They said, 'Our feet are turned toward the West—they are never to turn around.' Now mark what our forefathers told us. 'Your elder brother will settle around you —he will encroach upon your lands, and then will ask you to sell them to him. When you give him a part of your country, he will not be satisfied, but ask for more. In process of time he will ask you to become like him. He will tell you that your mode of life is not as good as his—whereupon you will be induced to make great roads through the nation, by which he can have free access to you. He will learn your women to spin and weave and make clothes, and learn you to cultivate the earth. He will even teach you to learn his language and learn you to read and write. But these are but means to destroy you and eject you from your habitations. HE WILL POINT YOU TO THE WEST, but you will find no resting place there, for your elder brother will drive you from one place to another until you reach the western waters. These things will certainly happen, but it will be when we are dead and gone. We shall not live to see and feel the misery which will come upon you."

So long ago did the world begin that nobody now knew when or how. This much was known: first came the animals, then the plants; man was last. Life on earth began when *Galunlati,* the world above this one, where the birds and the animals first lived, became overcrowded and they all migrated here. Those were not the creatures known to us but were all bigger and far more intelligent than ours. They all spoke the same language as did man, had their common councils, and, like men, were fond of playing ball. The time came when, for reasons nobody knows, these superior creatures deserted the earth and removed themselves back to *Galunlati,* where they still reside, leaving here behind the stunted, dumb, puny imitations that we know.

The first man and woman were brother and sister. Who made them and put them here has been forgotten, is a mystery. The woman conceived the first child when her brother smote her with a fish. In seven days, and again every seven days thereafter, like a hen laying eggs, she gave birth, until this world was in danger of overcrowding, and then the matter was regulated as we know it.

Even so, people multiplied so rapidly that in course of time the animals found themselves crowded for space. Meanwhile, man invented the bow and arrow, traps and snares, knives, spears, hooks and fishnets. The animals convened to take measures for their safety. It was then and there that all the illnesses and ailments that afflict mankind were invented: fevers and chills, rheumatism, toothache, blindness. So venomous was the atmosphere of that convention that *Tuyadis-kalawtsiski,* the Grubworm, the very one whose job it had been to marry people, and whose hatred of them now came from his being stepped on by their innumerable get, rolled on his back in glee over a proposal that menstruation be made fatal to women, and has never since been able to get on his feet again. Had not the plants, which were friendly to man, offered themselves as healing herbs (for diseases invented by the Rabbit the weed called rabbit's ear, for yellow bile the yellowroot, for forgetfulness the cockleburr, for nothing clings like a burr), humankind would have perished from the earth.

It was in those early times that the animals acquired their features and their dispositions. Insufferably vain of his bushy tail, *Sikwautsetsti,* the Possum, got it shaved by the Cricket, who pretended to be grooming it (the Cricket was a barber by trade), and ever since he has been so embarrassed to be seen that he lies down and grins a silly grin. In one footrace with *Tsitstu,* the Rabbit, that mischief-maker and arch-deceiver, himself so often deceived, the Deer won his antlers, and in another, the most memorable footrace ever run, the one against the Tortoise, *Tsitstu* got his lasting comeuppance. The Tom Turkey got his beard, a scalp that he cozened the Terrapin out of, and the Turkey Buzzard, who had formerly boasted a fine topknot, was rendered bald for his proud refusal to eat carrion, thereupon lost his self-respect, and now lives on carrion.

There were spirits then in all things, large and small, moving and stationary. Everybody and everything spoke in a universal tongue. The woods were full of voices. In every creature, every tree, every rock, every mountain, every brook there resided a spirit. Some were evil spirits, some good. There were the *Yunwi Tsudi,* the Little People: cave dwellers, music lovers, wonder-workers, good-hearted creatures who found lost children and restored them to their parents—and there were the underwater cannibals whose diet was children's flesh. All alike were departed now, powerless any longer to cheer or scare, dispelled by the missionaries. Exorcised. Explained away. Scorned away. Now a tree was just a tree, a rock just a rock, and now when you went for a solitary walk in the woods you had only yourself to converse with.

To think there was a time, and not so long ago, barely beyond living memory, when, instead of being tales told for the entertainment of children, these were the living faith of a people—your people! To think this as the night in the *asi* ended with the rising of the sun and your rising to go forth and salute it and go to water to wash away your sweat was to—was to what? To smile? To blush? To thank your lucky stars that you were born when you were, emancipated from primitive superstition? Or to yearn with your whole heart for such sweet simplicity, such happy harmony among all things that be, to come again, knowing that it never could?

From savagery to civilization in half a generation, from universal illiteracy to universal literacy in their own tongue through the alphabet given to them by their own living flesh-and-blood Cadmus (would that he also had the power to grow armed men from dragons' teeth!): that was what the Cherokees had achieved. It was a feat without parallel in the long record of human endeavor, and the period coincided with that of the childhood which Amos Ferguson—Noquisi—*Ajudagwasgi:* Stays-Up-All-Night—was now putting behind him. It was as if his childhood and that of his people had lain until now ripening in the womb of time.

It had been, for the most part of it, a happy childhood—

doubly happy, for it had been two childhoods in one, and whenever one of them turned temporarily unhappy there was always that other one to take refuge in. Until it became the worst of times, the worst of places, it had been the best of times, the best of places, to be a boy, to be two boys in one, red and white. No matter what the day of the week or the season of the year, deep inside himself he was always that secretmost self with its own unutterable name, whatever that happened to be at the time, but depending upon the day and the season he was one or the other of his two known selves. When school was in session, on weekdays, he awoke as Amos Ferguson, and put on shoes; on Saturday he awoke as Noquisi, and put on moccasins. The proportion of six days to one just about corresponded to his mixture of bloods. His white blood was the milk of his being, his red blood the cream, and on Saturday it rose. But without milk there can be no cream, and while it was that rich side of him that took him out of doors, on pleasure, and that brought him, at his grandfather's knee, tales of olden times, appealing to that love of the past, that conservatism and longing for stability common to all children, school was no drudgery to a child whose schooldays were those when his entire people had enrolled along with him, and were garnering the new knowledge as though it were manna from heaven. For that was what had happened, and even now, despite everything, was still happening. For the Cherokees it was a time of overnight emergence from the stone age to the age of iron, from benightedness and inconvenience to enlightenment and comfort. The first products of the Industrial Revolution had reached them. Later on would come the iron horse, the factory smokestacks, the pollution of the water and the spoliation of the land, but for now it was the small material blessings that make life a bit less brutish and, perhaps, a bit less short. Knives and hatchets of steel instead of stone. Instant fire: you could not know, you who took it for granted, what a convenience that was! Needles—a small miracle! Eyeglasses! They

showed the world to people condemned to grope their way to
the grave from the age of fifty, forty—from birth. They put an
end to the barbaric practice of abandoning such people to die.
Instead of having to stump through life lame after breaking a
leg and having a witch doctor mumble over it, now it could be
set and splinted and mend straight again. Imperfect as was his
administration of it, the white man brought representative
government, trial by jury, condign punishment, and replaced
the code of blood revenge, the endless family feuds. Freed from
superstitions that answered none of one's questions about life
but only threatened one with curses and blights, they were
healthier in mind. One went to school each day filled with
expectation, and brought home to the hungry family what one
had learned like food for the table. Revelation upon revelation
it had been. With the rapture of children at a fair, a nation of
twenty thousand gaped in wide-eyed wonder at a world in
which the things that had always mystified them were suddenly simplified and the deep mysteries for the first time revealed. "Amazing Grace," they sang—it had become almost
the national anthem—"how sweet the sound/ That saved a
wretch like me,/ That once was lost but now am found,/ Was
blind but now can see." And there was that coincidental acqui-
sition of their own alphabet. What no white man had ever
done one of theirs had done. As well as the whites, The People
could now communicate with others of their kind who were
out of sight. (Blood was forever being talked about in those
days: white blood, red blood, full-blood, half-blood, mixed-
blood, and all his life long, even into extreme old age, he would
retain some measure of his childish wonder that his, when let,
ran red. He expected it to be pink, barely pink, nearly white.)
On Saturday afternoons the horse was harnessed to the surrey
and his father and mother rode in it while he, in his moccasins,
his turban and sash, rode alongside on his pony and they went
out to the farm to visit his father's people. Being Noquisi on
Saturdays was no holiday. He had as much to learn as did

Amos Ferguson. At school Amos absorbed his indoors education; around the farm, in the woods, along the rivers and, like this, listening to his grandfather, Noquisi absorbed his.

To accompany almost every thing Indians did there was one of the old tales for a man to tell and retell, a child to listen to and listen again. Giving Noquisi lessons in the art of chipping arrowheads (Never mind that they had guns now. Guns were fine but the bow too still had its uses. While a white man was measuring and dispensing powder from his powder horn and fumbling for a patch and ramrodding it down the barrel of his rifle and finding a ball and ramrodding that and fitting a cap to the nipple and shouldering his arm and taking aim, an Indian could loose a dozen arrows. Besides, a gun made a hunter out of anybody; with a gun any fool could kill game, even a white fool.), his grandfather told him about Flint. Of how all the animals hated Flint for his having caused the death of so many of their kind, but only one, that wily little rascal *Tsitstu,* the Rabbit, had the courage to approach him, the cunning to undo him. Of how *Tsitstu* had inveigled Flint into paying him a visit, had dined him to such satiety that he dozed off, whereupon *Tsitstu* drove a stake into him, causing him to burst into pieces (one of which, striking *Tsitstu,* cleft his nose), and that is why we now find pieces of flint scattered every-where, yours for the picking up. Actually it was as though Flint had burst into finished arrowheads, so many were there to be found scattered everywhere, yours for the picking up: the legacy of generations of Cherokee hunters, warriors. Like every boy, Noquisi had a basketful of them.

That was last year when on Saturdays out at the farm Grandfather was always to be found in his toolshed at work on the bow and arrows which he had been taken with the notion to make.

"Getting ready to go on the warpath, Agiduda?"

Under the present circumstances it was not very funny even to the boy's father, who had asked it. To the old man it was not funny in the least. He responded with his most Indian grunt.

It was plain to see from the care going into its making that this was to be the bow to end bows—or else to bring them back. Grandfather turned out to be an expert bowyer. The wood was seasoned Osage orange, but the Osage were traditional enemies of the Cherokees and even now were harassing those of them who had given up the struggle and already gone west, so better call it by its other name, *bois d'arc:* wood of Noah's ark. Close-grained, almost unworkably dense it was, so that the shaping of the stave with drawknife and spokeshave took weeks. Perfect symmetry of the two limbs was the goal, thus their tapering proceeded simultaneously, cautiously, with almost imperceptible progress from week to week—wood once removed could not be replaced. When shaped, the limbs were tillered: balanced so exactly that, when drawn, the bow bent in as perfect an arc as the crescent moon. The final finishing was done with the cutting edge of a piece of broken glass, the shavings as fine as eiderdown. Endless hand-rubbing with oil made the yellow wood gleam like gold. The bowstring was plaited of gut, the handle woven of leather, the tips carved of antlers. A dozen arrows, each requiring days to true up straight and fletch with feathers all from the same side of the bird, in a quiver of hide decorated with dyed porcupine quills, completed the outfit. Only now, after months of labor, was it finished, so that much as he longed to, he being already a better than fair shot with his own miserable boy's bow, and more than an apprentice in the patience and stealth and immobility on the trail and on the game stand which hunting with the bow and arrow took, Noquisi did not dare ask Agiduda to make one like it for him.

Now when his week in the *asi* had ended, Amos Ferguson could go and get himself baptized by the new minister, meanwhile he was Noquisi full-time.

He was hearing little that was new to him. The recent and

ongoing occurrences affecting the elders affected the children too and were common knowledge, a common threat. What he was hearing in this old, all-but-forgotten tribal rite was more in the nature of a review of all that he knew, lest he forget it in the press of events soon to overtake them. He sensed that his grandfather wanted in these nights together to tell him once again, as though for the last time, who and what he was, for a way of life was threatened, might be coming to an end—if, indeed, the end had not already come.

They talked of the old-time festivals, six to the calendar year, when The People assembled like so many grains to make one ear of corn, some of them traveling for days to get there. They celebrated the appearance of the first green of spring; the heading-out of the maize; its harvesttime; the first full moon of autumn and the advent of the hunting season. Greatest of all the celebrations was *Ah tawh hung nah,* the new year. Life itself began afresh then. Old clothes, old furniture, old utensils, everything old was brought to be thrown on a communal bonfire in the village square. The fire in the council house was ceremoniously extinguished and a fresh one kindled. In every home the fire was extinguished and a fresh one lighted from the embers of the council-house fire. All was swept clean, all freshly coated with paint. The people purified themselves with the black draught and by bathing in the river. All was pardoned. Murderers came in from hiding and sat beside the survivors of their victims, who had been sworn to avenge them with blood. There were ball games and footraces and shooting matches and trials of strength and all week long there was dancing day and night. Something nobody but an Indian could know was the brotherhood, the simultaneous sense of community and self, the ecstasy of belonging to one's tribe—and the sorrow of seeing it riven into hostile halves.

They talked of real, historical people, their chiefs and their champions, of actual events, of the time when their young men lived only for war, of their battles against their blood enemies the Senecas, the Shawnees, the Creeks, and while in their present-day powerlessness they thrilled to the tales of their former ferocity, yet they counted their blessings in being free from the fear of the war whoop in the night, the scalping knife, torture and death at the stake. Their pride in their one-time bloodthirstiness was tempered with shame, for they had been taught, both man and boy, to believe that this was not bravery but barbarity.

If there were gaps in the telling of the story, there were also gaps in the listening. For it was a nightlong lament, a dirge, and even the eyewash of owl-feather-water was not proof against the old man's unbroken, low monotone, the darkness, the heat, the flickering flames, the cross-legged immobility relieved only by getting up stiff-kneed from time to time to add sticks to the fire, and the boy often dozed off despite himself. These lapses from attentiveness he laid to the white blood in his veins.

At break of day the fire was banked and, carrying their clothes, the man and the boy strode through the woodlot down to the river, both of them glistening with sweat as though they had already bathed. At the water's edge they offered up to the Great Spirit a prayer of thanksgiving for the new day. After bathing, they stood in the risen sun to dry themselves. Then they dressed, wrapping their turbans around their heads, slipping on their beaded moccasins, and returned through the woods, along the edge of the fields and past the barns and the slave quarters to the house.

Always before, until this year, there would have been cordwood for the coming winter stacked between standing trees and mounds of yellow sawdust on the sites where it had been sawed to fireplace length. The cotton fields that stretched out of sight would ordinarily have looked two feet deep in snow at this time of year; now they bore the stubble of last year's crop, brown stalks and empty bolls.

The slave quarters had stood vacant since spring.

"I am not freeing you," their master told them that day when he had them assemble. "Rather, I am letting you go. To the head of each family, and to each of you single men and women, I am giving this paper, stating that you belong to me, David Ferguson, of this place and of the Cherokee Nation West. That way no man may seize and claim you as his. You too are God's children. May He watch over you one and all."

The floor-to-ceiling windows were shuttered now and the house was beginning to need painting. Only beginning, for it was always painted every fifth year and was now overdue just one. The coat of white that it would have been given last summer would have been the tenth.

But for the kitchen, the downstairs had been stripped, the furnishings, accumulated over those fifty years, sold for a hundredth part of their worth, hauled away by the wagonload. Gone from the hallway were the marble-topped pier table with the ormolu mounts and the tall, ornately framed pier glass that hung above it. The caned Recamier settee, the many-branched sconce, the life-size Venetian blackamoor in his ruff collar and doublet: gone. The floorboards were bare where the long Turkey-red runner had stretched.

In the library the books remained in their places on the shelves. Of these Grandfather was determined to take with them as many as possible, for there would be none where they were going. But the deep armchairs, the leather-topped tables, the carved mahogany sofas, the paintings, the patterned carpet, so soft underfoot: all gone.

A coat of dust upon the floor where once had lain an Aubusson, where once had sat sideboards with rosewood veneers figured like flames, marble-topped gueridons upheld by kneed legs with paws, capped with rams' heads, a many-paned cabinet—Noquisi's particular joy—containing the collection of

colorful porcelain figurines: harlequins, dwarfs, mythological
and biblical characters, old-world shepherds and shepherd-
esses, an orchestra of musical monkeys, the mantelpiece garni-
ture of delftware vases, the bronze clock with its statue of
General Washington—a coat of dust with nothing but bare
floorboards to lie upon was the only thing furnishing the drawing room now. Before long all would be gone: house and land,
barns, sheds, cabins—the domain of its new owner, the white
man holding the winning ticket in the Georgia State lottery for
this piece of property of the dispossessed and deported Cherokees.

August 9, 1807. It was with this date in the collective
diary of The People that Agiduda located the origin of the
current and ongoing state of affairs that began the story still
unfolding, its final chapter still remaining to be written.

It was not for having stomped his pregnant wife to death
that on this day Doublehead, petty chieftain of the Chi-
camauga towns, was brought to justice. Nor was it for having
massacred the thirteen women and children of a family of
white settlers named Cavett. That first act was a private, family affair, to be settled between the chief and his late wife's
menfolks; the second was, or had become so through the influence of white men's notions, an excess to be frowned upon—
what Doublehead had done to wind up that day with a tomahawk buried in his skull so solidly that, to get it out, his killer
had to set foot on his brow and tug with both hands, was to
commit what to the Cherokees was the capital crime. Their
only crime at the time, for this was the year before they had
formed a government and decreed a uniform code of law.

The day before, August 8, all day long Doublehead's appointed executioners had waited for him in McIntosh's, the
tavern in Hiwassee Town on Hiwassee River. His canoe was

beached there. He himself was off at a ball game and there he had been detained. After the game was decided, liquor had flowed, and, full of it, a brave named Bone-polisher had picked a quarrel with Doublehead. Fueled by firewater, words grew heated and Bone-polisher was provoked into calling Double-head to his face what everybody was calling him behind his back, a traitor. Doublehead drew his pistol and shot the man on the spot. He died, but not from the gunshot wound, and not before chopping off with his tomahawk one of Doublehead's thumbs. With his good hand, using his pistol as a club, Dou-blehead beat the man's brains out.

At McIntosh's tavern in Hiwassee Town still waiting for him when Doublehead came in that evening were The Ridge— since become Major Ridge, one of the nation's two principal men and the leader of one of the two factions into which it was now riven—and his deputies, an Indian named Saunders and another named Rogers, the latter of whom, years later and in another country, would figure again in this tale of destinies entwined. At point-blank range The Ridge shot Doublehead full in the face and left him for dead on the tavern floor. How-ever, with a severed thumb, a shattered jaw and a bullet lodged in his neck, Doublehead managed to take refuge in a barn loft. There at dawn on the following day, August 9, The Ridge and his posse, now including vengeful relatives of the late Bone-polisher, tracked him down. Battered as he was, he was still full of fight and he went at his assailants with pistol and dirk and then with bare knuckles. After being shot again, this time through the hips, he was tomahawked. For good measure, his head was then pounded to a pulp with a spade. So died Dou-blehead, and so would die any and all Cherokees guilty of his crime, selling tribal land without tribal consent.

Murder being the wanton killing of a human being, the death of Doublehead would have gone no more noticed by the white authorities than that of any other head of game had it not been that he was their kind of Indian, one who could be bribed into selling tribal land, and so The Ridge might have gotten into trouble over the affair. This was prevented by the tribe's declaring itself a sovereign nation with powers to treat on a footing of equality with other governments, and making Doublehead's punishment the law of the land, that particular statute framed by The Ridge himself. Georgia was enraged. Not for the hapless Doublehead, but at the uppityness of a band of savages in declaring themselves a nation within the boundaries of the state.

The boy and his grandfather would find breakfast waiting for them. His grandmother kept out of sight. After eating the boy went to bed. He was tired and his eyes smarted, yet for a long time he lay awake, going over in his mind the stories of the night. He felt himself to have been present at each scene, to have been a participant in each event. As much as the features of his face, these stories were a part of him, his birthright. As with the clothes handed down in families, he was now of a size to fill them out. When he was wakened for their next session, the sun had set and twilight was coming on.

Inside the *asi* the boy fanned the embers of last night's fire with a turkey wing and fed it wood. They stripped. Being a man now taught him a new awareness of his body, and seeing his grandfather's an intimation of its destiny. He would remember throughout all the many years until it came to pass wondering whether his would one day be so wrinkled. That would be in far-off Texas, where he would scratch his grandson and bathe with him in the waters of that red river that he had once seen redder with blood.

1814. If only! *Ai!* If only they had done this! *Ai!* If only they hadn't done that! If only! Agiduda was sick of hearing it. It made his ears want to throw up. "If only" was not just a lament too late, it was an admission of foolishness, of lack of foresight—even of hindsight! If only they had realized that in fomenting the Indians' petty and pointless intertribal wars the whites were exploiting them for their own gain, leaving it to them to exterminate themselves. If only they had realized they *were* Indians, all of them. Not Cherokees and Creeks and Chickasaws and Choctaws and Seminoles but *Indians*—brothers not just beneath but on the skin. In numbers was strength. What we needed, we Cherokees, each and every one of us, was cousins, able-bodied cousins—cousins by the dozens. But without seed grain does not grow. *Ai!* If only our grandparents had bred more!

If only in that year of 1814, on that day at Horseshoe Bend, Junuluska, the Cherokee chief, had seized his chance to kill that viper Andrew Jackson instead of saving the day for him! There was an act to cause the bitterest of regrets. To have killed men whom he mistakenly thought to be his enemies in the service and for the glory of one whom he mistakenly thought to be his friend. More than Jackson's day, Junuluska saved his life by tomahawking the Creek poised to kill him. If he had known that Jackson would one day drive the Cherokees from their homes, he would have killed him himself there that day on the Horseshoe, said Junuluska.

There at Horseshoe Bend, allied with the Americans against Britain's allies, the Creeks, there where none of them had any business being, were some seven hundred Cherokee warriors, including the one who would distinguish himself the most, the one without a drop of the blood in his veins but no less, maybe more, of a Cherokee for all that, whose career as a man of destiny, for all its later ups and downs, was to have its dazzling debut in the bravery and bloodshed of that day: *Kalunah:* The Raven, sometimes *Ootsetee Ardeetahskee:* The Big Drunk—best known as Sam Houston. Fighting alongside him that day, his future father-in-law. Not the first one, nor yet the third one, but the intervening one, the red one: John

Rogers, one of The Ridge's deputies in the execution of the traitor Doublehead.

Then newly commissioned in the United States Army (he would thereafter take his service rank as his given name) Major Ridge was there that day. Who among the fighting Cherokees was not there? John Lowrey, Gideon Morgan, George Fields, John Drew, George Guest (when not known as Sequoyah), Richard Brown, George Hicks—Cherokees to a man, every mother's son of them, their peculiar names notwithstanding, and all were on the battle roll. Even the least likely of the lot was there, little Johnny Ross. Least likely of *armed* warriors, that was to say—though more of a fighter than the rest all put together. Passive resistance would be this one man's brainchild, and by his genius at waging it he would almost succeed (he still had not given up the fight, even this late in the day when all seemed lost) in defeating an enemy of overwhelming might and unscrupulous ruthlessness, meanwhile restraining by his persuasiveness (though obliged to speak to them through an interpreter, so little of the red red blood did he have in him) one of the most warlike people ever known and one now provoked beyond human endurance.

The battle plan that day was for a slaughter. For the taking of prisoners provision was not made. The thousand defenders were besieged in their compound. Flight could be in one direction only, by water, and there on the bluff overlooking the river sharpshooters lay in wait to pick them off. Though the odds against them were two to one, the Creeks in their stockade held out all afternoon against cannon and musket fire, and might have held out longer but for the example set by Sam Houston, who, though at that hour severely wounded by an arrow in his thigh, led the charge of his Cherokees to the walls and over them, where, in the mopping-up, he was shot twice in the right arm. He was twenty-one by less than a month.

Out of that thousand, one hundred-odd was the outside

number of those reckoned to have escaped with their lives. To the last man, the rest, asking for none, knowing that none would be accorded them, were accorded no quarter.

By the next morning's light a detail was sent out to count the dead. The sight they saw should have assured them that they need have no fear of being charged with inflating the size of their victory. However, to forestall any innuendo that a single one of their fallen foes had been counted more times than one, the precaution was taken of cutting off its nose as each body was counted. Five hundred and fifty noses was the tally. Meanwhile, until the process of decomposition bloated them and floated them to the surface, the number of those potshot in the river as they tried to swim to safety could not so precisely be stated. Conservative in this as they had been conscientious in their count of those on the ground, they estimated it at just around 350. The Indians, as was their wont, scalped the dead bodies; the whites, as was theirs, flayed them in strips for leather to make themselves souvenir belts and bridle reins of Creekskin.

It was his victory at Horseshoe Bend that first brought Jackson to national attention, that set him on the road that would lead to the White House, to the Cherokees' woe. That it was also then and there that their best friend, Sam Houston, first came to Jackson's favorable notice, leading to his lasting patronage, would avail them nothing. On the question of Indian removal the two men did not differ, they agreed, albeit for opposite reasons, Jackson because he wanted to get rid of them, Houston because he wanted them.

The true casualty figure at Horseshoe Bend was forty thousand: men, women and children, the entire Creek and Cherokee nations, might-have-been allies against their common enemy. If there be such a thing as justice in this world, then of what was about to befall them The People had brought much upon themselves.

But first, from out of a chronicle of ever-deepening darkness, a blaze of brilliance. 1821. Already inclined that way by their tribal bond, the Cherokees were unified into a single soul by the public demonstration (out of the mouths of babes, this one Sequoyah's six-year-old daughter) of his alphabet. They were like Adam first opening his eyes upon the newly created world, finding his tongue and giving names to all that it contained.

At a stroke, Cherokee utterances, theretofore as perishable as the breath they were borne upon, were thenceforth and forever fixed, transmissible, infinitely reproducible, and the living and the dead and the yet unborn could communicate with one another at global distances and across the unopposable onrush of time.

The Choctaws, the Chickasaws and the Creeks had sold out, the Seminoles had fought in the field, or rather in the everglades, the Cherokees had fought to save themselves in the white man's courts and to transform themselves in his schoolhouses. Told that their way of life was not good, they had changed it. Led by those of their own with a foot in each of the two worlds, the mixed-bloods like the Rosses, the Fergusons, they evolved overnight in their bid for acceptance. This was just what those who wanted their land did not want. In the eyes of the outside world it refuted the charge that they were unregenerate savages, subhuman, varmints—even, or perhaps especially, those the most white—as though the ermine were to be told, "You are a weasel. That black tip of your tail gives you away."

Education was nothing new for well-to-do mixed-blood families like the Fergusons. To prepare him for the College of

William and Mary, Agiduda's early schooling had been acquired at an academy in Philadelphia. Noquisi's father, Abel, had been taught at home by a succession of live-in tutors. But the mission schools were open to all, to the children of the most backward, the poorest, the darkest-skinned. Universal education would break down class barriers and be another tribal bond.

Then came the summer day when the village was roused from its early afternoon torpor by the roll of a snare drum and the shrilling of a fife. What people saw from their doorways was a squad of the Georgia Guard marching down the main street. There were five of them, one, an officer, on horseback, one driving a wagon, and three—the musicians—on foot. The measure they marched to befitted a firing squad. It was their second visit. The outcome of the first, some months ago, was widely known, and this one had been expected in consequence ever since. Though they went in dread and suspense, every inhabitant of the village, bewitched as the children of Hamelin, turned out to follow them up the street to the parsonage.

The minister had heard them coming and stood waiting outside his garden gate. His wife looked on from the front porch. The squad halted ostentatiously, the music stopped, the officer dismounted.

"Henry Wentworth?" he demanded.

"Your servant, sir," said the minister.

"By the authority invested in me I arrest you, Henry Wentworth, for the high crime of treason against the sovereign state of Georgia."

What the minister had done was refuse to swear his oath of allegiance to the newly amended constitution of Georgia. The amendments provided:

That the Cherokees' tribal government be abolished.

That the Cherokees be forbidden to assemble for any purpose, including religious.

That any Cherokee who advised another not to emigrate to the west be imprisoned.

That all contracts between Cherokees and whites be nullified unless they had been witnessed by two certifed whites.

That Cherokees be forbidden to testify in court against whites.

That Cherokees be forbidden to dig for the gold recently discovered on their land.

"Sir," said the minister, "I am a citizen of the Commonwealth of Massachusetts, and as such—"

A blow to the head from the officer's fist knocked the minister to the ground. He fell face-forward, landing on his hands and knees. His wife screamed and the crowd of onlookers emitted in chorus a loud *"Ai!"*

"Call yourself a white man?" the officer snarled. "You're a disgrace to the race!"

He gave a nod to the driver of the wagon (it was evident that this had been rehearsed with an audience in mind), who leapt down from his seat, whip in hand, and commenced lashing the minister across the back. The blows were heavy, but though the first one wrung from him a deep-drawn groan, thereafter he held himself to a whimper. The crowd wailed and mothers clutched their children to them.

When the beating was concluded the officer flattened the minister with a foot planted in the small of his back. The driver manacled his hands, then snapped a trace chain around his neck. He was ordered to his feet. He shivered and his jaw trembled out of control. The tears from his tight-shut eyes made it appear as though they were being squeezed dry.

The chain was fastened to the tailgate of the wagon. The officer remounted. The musicians climbed into the wagon bed and the driver resumed his seat. He whipped up the team. To get to the nearest jail they had a hundred miles to go.

Thus ended Amos Ferguson's formal education.

In the same year, 1828, when the United States elected its seventh President, the Cherokee Nation elected its first one, John Ross. His determination was to keep his people where they had always been. He was Jackson's equal in tenacity of purpose, his superior in wiliness, his inferior only in the size of his following.

Though surrounded by their white enemies, The People were not without white friends. The trouble was that their friends were distant and dispersed while their enemies were united and near at hand. Those bent upon their dispossession had power, but those northern clergymen, philosophers, editors and statesmen, the conscience of the country, whose admiration for their advancement and whose sympathy for their plight the Cherokees had won, had powers of persuasion. John Ross's hopes were based upon an appeal to the better nature of the American people as a whole—when that failed, upon an appeal to their courts and their self-proclaimed guarantee of equal justice for all free men.

But you can hire the best lawyers in the land, fight your case all the way up to the Supreme Court, win, and have it decreed that you are, as claimed, indeed a sovereign nation, within the bounds of the state of Georgia yet beyond its laws, then still lose your case when the President, sworn and empowered to uphold the rulings of the Court, declares, "Chief Justice John Marshall has rendered his decision. Now let him enforce it."

His week in the *asi* marked Noquisi's coming to manhood, but his childhood had really ended a year earlier and not here at home but in Tennessee. His ended along with that of every Cherokee child out of its infancy. Herod himself had not more sweepingly bereft a people of its children than had Andrew Jackson, "Old Hickory."

It was at the last full assembly of the nation, or rather, the last unenforced one. The Ferguson family went provisioned for six days on the road and two days on the campsite, with a tarpaulin for a tent and with bedding for all, traveling in a wagon drawn by a span of white mules, theirs but one in the caravan on the road, for the call had gone up every mountainside and down every glen in Cherokee Georgia, Alabama, the Carolinas and Tennessee—throughout the twenty million acres left to them, and which they were now being pressured to leave.

Newcomers joined the caravan at every crossroads. Some leading livestock meant to be slaughtered and cooked on the campsite, they came in farm wagons, in buggies and shays, in oxcarts, in closed carriages driven by slaves, on horseback and on foot, their faces powdered by the dust of the road. Converging from all points toward their destination, they were awed by their numbers, uplifted by their singleness of purpose. Like the smoke signals of old, like the relays of the tom-toms, the call had gone out, carried by riders and runners, and the Cherokees had issued from their lairs in all the variety they presented at this time of transition and evolution: varieties in color, in features, in dress, in deportment. Their oneness of mind contrasted with their diversity of appearance. Among them were people who might have been mistaken for the very oppressors whom they were convening to resist: whole clans of blue-eyed blonds, fair-skinned, freckled, who called themselves Cherokees and who would have fought anybody who called them otherwise, unpropitious as these times were to be one. Among others, within one family, was a gamut of shadings as broad as in one of those specimen apple trees onto the trunk of which have been grafted several varieties of the fruit. Then, down from the tall mountaintops and up from the far-off coves, came those colored and featured like the stones of their native streams: the root stock, the undiluted essence of the tribe. With pigtails and without; bearded and beardless; turbaned, plumed and hatted; shoed, booted and moccasined; in the homespuns and the calicoes of their white counterparts and also in buckskins and blankets; gaudy and drab—Cherokees all. Men in claw-hammer coats of black broadcloth, gold chains with watch fobs spanning their flowered silk vests, looking like aldermen, conversed with men in buckskin leggings gartered and tasseled above the calves, in bright, embroidered and beaded tunics and sporting necklaces of bones alternating with the skulls of songbirds. Nor was it always the lighter-skinned of the two whose measurements were kept on file by the Baltimore gentlemen's tailor. As outlandish a sight to Noquisi as it would have been to a boy of that seaboard city was the occasional exotic with an ornament in the septum of his nose and pendants in his ears that stretched the lobes almost to his shoulders. Of these specimens the most striking was one bandoliered, breast-plated, shaven-headed and turbaned, long-lobed and ox-ringed, and yet the name of this atavism, this throwback, was George Lowrey, and he was nothing less than the nation's Vice President, and a very able statesman he was, highly respected in Washington. The contrast between him and his chief, sandy-haired, frock-coated, diminutive John Ross, the perfect picture of a small-town banker, presented the two extremes of present-day Cherokee-hood. Of the two, it was Ross who was the more adamantly Indian, throughout his every cell and down to his very marrow.

All night long, undeterred by the rain that had begun and now had turned the roads into sluices, they kept coming. Places were found for them by firesides and food shared with them, and all who could be were crowded to sleep inside the tents and the covered wagons; even so, many spent the night in the open, including John Ross, who refused all offers of shelter. When day broke the following morning there stood revealed the largest gathering of Cherokees ever assembled. Five thousand strong they were. Or was it five thousand weak?

Beneath the vast open-sided shed and outside among the dripping trees people clustered for low-toned conversations, the women along with the men, for they were not excluded from tribal deliberations as were the women of other tribes; on the contrary, their opinions and advice were sought.

The children, too, were there: little pitchers, big ears. They had been sent off to find others to play with but they soon drifted back to their bases. A word, one essential to their striking up acquaintance and getting on with one another, was now missing from their vocabulary, whether they spoke English or Cherokee, or both. It was the word most often on children's lips. The word was "let's." It was with this word that play was begun, projects proposed, it was the "open sesame" to the world of make-believe; now none but the youngest of Cherokee children had any heart for play, and while they might all long to escape into make-believe, the real world was too much with them. They had had to assume worries that fitted them as did their parents' clothes when they put them on for fun. They had been hearing of these worries since their earliest years. Indeed, they were often the first to hear of them, for in many families the child had to interpret the latest news for parents who spoke no English. Thus when the meeting was gaveled to order, these miniature members of the tribe stood to listen along with their elders, and just as gravely.

On the speakers' platform, on one side of the Commissioner of Indian Affairs, sat Major Ridge, looking like an elderly lion with his grizzled mane and his fixed, fierce frown, and on the other side sat little Johnny Ross, *Tsan Usdi,* also known affectionately by his childhood pet name, *Guwisguwi:* Swan Song, with that equally fixed faint smile of his. A figure of towering authority, every inch of him, the one looked; few inches of anything much at all, the other. Lowrey too was

there, as were Ridge's son John and his nephew Elias Boudinot.

The business of this gathering was to hear the government's latest—and last, sternly warned the Commissioner—
offer to them. It was four and a half million dollars—up from
three and a half, owing to the good offices of the Ridges. This
for twenty million acres of prime farm and forest land, spread
over five states, and for their houses and improvements standing thereon.

Not only was this a good offer, they themselves knew—
who better than they?—what their alternative to accepting it
was. Thereupon the Commissioner went into a recitation of
their woes. Squatters had overrun them, had settled on their
lands, stolen their crops, their herds, their livestock. Their
fences had been torn down, their barns and houses broken
into, burglarized. Traders had corrupted them with whiskey,
gamblers had cheated them. They had been falsely arrested.
They had been bullied, beaten, hunted like wild animals, mur-
dered in cold blood. The list was long indeed of the Cherokees'
tribulations which the government, represented by the Commissioner, was sworn to protect them against.

Major Ridge's speech was, in substance, an echo of the
Commissioner's, though it seemed the other way around, for
Ridge was original in style, he was eloquent. He spoke in
Cherokee, his only tongue. He was a master of it, the nation's
greatest orator, perhaps its greatest ever, and to them, as to all
Indians, oratory was an intoxicant. They nodded now, they
swayed, they rocked, they grunted. But when he concluded by
saying that their only hope was to leave their homeland and go
beyond the Father of Waters, they stood still and silent.

Ross's Cherokee was rudimentary. As only a portion of
his people understood English, for many of them their leader
spoke to them always through an interpreter. However, nothing much was lost in translation, for it had no style to begin
with. And anyway, in what Guwisguwi had to say on the sub-

ject of their removal there was never more variation than in
the song of the swan.

"Very well, then," said the Commissioner when Ross sat
down, "without further ado, all those in favor of accepting this
treaty, signify by saying aye."

Not a voice was heard—not even a Ridge's. While thousands of pairs of eyes, like so many double-barreled shotguns,
watched, they exchanged warning glances one with another.
The two hundred-odd whom they had induced to go west were
already out there. Left to uphold their point of view in the old
country were they themselves and hardly anybody else. The
framer and the one enforcer of the law against the sale of tribal
land knew what would have happened to anybody who piped a
note to puncture that thunderous silence, or even so much as
cleared his throat to do so.

Jackson's man on the spot was one Schermerhorn—John
F., formerly a Presbyterian preacher, now pursuing the more
lucrative trade of Commissioner of Indian Affairs, known to
the Cherokees as *Skaynooyanah,* a nickname always good for a
snicker: the Devil's Horn. He it was who had deceived the
Seminoles into signing a document which, when it was explained to them that with it they had thereby conveyed to the
United States their native Florida, agreeing to vacate it and
emigrate to the west, had sparked the lively little war now
waging down there, with the palefaces getting the bloody hell
beat out of them in those malarial mangrove swamps where
the Indians rose up, struck, then sank from sight like their
brothers the alligators. As regarded Cherokees, there was
scarcely a one of any standing in the tribe whom Skaynooyanah had not attempted to bribe. Upon the failure of his
mission in Tennessee he ordered the nation, every living head
of them, to convene again, this time in New Echota, Georgia,
theretofore the place of all places forbidden to them to assemble in because it was nothing short of their shrine, the former
capital of their short-lived, now outlawed, government, for rat-

ification of the treaty. One man, one vote; and to make sure
they exercised their democratic right and responsibility, he
ruled that all who failed to appear be counted as having voted
in favor. Thus, adding the two hundred-odd who showed up
on the appointed day to the eighteen thousand who stayed
away, the Cherokees, whose feeling for their homeland
equalled that of the Jews for theirs, elected unanimously to
relinquish it and be herded en masse to the place known to
them always as the Land of the Setting Sun, Land of Darkness, Land of Death.

The time: late at night. The scene: the home of Elias
Boudinot, Ridge's nephew, in the former Cherokee capital,
New Echota. Guests are expected, nineteen of them, they will
arrive momentarily, yet the house is in darkness except for the
parlor, and this is lighted by only a single candle and the
flickering of the fire in the fireplace. Gatherings of more than
two Cherokees are outlawed in Georgia; however, that is not
the reason for the secrecy of this one—rather the opposite.
This one is so hugger-mugger because it has the blessing of the
state authorities. For those stealing their way here the night
holds dangers far more to be feared than the Georgia Guard.
These men will arrive on foot, singly, glad to get indoors, and
yet they will not welcome one another's company, for, with
one exception among them, each must suspect the other's motive in being here, and fear that his own is similarly suspected.
They will one and all be anxious to get the business over with
that they are here to do, and disband and again go off each on
his separate way into the night, grateful for the cover of darkness.

It was said to be Ridge's son John who first changed
course. He was now as fanatically in favor of removal as he
had formerly been opposed to it. His present attitude was per-

haps most clearly evidenced in the name given to his newborn son: Andrew Jackson Ridge. No fear did the west hold for him. He would have been out there ere now were it not that he was determined that everybody else go along with him. To see that they did so was what he, the first of the guests to arrive, was here at his cousin's house this December night to do.

At least one among those participating would talk about the gathering afterwards, and for publication. As reported in an area newspaper, after reading the treaty aloud while the Indians sat in the shadows smoking their pipes, the Reverend Schermerhorn laid it on the candlelit table. For some time longer the Indians smoked on. None was eager to be the first signer. Presently, one named John Gunter rose and went over to the table. (It was mere coincidence that the measure used by land surveyors was known as Gunter's chain.) Taking up the pen, Gunter dipped it in the ink, saying, "I am not afraid. I will sell the whole country."

And so he did, and so did they all. Twenty men, twenty puppets, appointed to represent their nation by the government they were treating with, but unaccredited by their own people, sold the land that had been theirs since before their records of themselves began, the resting place of their ancestors, the land of a people to whom every tree, every rock, every least animal, every insect had a soul and was a fellow creature, land so alive, so sacred, they went down on their knees and begged its forgiveness before cutting a furrow in it.

As to which of them had talked, a good guess would be Andrew Ross. He would have been unashamed of his part in the transaction. Sad, fearful of the consequences, but unashamed. He was the one who would have had no misgivings about having done his selfless, inescapable, if unpleasant, duty. He was the one among them who would have harbored no suspicions of the purity of the others' motives, for he judged them by his own. To the diehards, the holdouts—and that included nearly the entire Cherokee nation—what they were doing would be an unforgivable betrayal. As John's brother, Andrew Ross would be the hardest of all to forgive. His very own blood brother! On no other ground but that of a principled difference of view could he ever again have looked John in the face—or for that matter, any other man, red or white. He would forevermore be known by the company he had kept; imperishable parchment he was about to put his name to, the name of his family, of his ancestors and his offspring. He dared not believe but what the rest were as personally disinterested as he was in the transaction.

Let his not be the last name to be affixed, looking as though he had hesitated, had feared, had scrupled to put it there. In fact, it headed the list, for he wrote it in the space Gunter had left blank above his. He was a brave man to do what he was doing, but he had needed a reckless fool to embolden him. The others all needed Andrew Ross. That name, so little to be expected, so out of place in that company, was the imprimatur which that document had to have on it were it to be anything more than a scrap of sheepskin.

It was further reported, though not in print yet just as widely circulated, that as his "X-His Mark" dried on the page, Major Ridge was overheard to say, "I have signed my death warrant."

A petition to Washington was circulated to protest that the Treaty of New Echota signed by the Ridge party did not represent the will of the people. The petition contained fourteen thousand signatures. It was scoffed at by some because it was shown to include the signatures of dead people and of babes in arms. But what was wrong with that? The spirits of the dead lived on, and they grieved at the prospect of separation from their loved ones. As for the babes, were they not affected, were they not to be represented, were they to have no say just because they could not yet write? They would have signed if they could. As they could not, it was their parents' bounden duty to sign for them. The petition was ignored. Back from Washington came the order to proceed with the provisions of the treaty and prepare for the removal of the Cherokees.

Now it was the eighth day and outside the *asi* the sun was rising. To the best of his ability, the old man's tale was told. Awaiting Noquisi was the world he had detailed. Things had come to this—remarkable fulfillment of Indian prophecy!: their homeland had been sold out from under them by none other than Major Ridge, the man who wrote the law against doing what he had done and enforced it the one time ever with his own bloody hand, and now the Cherokees must prepare themselves to be uprooted and moved west to the land of the setting sun, the land of darkness, leaving behind them the bones of their ancestors, there to settle in deep discord. Even into the Fergusons' own family, as into the nation's first family, the Rosses, the division extended. It all but paralyzed his old tongue to say it, but his own son, his Abel, Noquisi's father, was of that party, Ridge's party.

Actually father and son were of one mind on the matter, or rather both were of the same divided mind, and when they argued it was not with each other but each with himself. This heated their exchanges, for no opinion is more exasperating to a person than one of his own which he finds himself unable to defend. Add to this the frustrated longing to be convincingly refuted in the opinion one is espousing and the self-dissatisfaction is compounded. The hearts of both men were with Ross, the minds of both with Ridge.

Recently the final blow had fallen, the ultimate irony: the earth itself, that Cherokee earth so precious to them that despite the missionaries' teaching it still spoke to them through every rock, every brook, every leaf of every tree a tongue, had betrayed them. Precious indeed! Buried in its bowels, unknown

to them, and only now, at the worst possible time, brought to
light, the element that the white man coveted most, that drove
him raving, murderously mad, that brought out the very devil
in him: gold. The misery foretold of old, they, man and boy,
had lived to see and to feel.

Magnified by his spectacles, the tears brimming, the old
man's eyes glistened in the light of the dying fire, overflowed to
mingle with the sweat of his face.

"Do not despair, Agiduda," said the boy. "All is not lost.
As long as we have Tsan Usdi there is still hope."

"He is the hope of us all," said the old man. And then:
"But as for me, Sgilisi, you are my hope."

"Oh, Agiduda!" the boy cried aloud, and pressed his
sweaty body against his grandfather's. To himself he said, "*Ai,
me! Then I fear all is lost.*"

Having greeted the sun and gone to water, the boy—now
the man—was served the traditional meal of partridge and
cornmeal mush. As a warrior he would have need of the
stealth of the partridge, its natural camouflage, its ability to lie
so closely concealed that no hunter suspected its presence—
then that burst from cover with drumming wings that stopped
his heart with fright.

Noquisi—Usgasedi—loped his pony home that afternoon
with the bow and the quiver of arrows bouncing painfully,
pridefully against his grated back. Meant from the start for
him, they were his grandfather's gift to mark the occasion of
his becoming a man. It took all his strength to brace and string
the bow; to draw it to the full length of an arrow was beyond
him. To achieve that now would be his aim and the measure of
his manhood. He must grow big and powerful, and the way
things were going he must do it in a hurry. An allotted life
span later and a world to the west, he would still remember

and would relate to his grandson, who in his turn would relate it to his son, how all the way home voices had called to him, saying,

Noquisi, be nimble!
Noquisi, be quick!
Noquisi, jump over the candlestick!

Part Three

"Ai! So now the handwriting is not just on the wall—it is on the very trees," said Abel Ferguson. "Tell me, Father, after this are you still determined to hold out here?"

For some time following Amos's report he had said nothing, restrained by the presence of their guests. But his exasperation would out. His tone was such as almost to make one think he relished this confirmation of his worst fears, his direst predictions.

"We will discuss it tomorrow," said his father.

"Tomorrow!" said Abel scornfully. "Here there is no tomorrow for the likes of us." Then he was ashamed of having shown to strangers disrespect for a parent. "As you say, Father."

Unknown men were in their woods. Georgians. Three of them. Two of the three carried a long link chain between them and of those two one carried a paint bucket. One stood still while the other one, him with the paint bucket, paced off the length of the chain. Exactly twenty-two yard-long paces it was, Amos had observed. Where the chain fetched him up, this man slashed the nearest tree with the hatchet hung in his belt and on this raw slash he painted a number. The third man stood guard with a double-barreled shotgun. A fine guard! Never for a moment did he suspect that they were being followed and watched, and by somebody near enough—phew!—to smell them.

This ill-timed allusion to the offensive body odor of whites reddened the faces of all the family with embarrassment, and Amos could have bitten his tongue. Fortunately, the Reverend and Mrs. Mackenzie seemed to think it was meant to apply to the men in the woods personally and took no offense themselves.

For this party in commemoration of the baptism, the Mackenzies had ridden with the Fergusons out to the farm. Dressed white for the day, Amos rode his pony. He had gotten to the farm ahead of those in the buggy. He was in the barn lot feeding and watering the pony when he heard the sound of the hatchet in the woods and went to scout it out. He left his shoes behind. It turned out that he had little need for his stealth. *Yvwunegas* all had poor ears, no eyes in their heads at all. To the momentary sense of superiority one always feels over anybody whom one is observing unsuspected, Noquisi (he was Noquisi now, despite his clothes) added his own abiding sense of superiority: that of the Indian for white men. This superiority turned to contempt when the objects of it proceeded to do what these did.

The man holding the hind end of the chain called, "John?"

Both of the other two answered. However, before he could do so, the one with the paint bucket was obliged to empty his mouth of tobacco juice. Noquisi could hardly believe his eyes.

"John *Yoder*?"

Here the man was, in enemy territory, and yet, ignorant, incautious fool that he was, the one with the paint bucket answered to his name!

Noquisi let the party move on, then emerged from hiding. Whether or not he was actually going to do what it had now been put in his power to do would be decided later, but here

was an opportunity not to be passed up, and so, to impress his
enemy's name upon his mind, he repeated it to himself as he
stirred the end of a stick in the gob of spit on the ground. He
wrapped the paste in a leaf.

"Sir," said the Reverend Mackenzie to Grandfather when
Amos reported the presence of the men in the woods, "if this is
some matter requiring your immediate attention—"

"No, sir, it is not. I know what it means, but while I don't
like it, there is nothing I can do about it."

It was that "while I don't like it" that sealed the fate of
John Yoder.

To make his Scottish guests feel more at home, Grandfather had greeted them dressed in his kilt and sporran. He
looked like the chief of his highland clan, or rather, he would
have had he not also worn a fringed and embroidered buckskin
shirt, a red-and-white polka-dot turban and his best beaded
moccasins. He met them on the verandah, where he served
them home-brewed beer in stoneware bottles fresh from the
springhouse and frosted with sweat on this hot day, along with
cracklings of pork rind and salted crawfish tails. His own man
now, Amos drank along with the rest.

Now the meal had been served and grace said over it. To
eat it, all were seated on the dining-room floor. Their plates
had been filled out in the kitchen, but instead of seating them
at the table there Grandfather dispensed cutlery to them and
led the way down the hall. The family, bringing up the rear,
exchanged wondering and worried looks. At the dining-room
door Grandfather stood aside and ushered in his guests. They
were too polite to exhibit any hesitation. Perhaps they supposed that they were meant to pass through this empty room
en route to another. There where once on the great mahogany
table silver had gleamed, crystal sparkled, china glowed, where
family portraits looked down from the dark, unfaded squares
on the papered walls, Grandfather spread a handkerchief on
the bare floor, seated himself beside it and invited Mrs. Mac-

kenzie to take her place upon it. The rest of the Fergusons straight-facedly followed his example, for the will, the every whim of the head of their house was law.

It was pride, that flinty, unyielding Cherokee pride. Never admit defeat, not even in defeat. Especially not then.

When he had finished his meal Amos asked to be excused. He could never be kept indoors for long when he was out at the farm and the weather was fair. He said he was going fishing.

And he did dig worms in the barn lot. He set off with a cane pole. But while he had a use for the worms, the pole was just to throw anyone off his scent. What he was about to do a boy of his clan, the Wolf, two years older than he, said to have witch doctors for relatives, had offered as a great favor to teach him. To find a safe place to talk, deep in the woods, they had walked for miles; even so, they had spoken in whispers. For this was powerful medicine. Not until they were alone would the boy even pronounce its name: *Ditalatliti*.

He had memorized the spell, had collected the requisite ingredients and made up a kit, had searched and found a suitable place, just in case the need to do it should ever arise. The way things were going these days, with enemies on every hand, you never knew—better be prepared for the worst. This kit of his, in its deerskin drawstring pouch, he kept hidden in the barn loft. There he had gone from the house to fetch it, taking care not to be seen and to do all his thinking in Cherokee. Whenever he was about to do something of which God would disapprove, he thought in Cherokee, the language from the time before the coming of God. In the loft he took the red sash from the pouch and wrapped it around his waist, for no important enterprise could hope to succeed unless from the outset one wore something red.

Thinking that he would never have dared do what he was doing had Agiduda not scratched and toughened him and made him *usgasedi,* he left the fishing pole at the *asi,* then went along the riverbank and through the woods to the tree that had been struck by lightning. There he took from his pouch the tube made from a joint of *kanesala,* the poisonous wild parsnip. Into this tube he put first the paste made of dirt and the man's spit, then a paste made from seven earthworms which he ground on a stone, then a splinter from this same lightning-blasted tree. At the base of the tree he dug a hole. Into the hole he put the one black pebble and the seven yellow ones along with the tube and covered everything with the square of black cloth. Then he filled the hole.

He recited the spell. He was fearful of unleashing the powers he was invoking, more than a little fearful of himself. Knowing that what he was practicing was denounced by missionaries as black magic, he spoke in the language of the vengeful, merciless old red gods to whom he was appealing and for which the jealous and watchful white God, whose wrath he knew to fear, needed an interpreter. However, in relating the incident to his grandson, in Texas, all those many years later, having in the meantime tested the wrath, as well as the mercy, of that great God and found him impotent in the one and arbitrary, if not racially prejudiced, in the other, he had no hesitation about translating it into His tongue.

What he said was, "Hear me! I am going to trample on your soul. I know you. You are of the clan of Yoder. Your name is John. I have buried your spit. Your soul I have buried. You are covered with the black shroud. You are on the path that leads to the land of darkness. Your soul will yellow and then will blacken. It will be poisoned. The worms will devour it. It will turn blue and fade away, nevermore to be seen. I have spoken."

He concluded the ceremony by building a fire on the spot, watching it burn out, and scattering the ashes.

Pleased with his day's work, Noquisi, before becoming Amos again, cut a gourd from the vine trailing the picket fence on his way back to the house. It was a good omen. In time the gourd would dry and the seeds inside it would rattle. Just so, but much sooner, would the soul of his enemy wither within him. The irreversible process had already begun. Even now the spell was doing its deadly work. It could not be stopped, for nobody knew about it. Had he known what he was doing by both spitting and revealing his name, John Yoder might have hired his own medicine man to protect him against the peril he was in, but then, if he had known he would never have done it in the first place—ignorant *yvwunega!* His ailment was one that no white doctor, not even the chief of King's College in New York, where Noquisi's father had trained, could diagnose and cure. A week from today that careless fool John Yoder would be dead. Then at least there would be one less surveyor to parcel Cherokee land for the Georgia State lottery.

The old Amos Smith, in recollecting for his grandson, Amos III, his long-lost Cherokee childhood, spoke of his good fortune in having had a doctor for a father. No other boy got to know his place and his people as he did in making house calls around the countryside accompanying the only doctor within hundreds of miles. No other basked in reflection from the gratitude, the adoration, of people cured of illness, relieved of pain, saved from deformity, spared from death, from the untimely loss of loved ones—a people, even the most advanced of them, still retaining vestiges of their traditional awe and veneration of medicine men and their magic, their occult powers. And he had had not just any doctor for a father, but one uniquely qualified by the combination of his college training and his folk heritage of the curative virtues of plants.

He was his father's groom and liveryman, his pharmaceutical laboratory assistant, his herb-garden helper, occasionally his surgical team, oftentimes his interpreter—for the doctor's Cherokee was nowhere near as fluent as the boy's, and frequently their calls took them into outlying areas where that was the only language spoken—his sometime nurse's aide in the three-bed hospital which a wing of the house in town had been made into.

A rider or a runner from out in the country would come with the message that some person was too sick, or too badly injured, to be transported. While his father packed his medicine bag, Noquisi harnessed Arrow, the dapple-gray gelding whose groom he was, hitched him to the buggy and packed it with garden tools. The foot messenger rode in the bed. They left never knowing when they would get back.

Like the varicolored concentric rings of a target, the complexions of the people, lightest at the center, grew ever darker the farther out from town into the countryside you drove, until, high in the hills or deep in the valleys, you reached the root stock, the source, the pure, undiluted bloodline. The Old People, Noquisi called them, although among those out in the hinterlands where intermarriage had seldom reached or from which those of mixed blood had left, drawn to their own kind in and around the settlements, were to be found young people too. On a call deep in those parts they just might find a medicine man or a witch doctor, an exorcist of evil spirits, at the patient's bedside practicing his arts while awaiting the coming of the doctor. These colleagues of his he treated with full professional courtesy as consultants in the case. They did no harm; on the contrary, they did good by distracting the sufferer's mind. Moreover, he declared, much of his own herbal lore —some of it spurious, to be sure, but much of it time-tested and proven—had come to him from them. It was there among those outer rings, in the performance of his pastoral duties, that the Reverend Mackenzie would find the Indians of his expectations. And he, too, often took along his young friend Amos Ferguson to serve as his interpreter.

Sometimes the distance from town was too great, or the patient too sick to be left so soon, for them to return home the same day. In some of those one-room, windowless, smoke-filled cabins they slept on the floor alongside the family members. The people asked to be told the latest news; when they heard they groaned. Time was when the doctor had taken home with him meat, meal, molasses, game, wild honey, nuts. Now fewer and fewer were able to pay him even in barter. Gravely ill patients, if they were able to travel, were brought back to the hospital to be attended there.

The garden tools were for the trip home, for along the way father and son were both on the lookout for plants for the pharmacy, or for transplanting in the herb garden. Some places they knew always to stop at in season. On one road was a field where pennyroyal grew, a simple cure for many ailments, its oil an excellent insect repellent. There was a certain field of mustard, for making plasters; another of flax, its blossoms the bluest of blues, its oil used in poultices and for bringing boils to a head. They knew the whereabouts of a toothache tree, rare in those parts, the nodules of its bark better even than cloves for deadening the pain. Wormwood, a garden escapee, they collected to be rendered into a vermifuge, mint for colds and coughs, licorice root for sore throats, larkspur for the ridding of head lice, hellebore for a sedative, Indian hemp for an anaesthetic, thorn apple for the spasms of asthma, willow bark for a tea to alleviate the miseries of rheumatism and headaches. Syrups, salves, creams, lotions, ointments, tinctures in flasks and crucibles cooking on the stove made of the laboratory by turns a perfumery and a pestilence—and always a fascination, an enchantment, a place where a profession was play. Had he not made himself so useful there, the boy would have made himself a nuisance. The path he had marked out for his own in following in his father's footsteps ran as direct as the flight of an arrow. Now that the mission school had been closed, he was studying the textbooks his father had been taught from by his tutors when he was a boy. He would follow him next to William and Mary, and from there to King's College in New York. Such at least had been the plan before the late worsening of the troubles. Now . . .

Now what had been the satisfaction of curing people of the expected illnesses and the unexpected accidents of life turned more and more into the sorrow, the terror, the impotent outrage of treating people set upon and savaged. The doctor was called in to perform surgery upon a man shot in the back by a settler, to treat another one clubbed nearly to death. He was called in to assist at a difficult delivery, and he learned that the husband's cattle had been stolen, his barn burned. One patient's neighbor had been forced from his house at gunpoint, was subsisting now, he and his family, like wild animals in the woods. The doctor was torn between leaving his boy at home nowadays as he made his calls and sparing him these impressions, or taking him along so that he would never forget them, would pass them on to his last living descendant.

The boy thus got to see the land and learn to love it; he saw his people and learned to love them—to love them for their endurance and their obstinacy, their resistance to deportation. He saw the desperation that turned them for hope and consolation to the Reverend Mackenzie's teachings. His father loved the land and the people, too, but the more he saw of the ravages to the one and the trials of the other, the more convinced he was that to emigrate was now their only hope of survival. It was this exposure of his to the ever-worsening conditions, an exposure greater than any other man's possibly excepting John Ross, that inclined him toward the Treaty Party. Meanwhile, however, he did not discourage his son's attachment to his grandfather; on the contrary, he fostered it, although it made the boy a partisan on the other side in the running dispute between his father and himself.

Dr. Ferguson and his family had suffered no molestation, neither by the authorities nor by the settlers. The district's only doctor was far too precious to his people—and also to the settlers and the authorities, who, when they took sick, found themselves able to overlook his drop of Cherokee blood. It was understood that any mistreatment of him would have met with the terrible Indian retribution of two eyes for an eye. John Ross, when he was abused—arrested without charge, clapped into a one-room jailhouse where the body of a man (if a Cherokee could be so called) still hung from the rafters two weeks after his execution, run out of the state, his home confiscated —had restrained his people from retaliating; Dr. Ferguson would have been unable to do so. But they themselves could turn against him, and when his inclination to emigrate became known, they did. No harm did they do him, and it was illegal for them to attempt to dissuade him, but they turned against him.

Dr. Ferguson did not feel that he would be abandoning his people. Like it or not, they would all soon be joining him in their new home in the west. There they would have the same need for him as they had here. He would be waiting for them with a pharmacy, a surgery, a hospital all set up. Indeed, rather than abandoning them, by going ahead he would be rededicating himself to them.

However, the diehards who felt that anyone who went was deserting them were resentful of their doctor for even talking about going. That he was the son of one of their most respected leaders was no mitigation; on the contrary, it was a betrayal of that leader, and thus doubly a betrayal of them all. It had become heresy to think differently from Tsan Usdi. The more prominent the person who did so, the greater the outcry. Anyone who was not with them was against them. Any break in their ranks reinforced the enemy.

"It is not that I think the cause is wrong and deserves to lose," the doctor declared. "I think as you do, that it is right and deserves to win. But anybody with eyes in his head can see that it is lost. We are outnumbered and we have been outfought. Now is the time to make the best we can of things before they get still worse. However, if it turns out that you were right to stay and I was wrong to go, if conditions here improve and the outlook brightens, I can always come back. All roads lead two ways."

He likened himself to Noah. The flood was coming and he had been forewarned. He had been chosen not because he alone among men found favor in the eyes of God but rather because he was better educated than most, knew more of the world, could see where things were tending, was clear-eyed enough to recognize the inescapable. He had been told to build his ark, provision it, take with him the wherewithal for starting life over after the waters had receded. If his kind was to survive, he must prepare the way, find his Ararat and send out the dove. He would have a home ready and waiting for his old father and mother.

"Is this the only spot of earth that we can live on?" he asked. "Is this the only air our lungs can breathe? Are we so dependent, so delicate, so unadaptable?"

"You speak like a white man," said his father. "To them one place is the same as another so long as it yields a profit. For us the earth is more than a provider. It is our mother and father. All its creatures are our brothers."

"What you are describing, Father, is a backward and primitive people. Yes, I have seen what it means to them to be evicted from their homes and driven off their land. I have seen grown men and women kneel and kiss the ground. I have seen them stroke a tree and bid it good-bye. A touching sight. It brought tears to my eyes. Both of them. With one I wept for their sorrow and with the other for their childishness.

"What is home? Our first one is our mother's womb, but there comes a time when we outgrow it and the cord is cut. Then it is our parents' house. Precious. Never to be forgotten.

But there comes a time when we leave it, like the birds their nests, to make a home of our own. Those who do not do so, who spend their lives with their parents, we feel have never quite grown up but have remained children. Maybe leaving here and going to a new country will be the thing to make our people grow up, become independent.

"This place is no longer our home. It is our prison. We have been deprived of every freedom. We may not plan anything for our protection. We are forbidden to speak to one another in numbers of more than two. Our newspaper has been suppressed. Our children are growing up in ignorance and superstition. We are losing the advancements we have made and reverting to savagery. Out there we will be free to take up where we were interrupted."

The appearance on the family farm of the lottery land surveyors that day in celebration of his son's coming to manhood only crystallized into a decision sentiments long felt by Dr. Abel Ferguson. Here there was to be no manhood for that son of his.

On a morning not long afterward, Noquisi was sent out to the farm. There he left his pony, driving back to town with a wagon and team. He felt himself being watched with hostile eyes from every house he passed along the street. For although the doctor had announced his intention to nobody outside his family, all the world knew about the wagon train then assembling and being provisioned, its departure date set.

The job of packing the household goods was Noquisi's and his mother's. It took them a week, not because so many of their belongings went into the wagon but rather because so many of them, each requiring consideration, reluctant rejection, did not. The items of bare necessity for life, those permitting one no choice, declared themselves unarguably; from each of those little personal possessions that lighten living came its mute appeal. One had to be firm. Room for pots and pans, no room for playthings. Several times his mother came upon the boy handling something of his that she knew he treasured, and more than once she said, "I'm sure we can make space for that, Noquisi." He refused, irritably after a while. She desisted when she realized that he was putting his childhood behind him and that his pride in his manhood more than compensated for any sorrow he might have felt. If she herself sometimes weakened and wept over parting from the home she had made, Noquisi was never allowed to see it. "What many of us never had I reckon we can learn to get along without," he heard her say to his father. Mainly the wagon contained medical supplies.

Of all the many people whose ailments he had treated, whose broken bones he had set, whose wounds he had stitched together, whose aching teeth he had extracted, whom his wife had nursed, none came to see the doctor off. At the edge of town, in the open door of one house, just one, a little girl, stood to wave good-bye. As she did so she was yanked inside by her mother.

They rode on for a little way, then the doctor reined the team. For a while he sat silent. Then he said, "I delivered that child. Without me, the mother might have died and the child too.

"I know that what I am doing is right and that it is only a matter of time before they must all follow me. I know that I am right. That is what worries me. A person in the wrong can never forgive the person in the right."

At the crossroads a mile outside of town they were met by the old folks. Their good-byes were kept brief because their separation would be brief. They would be reunited all too soon.

While his parents proceeded on their way, Noquisi rode home with his grandparents. Entrusting him to their keeping would make this temporary separation of the family seem less of a separation. He was being left with them because he was a man now and would be a help to them both here and on the road when the time came. And because, pale of face though he was, Abel Ferguson had the Indian sense of the strong bond between children and their grandparents. Indeed, it was the parents' duty to relinquish the child to them, that they might enjoy him in the time left them.

For a while the drawings of the Georgia State lottery for the redistribution of Cherokee homes, farms, shops and stores were suspended. They had been suspended after it came to light that the supervisor of the lottery, one Shadrack Bogan, had, for a consideration, rigged them. Five winning tickets, all for highly valuable properties, were found to be fraudulent, forged by Bogan's hand. There was no knowing how many more such had gone undetected, how many of the certified winners occupied their holdings through downright thievery.

Now that a new supervisor of the lottery had been appointed to succeed the discredited Bogan, the gaming wheels were spinning as before over in Milledgeville and Cherokee holdings were again being awarded to the deserving, including the five known frauds, which were resubmitted and redrawn. However, following the Bogan scandal there was considerable erosion of the public's trust in Georgia's lottery. But where there's a will there's a way, and there's more than one way to skin a cat. There existed ready-to-hand an alternative procedure by which settlers might acquire Cherokee homesteads, one that left nothing to chance. Noquisi was taken to observe this procedure at work. It was a sign of the times they were living in that his grandfather wanted him to see and remember, to tell his grandchildren about, if, God willing, he lived to have any.

To go into town on a Saturday was a risky thing for them to do, for although, among the many white strangers now there, they might easily have "passed," Agiduda, unmoved by Grandmother's arguments, her pleas or her tears, *would* wear the turban, the sash and the moccasins he had defiantly adopted late in life, and if he would, then so would Noquisi. It was on Saturday that firewater flowed in the town. To sell liquor to an Indian was illegal. They were not permitted to enter the taverns. In some cases it was hard to tell who was an Indian and who was not. So—in great quantities—liquor was bootlegged: the bottle produced from out of the leg of the seller's boot. Many Cherokees, dispossessed, homeless and despondent, were now drowning their sorrow in drink. Sometimes the drink turned them sullen and resentful, and a sullen Indian was one just asking for trouble. For an Indian to find trouble he never had far to look, and when he did, then every Indian in town at the time was in trouble. All this notwithstanding, the Fergusons went into the county seat.

It was to attend a session of the district court that the boy was taken by his grandfather to town that day. Had things been otherwise than they were, had there been any counterattractions, the court sessions would have been the place's feature entertainment; as things were, they were its only one. However, no loss was felt; they filled the gap. A bearbaiting, a public hanging would have had to compete for custom when court was in session. To see the jurors retiring to deliberate, and then returning in under a minute with a verdict of guilty as charged, was worth the price of a ticket, and it was free. And when, through their interlocutor, the foreman, they put long legal questions couched in mumbo jumbo to His Honor, the judge, they were as good as a minstrel show. It was said that somebody had once opened and looked into the copy of the Bible upon which witnesses, whether right- or left-handed, or even ambidextrous, placed their right hands while swearing to tell the truth, the whole truth and nothing but the truth, and had been shocked to find that it really was a Bible. Most likely because no book more appropriate to the tenor and atmosphere of the court was procurable locally.

Among the pool of prospective jurors a spirit of civic-mindedness prevailed. No venireman ever asked to be excused from duty, not even those working in the gold fields, for whom the per diem allowance of a few dollars and all you could drink was a financial sacrifice. Jury duty was a chance to shine, a challenge to put on a performance for an appreciative but demanding audience. Deliberations were never protracted, there was never any wrangling, a verdict had already been arrived at before the choice was made of twelve good men and true.

Nonjury cases were every bit as entertaining, for the judge was a one-man show. His way with the gavel, his bullying of witnesses, his comically straight face, his steady sipping from his glass of water, the proof of which could be sniffed as far back as the fifth row of spectators' pews, had gained him a following. He was judging the case the Fergusons went that day to hear tried. It was one in which the plaintiff sought a court order for the eviction of a family illegally occupying a house belonging to him. The head of the family was the man from whom the owner had bought the house. He had been served notice to vacate but the notice had been ignored. As proof of his ownership of the house, the plaintiff produced the deed of transfer, signed by the defendant, and two witnesses who swore under oath that they had been present at the transaction.

That they knew the outcome of the trial beforehand did not lessen the spectators' pleasure. It was like seeing a favorite skit performed again. This one was far from the first such case they had attended, and all ended alike. They were not there to be surprised by the plot, they were there to enjoy the action and to see a demonstration of blatant impudence.

Questioned by his attorney, the defendant on the stand

claimed that the signature on the deed purporting to be his was not his signature, examples of which he executed and entered in evidence; that he was barely acquainted with the other party in the case; and that he had never until now laid eyes on either of the witnesses. He was then questioned by the plaintiff's attorney.

"You had, I believe, a mixed-blood grandmother, part Cherokee?"

The man on the stand was silent. His conflict of mind was plain to see. He was torn. He wanted justice, wanted to keep the home that was his, yet he was remembering some of his grandmother's many acts of love and kindness to him. She was his mother's mother. Now, poor soul, she was dead. One day her spirit and his would meet again. In the end—swayed also by fear of being prosecuted for perjury—he was unable to disown his grandmother.

With that the plaintiff's attorney rested his client's case. He moved that this man's testimony was inadmissible in this court. The judge's ruling was mandatory: the order of eviction was issued forthwith.

"*Next* case!" said His Honor. It was his punchline, and it never failed to draw from the crowd a great guffaw. The merriment was enlivened by his mock-serious attempt to gavel them to order.

It was not long afterward that Sonny Slocum, whom Amos had known all his life, whom he had sometimes played with despite the gulf in their social standings, the Slocums being little better than pore whites, got wise to this trick and stole Amos's pony. The pony was stolen while grazing in the pasture, wearing only a halter. Later Sonny came over and offered a dollar for the saddle and blanket and the bridle. It puzzled him that his offer was refused.

"Why, Amos, you ain't got no more use for them things," he complained.

Early one morning in February a man appeared on the place. Who he was, how he had gotten there, when he had arrived, there was no accounting for. It was as though he had sprung from the ground overnight like a toadstool.

When first seen, he was standing down by the barn lot gazing up at the house, his putty-colored hat pushed back on his head. He watched Agiduda's approach with his arms folded across his chest. He was a tall, gaunt man with several days growth of rusty-red whiskers on his face and throat, rising almost to his eyes. Between this and the shock of hair that grew low on his forehead he peered out at the world as a poodledog does. By spitting on the ground he gave away his race.

"Drawed you a nice place there, neighbor," he drawled. His breath visible on the frosty air seemed to be the fumes of envy and resentment. "Warn't quite so lucky in the draw as that myself. But you can keep your fine big house, mister. I got me a gold mine." He spat again, this time venomously, turned his back and stalked away. He covered ground with a stride that was long and stiff-kneed. He disappeared into one of the former slave cabins, where, apparently, he had already made himself at home.

On that same morning of his sudden appearance from out of nowhere, the new owner of the 160-acre lottery parcel adjacent to the Fergusons' remaining land fell to improving his property. Not only had he himself materialized unobserved, mysteriously conveyed, he had brought with him tools—at least, an axe. The steady sound of it at work in his woodlot reached the house daylong. You would have thought the man had undertaken single-handedly to clear the land for crops, and to get the job done before nightfall.

For several days, from sunup to sundown, the sound of

chopping continued, as persistent as the hammering of a woodpecker. Then, although the Fergusons were early risers, they awoke one morning to find, on the line dividing their shrunken property from that of their new neighbor, a row some six feet long of palings driven into the ground to form a fence, or rather, a wall. As contiguous as teeth they stood. The man was erecting a stockade, and such was his urgency to get it done, he was driving stakes into ground still only partially thawed. To put up this first section of it he must have worked by the light of last night's moon.

The Fergusons watched him from a window. He pounded the stakes into the ground with the flat of his axe. Infinitesimal was the penetration into the grudging ground that each stroke gained him; a quarter of an hour's work advanced his project by mere inches.

"What kind of livestock is he meaning to fence in that he needs a solid wall like that for?" Agiduda wondered aloud. "Cattle don't require it. Sheep don't."

"Even hogs don't," said Noquisi.

"What can he have in mind?"

The man worked with the persistency, the concentrated single-mindedness, or mindlessness, of an insect at its one instinctual function. To him the Sabbath meant no more than to a pissant. It was doubtful that he knew when it fell, all days of the week being alike to him. He would run out of saplings, and then for the next several days his axe would be heard again in the woodlot. The tick of a clock could hardly have kept up with it. Then he would be seen plying between the woods and his work site carrying saplings in bundles on his back. After a stake was driven in place its tip was sharpened to a point with a drawknife.

What was fueling all this activity was another mystery. Sheer willpower, he seemed to be going on. Perpetual motion. The man took off from work for a spell occasionally, but hardly long enough to have gone into town, on foot, to trade.

A shot sounded from time to time in his woods, and there were still some nuts from last year's crop on the ground, but no roots at this season and certainly no berries. Flour, sweetening, fat: what he was doing for these white man's staples God only knew. He could have set a trotline on his stretch of the river and, breaking the ice, have run it mornings and evenings. No team, not even a saddle horse, was anywhere to be seen on his property, yet he must have arrived by some conveyance well-provisioned.

Chop, tote, pound, sharpen: daylight to dark, rain or shine, seven days a week: after a month of it the fence stretched fifty yards. Then work stopped. The man disappeared from sight. Silence fell. No more saplings came out of the woods.

"Wore himself out," said Agiduda. "He needs to rest up before turning the corner with that thing. A week in bed, I should think."

But the fence was carried no farther. It was left a straight line enclosing nothing, starting where it did, running its length, then terminating. Anybody could have walked around either end of it.

Just one finishing touch was applied to it. One day soon after work on it was abandoned, or, as it turned out, completed, a sign appeared midway on its outside. There was no need to get closer than the house to read it. What it said was, "KEEP OUT. Mr. O. J. Blodgett, Sole Prop."

After his fence was finished, nothing more was seen of Mr. Blodgett. He got an early start on the day; smoke was already rising from his chimney no matter what hour the Fergusons got up, but what he was doing with his time there was no knowing. Then one spring morning at break of day he was seen issuing forth with a pick and shovel over his shoulder. Had he been serious, was he speaking literally, in saying that he had gotten himself a gold mine? If so, he was wasting his time even more senselessly than in putting up his pointless fence. The gold fields were confined to a distant part of the Cherokee territory.

Meanwhile, provisions were running low, and as if that were not bad enough, Grandmother, in her anxiety, imagined them to be disappearing even faster than they were. She said nothing about this at the time for fear of revealing what she had long suspected, that her brain was going soft, and of pointing out what was already plain to see, her incompetence as a housekeeper.

First it was a ham. She had thought she had four of them left in the smokehouse. She could have sworn there were four. They had butchered in November. She had served a fresh ham at Thanksgiving and a cured one at Christmas. After that they had lived off the buck which was the first deer to be killed by Noquisi with his new bow. What Indian would eat hog meat when he could eat venison instead? To this day, some would no sooner touch it than would a Jew. So she had thought that of the original six hams she had four left. Now when she went to get one she found only three. When could they have eaten the other one? And how could she not remember their eating it? Cooking anything was an experience for her, not just memorable but painful; how could she have forgotten cooking that ham? Her brain was going soft. It had never had much use, and now it was going soft. She mistrusted her capacity to count to ten. She was ashamed of growing old and embarrassed to have it seen. Her ineptitude at the household tasks now asked of her added to this sense.

She who had never planned or prepared a meal, who had never been inside the root cellar except to take shelter there from cyclones, must now manage a house. Of quantities of foodstuffs needed in store, of methods of preserving this one and that, she had only the most rudimentary notion. How long different things took to cook, so as to have them all ready to serve together, how much seasoning to add: these things, second nature to most women, to her were a mystery. She had sat down to her meal and eaten it, and that was her only connection with it. The activity that went on in her parents' kitchen when she was a girl, and later in her own, no more concerned her than did the picking of the cotton or the shearing of the sheep.

In a kitchen Mr. Ferguson was as inexperienced as she was. But he had taken his turn as cook in hunting camps. He had never slaughtered a hog or a beef before, but he had killed and butchered many a buck, and there was not all that much difference. He had cooked a little for the fun of it, and now, seeing her struggle, he came to her aid, he made a game of it— two old folks playing house. And, indeed, the empty house had something of the air of a playhouse, especially with the boy living with them; they were camping out in it. Between them, Mr. Ferguson and Noquisi did the scullery work. It drew them close. Having these chores to do helped to some extent to take their minds off the separation of the family, the threat of dispossession and removal that hung constantly over them. Yet it shamed her as only an Indian woman could be shamed to see her man doing woman's work, and to have the boy see his grandfather thus humiliated in his old age.

No matter how she tried, she mismanaged everything, and now, under her supervision, a general collapse loomed imminent. The milch cow seemed to be drying up, long before the time for it—no doubt because she was such a poor milker. The hens' production of eggs had fallen off by fully half. Hardly a week passed but what another one disappeared from their pen. A fox must be getting into it, though she could not find the breach. A turtle it must have been that got one of the ducks on the pond. Apples, potatoes, squash, turnips, pumpkins, peas, beans, lard—she knew she was wasteful, that she

spoiled much food in preparing it, still she did not understand
how an old couple and a boy could consume stores at such a
rate. When spring came and the ground thawed and could be
worked, a kitchen garden could be planted, but could she hold
out until then?

Go the Cherokees must, sooner or later, and the sooner
the better, for conditions here worsened daily, and those the
earliest on the scene out there would have the first choice of a
place to settle—that was one of the arguments used by the
Treaty Party to persuade them to emigrate. Another was that
by going voluntarily they could pick their own departure date,
at a favorable season of the year, travel their own chosen
route, at their own pace, could provision themselves according
to their tastes, could go in dignity rather than be driven like
cattle, which was the alternative they were threatened with.
Yet none, or very few, almost none, went voluntarily.

Did they think that the threat was an empty one? How
could they think it? Had recent events taught them nothing?
Were they blind to the example of their brothers the Choctaws,
the Chickasaws and the Creeks? Where were they now? All
were gone, deported, and along the way, such were the conditions under which they were herded, they had lost thousands
of their numbers to disease, exposure, starvation at the hands
of swindling sutlers operating under government contract.
That same threat hung over the Cherokees. What made them
think that they and they alone of all the tribes could escape it?

Even those who asked the question, or who put it to
themselves, knew what made them think it. Their innate and
unshakeable conviction of their difference, always held, now
more than ever strengthened by the invention of Sequoyah's
alphabet, the success of their efforts to civilize themselves, the
consciousness that outside the American south, all around the

world, were thousands of people who believed them to be, and encouraged them to think themselves, superior to their backward, naked and illiterate red brothers. From the white man the Cherokees had learned many lessons, but despising Indians, all except their own, was not among them. In that the whites could have taken lessons from them. That the Cherokees had congressmen and clergymen, editors and philosophers crusading on their behalf whom the other tribes had not had, they took to be fitting and proper.

They had followed a different course from that of the other tribes, a course which, if it had not won, had still not lost. The Creeks, the Choctaws and the Chickasaws had crumpled under pressure at once, had sold out; the Seminoles had fought, and, through base trickery, now had lost. The Cherokees had litigated in the white man's courts. They had won there, and although the President professed himself powerless to enforce the high court's ruling against the state of Georgia, here they still were, unlike the Creeks, the Chickasaws and the Choctaws. Meanwhile their archenemy was nearing the end of his tenure in the White House. In the coming national elections there was a good chance that the other party might win. Its leader, Henry Clay, was a friend of the Cherokees. He would assert the power of the federal government over what Georgia called its state's rights. Meanwhile, working for them tirelessly, selflessly and brilliantly, they had their own Tsan Usdi. How could you lose all hope? To do so was to desert him.

The notice first appeared tacked to the door of the former Cherokee council house, now district headquarters of the United States Army, in the former Cherokee capital of New Echota, toward the end of 1837. Within days it was posted on trees throughout the territory. The message, in English and

Cherokee, was that on May 23 of the following year those Cherokees who had not yet removed themselves would be forcibly removed to the lands awaiting them in the west. The locations of depots to be built to receive them were given, and their cooperation was solicited in presenting themselves voluntarily for transport and thereby sparing the Army having to hunt them down. What Cherokee had translated the English and set it in the only existing font of type in Sequoyah's alphabet? For his family name, at least, most needed only one guess. Ridge.

The first sweep by the soldiers of Cherokee homes was for the confiscation of their arms. Not even the poorest cabin in the remotest part was overlooked. And because there was often no communication between the raiders and the occupants, the place was turned into a shambles in the search.

Such as they had were hunting arms. The loss of them was disheartening not because they were deprived of the opportunity of turning them upon people, they had no intention of doing that, but because of their attachment to them. Most had forgotten—had never known—the use of the bow and arrow; upon the household rifle depended the meat for the table traditional to them, their very concept of themselves. An object of beauty as well as usefulness, the product of skilled craftsmanship, purchased at sacrifice or lovingly handed down from father to son, his rifle was often the only possession that a man looked upon as personal. Together, he and it shared memories of many a head of game, and mutual respect, each for the other's trustiness. His rifle was the emblem of a man's manhood, its loss the loss of that attribute. That it should be thought that, even armed, they posed a threat saddened them with the sense of their present-day powerlessness. Agiduda doubted that his Joseph Manton fowling piece or his father's Pennsylvania flintlock would find their way into the federal armory. He suspected that they would remain in the possession of the Georgia State militiaman who rode off carrying them.

Like the condemned man on death row, the date for whose execution had been set, becoming his own cellblock attorney, the Cherokees tried to stop the clock, sending Ross repeatedly to Washington to argue their case, to delay. Yet on the homefront, meanwhile, the setting of the date seemed to have made little or no difference, hardly any perceptible impression. So the Reverend Mackenzie reports.

He had been unsuccessful, incidentally, in his efforts to have the town tavern closed on Sabbath mornings. It was there that the husbands and fathers of his congregation waited for them until services were over. Thus he was not reaching with his message of brotherly love those for whom it was primarily intended.

The concentration camps—log stockades requiring the felling of whole forests—were erected and their gates thrown open to receive the volunteers; they stood empty. On their walls appeared the words *TLA YIDAYOJADANVSI:* we will not emigrate. The Cherokees now had an added reason for wanting to remain in their homeland and resisting to the last all efforts to remove them: horror stories of the journey reaching them from those who had gone west, of the ruggedness of the land out there, and even of the hostility they had encountered from those of their brothers who had gone and settled there earlier, of being swindled by members of their own clans in the purchase of land, stock, provisions, seed. Their troubles had split them, had frayed the tribal tie, and pitted Cherokee against Cherokee. On his errands around the countryside, ministering to the sick and the dying, burying the dead, baptizing the living, marrying them, the Reverend Mackenzie found no evidence of panic, certainly none of widespread preparations to leave any time soon.

He found just the opposite, in fact. People burned off the brush and last year's stover and stalks and vines. They mended fences. As his friend David Ferguson said, speaking of his repairing his verandah, "Why am I doing this for the next owner? I'm not. I'm doing it for all its past owners. They kept it up for me and as long as I'm still here I'm responsible to them." They even cleared new cropland. The threat that they would not be here to gather their crops did not discourage them from planting; on the contrary, it was as if planting a crop were the guarantee that they would still be here when harvesttime came. The seeds they sowed were their link with that land they loved. The roots of the plants were their roots; the more of them the stronger the tie. Not ordinarily the most industrious of farmers, an occupation they for long resisted, the Cherokees that spring of 1838 were industrious as never before. The winds of change were blowing but they fanned into flames the embers of resistance. As do certain plants, hope flourishes in the poorest soil.

Surely people the likes of the Fergusons were not so simple as to think that by working the soil they sent their roots in it down deeper? Necessity in part dictated their zeal but they worked not just out of necessity; they took satisfaction in the work. Did this arise from a sense that this would be the last time they would ever till that precious soil? Or was it just the opposite of that: the novelty of their doing so for the first time? Was it a sense of belated self-discovery, a disavowal of the privilege and the pampering that had always been theirs and an identification in these troubled times with the masses of their people who had always fed themselves with their own hands? Whatever was their drive, they were always busy whenever Reverend Mac, as they had taken to calling him, and which he forbore to correct (it was not the "Mac" that he minded—he rather liked that; it was the "Reverend" without the "the" that was improper), dropped in on them that spring. Busy spading rows in the kitchen garden, sowing seeds, busy molding candles. It was plain to see that working together drew them together. They were grateful for the physical exertion; it kept them from brooding.

They were glad to see Reverend Mac, for he was almost the only person they saw those days. A siege mentality had gripped them, as it had everyone. This house that had once been open house to one and all—red and white and shades in between—now received few callers. Its size made it all the more silent; its emptiness was large-scale. Neighbors with news to relate came by night, spoke low, were brief and soon departed.

From time to time on his pastoral house calls out in the countryside the Reverend Mackenzie was accompanied by Corporal Willis Odum of the Georgia State Militia. His duty was to enforce one law, to check that the one man to whom it applied was adhering to it. Thus he was present at last rites, conversions, baptisms, always with the same expression on his face of disbelief and distaste. To the Corporal the Indians' Christianity was a pretense and a put-on, a fraud upon the Reverend Mackenzie above all. They were, he said, an open book to him. If so, said the Reverend Mackenzie to himself, it was the only book that was.

"Christians my foot!" he said. "Spawn of the devil. All this religious hocus-pocus ain't nothing but a way to get around going west. But they're going, them johnnycakes, every last one of them, and the sooner the better. You know, Preacher, you're lucky to have me with you out here in some of these out-of-the-way places. You could get bushwhacked and nobody'd ever know about it."

"I have never met with anything but friendliness and hospitality from these people."

"Had me a pet fox once. Raised it from a pup. Gentle as a hound. Run loose but never run off. Come when called. Eat right out of my hand. One day for no particular reason that critter turned on me and just look a-here at the scar. That's redskins for you. No more to be trusted than wild animals. Think you've got them tamed but they're fooling you and you're fooling yourself. It don't matter how little a part they are. One drop is enough to taint the blood.

"Unless we kept watch every minute they'd rise up and slit our throats to a man, woman and child. Our biggest mistake is in learning them some of our own ways. Makes them more dangerous than ever. You can put them in decent clothes, proper houses, make them look on the outside like human beings, but you can't take the Indian out of them. And don't never make the mistake of thinking you're the exception to the rule. They hate us white folks one and all."

"What about the ones over the years who have married among them, become their kin, been taken into the tribe?"

"Them ain't white men. Them are paleface Indians—the worst kind of all."

He posted himself outside the house of call. Thus he was never actually where he was supposed to be, present at ceremonies, only on sentry duty, and had no way of knowing how many undesirables were assembled inside or what went on. "Stinks in there worse'n that fox den I took that pup out from," he said. Besides, he was always expecting ambush, and that meant in the least expected places. That the savages had for so long remained peaceful did not reassure him. Indian vengeance matured like whiskey in the cask.

The Corporal was skeptical among all else of Cherokee vows of fidelity exchanged in the rites of holy matrimony. Sitting on the buggy seat and loosing a stream of tobacco juice, his parting words as the Reverend Mackenzie went up the path to perform the marriage ceremony were, "Now, remember, just one bride to the groom, eh, Preacher. More'n that constitutes unlawful assembly."

The boy and his grandfather were seldom apart during this time. They worked alongside each other. They took walks together. They spoke little then. Each was straining with all his senses to impress the scene upon his memory, to take it with him on leaving. Words were unnecessary between them. Each could read the other's thoughts.

On these walks their sense of their loss was expanded. For this was land which their people had forever tended with a care for it and for all the fellow creatures with whom they shared it, leaving in the field at harvesttime a portion of the corn for the deer and the migrant geese, not farming to the edges of their lots expecting from every inch a marketable yield, but leaving the hedgerows untrimmed, a tangle of protective cover for the small animals and the birds to feed and nest in. And beyond the bounds of their own parcel lay land that they were losing too: tribal land. For as his grandfather said to the boy, a white man thought that only his small plot of earth was his, and not that all of it was. And to him that plot of his was his enemy, begrudging him the living he must wrest from it in the sweat of his brow.

They tried even in their thoughts not to pity each other, for they knew that to be pitied made one pity oneself and weaken. But they did pity each other. The boy pitied his grandmother, for her attachment to her home was like that of the generations-old wisteria vine that clung to it with its many tentacles from the foundation to the eave. But he pitied his grandfather more, for because of his long life as a farmer and an outdoorsman he had as many roots in this soil as did the trees of the forest.

Although he was not getting much taller, as measured by the mark on his wall, it was during this period of inner ripening, of forced mental growth, that the boy's power of thought-reading rapidly matured. He had known to expect this. It was a faculty possessed by Cherokees—one they did not advertise to outsiders. Thus he had known from the time he knew anything that if he was to have any secrets from his grown-ups he must think about them only when he was off by himself, for such thoughts proclaimed themselves like smoke signals. He had had many startling but convincing proofs of that. As this power of penetration grew with age, he was not sure but that Agiduda knew what he was thinking even when they were apart. Not that he had anything to hide from *him,* for with age also came tolerance of youthful mischief. Now the current began to flow in both directions. Old, wise and wily as it was, his grandfather's mind, perhaps deprived of its distinctiveness from others of his kind because of their common predicament, became accessible to the boy. This new ability of his did not gladden him, it saddened him to find that he could enter and find there a mind caught and writhing in the same trap as all the rest. That was one of the most painful aspects of being included with all your kind in a common threat: it was to have no life of your own, no more individuality than a raindrop.

Their evenings were spent by the family with the grandfather reading aloud to them. That was how their evenings had always been spent. Thus it was an assertion that life went on as before. It was more important now than ever. The boy's education must not be neglected, nor must the old folks' minds be allowed to stagnate and they turn into the uncivilized savages that the whites proclaimed them to be. And it was a distraction from their troubles. Or would have been had the old man not veered in one direction like the needle of a compass to readings that reminded them of their troubles. He read them, "Breathes there a man, with soul so dead,/ Who never to himself has said,/ 'This is my own, my native land!' " He read them *Robinson Crusoe.* They were not entertained by the hero's ingenuity at surviving in adversity. They were appalled by the hardships of a civilized, social man, castaway, reduced to brute existence, aching with loneliness and homesickness and with the fear that he had been abandoned by God.

Their most recently finished book was *Paradise Lost.*

"If it had happened here it would never have happened," was Grandmother's comment on The Fall.

"How so?" asked Agiduda.

"Because there were no apples in this country until the white man brought them with him. And because no Cherokee woman would have been enticed by a snake. We all know they speak with a forked tongue."

They laughed together over this but soon fell silent, each listening to the echo in their minds of the poem's closing lines and thinking of the similarities and the differences between themselves and their original parents. On being expelled from their paradise, not all the world was before them, where to choose their place of rest. They would have no choice, they would find no resting place. Theirs was to be the land west of Eden. Nor would their steps be wandering and slow. They would be pointed directly toward the setting sun, and they would be in quick march.

Go they must, there was no escaping it, the date was set, and there was this powerful inducement to come in voluntarily to the stockade: if you did so you were allowed to bring with you whatever you could carry. You could ride in, on horseback or even by wagon and team, and with these you could make the long trek west. Wait to be hunted down and brought in and you would come as you were. You would come as you were and you would go west as you were: on foot and with nothing but the clothes on your back. It was like the favor of giving a condemned man his preference in the mode of his execution.

It was a time to choose from among your belongings the most essential, the things needful for making a new home, beginning a new life in a new place, and, among the inessential ones, those the most precious, without which life would be nothing more than bare existence, ones that would be links with the old life. It was a time to find white buyers and get the best prices you could for the things you must leave behind.

Agiduda would go to the library to choose among the

books. White buyers for these locally there were few or none, but so many could not all be taken. The bound volumes of *The Tatler,* for example, would seem to have little application to life in The Territory beyond the Mississippi among the coyotes and the wild Osage. And yet it might be just the thing to make life tolerable in that literary desert. He would dip into its pages. And for that day the choosing of books was over. *The Tatler*'s remoteness from his troubles made it appealing to Agiduda. Its urbanity and polish made him feel that his crude world was not the only world that men had made for themselves.

The departure date was like one fixed for your execution, and the inducement to come in beforehand on your own like an invitation to mount the gallows sooner than the date set by the judge. Who would hasten his own execution? Yet perhaps the condemned man who has lost his every appeal sometimes felt the temptation to get it all over with. To live for nothing but to watch the approach of your appointed end—was that to live?

But they had not lost their appeal. They had won it, had won it in the highest court of the land. They had shown that the Ridge party did not speak for them and that the treaty it had signed was invalid. Even now, powerful members of Congress were working in their cause. There were editorials, lectures, fund-raising events, protests, rallies for them in New York, Boston, Philadelphia. Good people everywhere were on their side. Something so monstrously unjust could not come to pass. It was not possible in the modern civilized world that a people whose only offense was their existence could be so mistreated. Tsan Usdi had not given up. It was for you that he fought on.

Then it was another day nearer to the appointed one and somebody stopped to say that Tsan Usdi was just back from his latest mission to Washington and that President Van Buren, Jackson's handpicked successor, who was as bent upon

Indian removal as Jackson ever was, had refused even to see him. You said to yourself, "The end has come. I *must* start packing." And you were so overwhelmed with sadness that you were unable to stir from your seat. The next morning you summoned up a bit of strength (there was a renewal of strength when all hope was lost, all illusions dispelled) and made a start on the job, and somebody dropped in with a letter from people who had made the trip and such were its terrors you said to yourself, "If they want me to go, they will have to come and get me. And they will have to drag me kicking and screaming every inch of the way."

Noquisi, or rather, Amos, served as the Reverend Mackenzie's interpreter for some of the wave of conversions to Christianity during this period. The Reverend Mackenzie ought to have rejoiced in this salvation of souls but his own soul was troubled by the tactics he was obliged to employ. The primitive mind required special handling in matters theological. The Indians looked about them and saw themselves losing and the white man winning in their unequal contest. This must be because the white man's was the more powerful god. So they would switch their allegiance, then with His help they would keep their homes and not be removed to the place they conceived of as hell on earth. The Reverend Mackenzie tried to warn them that prayers were not always answered, yet he found it hard to explain to them why not, when God was all-powerful, all-merciful, and you had kept his commandments. He tried to instill in them higher, selfless, spiritual motives for converting, but he feared he was not always successful, and he dreaded their disappointment and disillusionment, and their consequent anger directed at himself.

The case of one Corn-dancer taught him circumspection. Corn-dancer's god was no good. He had sacrificed to him

all his days, and what had it gotten him? Corn-dancer's enemies prospered while Corn-dancer suffered. He wanted to hear
more about the Reverend's god. He was prepared to listen
sympathetically.

The Reverend Mackenzie began by saying that he, Corn-
dancer, had a soul.

Corn-dancer snorted. He was offended by what he consid-
ered an insult to his intelligence and to that of his race. He
knew he had a soul. All Indians knew that—even the ignorant
Osage.

This soul of his was everlasting.

Another snort. To the everlasting souls of his ancestors
Corn-dancer had turned since childhood. Even the Osage—

For the salvation of this soul of his from the eternal
flames of hell he must believe in and worship this one and
only, this jealous god.

That a god should be jealous and insist on being the one
and only came as no surprise to Corn-dancer, but he knew a
good trade when he saw one. He grunted in agreement. Nor
did the Holy Trinity give his primitive mind any more trouble
than it had given Amos's childish one. In fact, the ease with
which it was accepted troubled the Reverend Mackenzie by
confirming his own reservations.

The old man listened, nodding and grunting with approval, as the Reverend Mackenzie expounded the Articles of
the Faith and the Ten Commandments. Of these, keeping the
seventh would cost Corn-dancer no effort at his age. As for the
fifth, he had always honored his father and mother—all Indians did, even the Osage. As Corn-dancer, in an untranslated
aside to the boy, observed, he found it rather revealing that
white people should have to be told by their god that they
must. He particularly approved of the fourth commandment,
which came out in translation as to loaf on Sunday. Best of all
he liked the last two; they suited his situation precisely. These
alone would have sold him on this god, but for one thing.

Every day the white man, whose god this was, bore false witness against his neighbor in the courts of the land, while the Indians were forbidden by law to testify against him. Coveting his red neighbor's house was what the white man was here expressly to do. Had this almighty god not the power to enforce his commandments upon his believers?

The Reverend Mackenzie assured Corn-dancer that such sinners as those would roast eternally in hell—unless, he felt obliged to add, they repented on their deathbeds.

Ah. In other words, just believe in this god and you were free to do all the mischief you pleased and leave your ill-gotten gains for your children to enjoy—as the sins of the fathers could not be visited upon them—so long as you said before dying, "I'm sorry. Forgive me." Corn-dancer understood now why this god was so popular. He was a good god for white men, not so good for the poor outnumbered Indians.

Finally, Corn-dancer could feel nothing but shame and contempt for a father—one supposedly all-powerful—not coming to the rescue of his only child when that child was tortured by his enemies and put to die at the stake.

And so Corn-dancer was lost and damned, much to the Reverend Mackenzie's sorrow, and his embarrassment before the boy, his interpreter. To these simple-minded arguments the answers were too complicated, he explained.

It was at this time that two men, one, after a period of eclipse, even of disgrace, now world-famous, powerful, the other always obscure, long assumed dead, reentered the life of the tribe. It turned out that they had been silent partners in a recent event that had changed the course of history, had redrawn the map, and brought the one to prominence and fame. Of this connection between them Agiduda learned at a meeting of Ross's cabinet just over the line in Tennessee. Although it then seemed irrelevant, it was information which was to prove in time to be of importance to the Fergusons, those left of them.

For some Cherokees there had always been alternatives to be feared even more than deportation to the land of darkness, and, over the years, bands of them had fled there. For them it was a refuge. Of these, some belonged to that small minority faction who resisted being civilized and clung to the old traditional tribal ways, others were fugitives from justice, some from red justice, some from white justice. Fugitives from justice of both colors was the first band ever to go, and they had kept going until they got clear out of America.

There were two versions of their story, a red one and a white one. Both were agreed that it took place at a spot in Alabama called Muscle Shoals, on the Tennessee River, on a day in June of 1794.

Down the river that day came a boat known to be laden with trade goods and with twenty slaves, a prize of war (not to mention the thirteen white scalps on board—as yet still attached to their owners' heads) to be coveted. And so (this was the white version) the Cherokee chieftain Diwali and his band boarded it, killed the six men of the crew, the three women and four children, and took captive the slaves.

News traveled slowly and by word of mouth in those days, for Sequoyah had not yet invented the alphabet, and, busy raiding white settlements here and there, Diwali had been on the warpath for some months and was out of touch with things. Now, nearing home, he was met by runners with the news that the war he had thought he was fighting had been concluded by a peace treaty some time past. The news of Muscle Shoals had preceded him and the event, committed in peacetime, had been condemned as an atrocity by the whites and repudiated by the Cherokees. Awaiting him was arrest and extradition and most likely the gallows and a hangman's noose. Diwali turned about and went west, settling his band in

Arkansas, where, over the years, the outpost was joined by others of The People, forced for one reason or another to leave their homeland.

Blood had flowed at Muscle Shoals that day, both versions of events agreed as to that; but according to the red version it was not an act of war but a private dispute over money and deception. Captain William Scott had trinkets to trade to Indians and he invited Diwali and his band aboard to inspect his wares. Plied with whiskey, they paid exorbitant prices for glass beads, mirrors, body paint.

When they sobered up, and saw how they had been swindled, the Indians returned and demanded their money back. They were refused. In the fracas that ensued, an Indian was speared by a boat hook and killed. It was then, and only then, according to this account, that Diwali attacked, and while in the fray the white men were all killed, the women and children were released unharmed and sent on their way downriver.

But his version might not be believed, not even by his own people. Flight to the dreaded west where none dared follow him was the prudent course for Diwali. Now he was seen by many Cherokees as their Moses.

Diwali: The Bowl, or Chief Bowles, as white people called him: at least half and maybe pure Scots, possibly the only Bowles spared, because of his tender age, in the massacre of his family by Cherokees and raised in the tribe as one of their own (like the convert more Catholic than the Pope, these grafted-on ones were often the most thoroughgoing Indians of them all, and the most ferocious haters of whites) was thirty-eight years old at the time of the events at Muscle Shoals. Today, in 1837, he was still alive, now eighty-three, and still out west, though no longer in Arkansas. Long a figure of legend, remote in time and place, he now reentered the lives of The People remaining, holding out, in the old country. His fortunes had changed radically; they had been completely reversed. Now instead of being an outcast, a fugitive, he was suddenly able, in this their hour of need, to offer them, all eighteen thousand of them, as well as all the other four of the so-called Civilized Tribes, the Creeks, the Choctaws, the Chickasaws and the Seminoles—any who wanted to come— the more the better—a homeland.

But that story first necessitated a digression, reversion to yet another time long ago and to a different place, the story of yet another Cherokee, he likewise controversial, likewise legendary, he the most improbable Cherokee of them all, a real cuckoo bird this one, hatched in a foster nest and finding his way to his true flock only when fledged, one long absent from tribal affairs but now come back, a prodigal son in reverse, returning from disgrace in triumph and glory—often an amusement to The People, occasionally an embarrassment, always a puzzle, predictable only in his unpredictability, now the most famous Cherokee of them all, not even excepting the sage, the living saint, Sequoyah—a Cherokee when it suited him to be one, the leopard who could change his spots. His story would lead in time back to the one about Diwali, for in this latest, world-shaking turn of events the two—old friends —maybe even one-time, overnight in-laws, after the hospitable Indian custom—had been allies, but first: back to the year 1809 and once again to eastern Tennessee and to that same river, the Hiwassee, where, two years earlier, the traitor Doublehead had met his bloody end at the hands of Ridge, Saunders and Rogers.

Not seen at the time for what it was, an event to change the world, to alter its very map: Sam Houston's running away from home, aged sixteen, to become an Indian. The flight itself was not adventurous. To become a Cherokee, which to him meant to dress flamboyantly (a lifelong vanity), to dally with those dusky, dark-eyed daughters of Eve, the easygoing Indian maidens, to indulge the taste for firewater (a lifelong weakness) he already had at that age, and above all to loaf, to lie on the riverbank and read of Greek and Roman heroes and day-dream, free from drudgery behind the dry-goods counter of his widowed mother's trading post and from the ignobility of being "in trade," so soul-soiling to him who felt himself predestined for great deeds and high places—to attain these heart's desires all the lad had to do was paddle the few strokes across the Hiwassee. He might have swum it. There, so near, was another world.

He was welcomed. With that casual, that almost promiscuous foster parenthood of the unprolific Cherokees, Olooteka, also known as John Jolly, chief of the village there on the opposite bank, took the youth into his home and adopted him. No doubt he was scratched and sent to water, spent his week in the *asi,* that would have been his one test to pass. *Kalunah:* The Raven, was the name he took.

Those were the days to be an Indian! The Cherokees' worries and woes were then but small clouds on the distant horizon. They were still themselves then. They had not yet stopped being Indians and begun aping their enemies in hopes of acceptance by them. A man's time was spent in the manly pursuits, hunting, fishing, trapping, idling. There was no grubbing in the dirt, no hoeing of weeds, no bending and stooping to gather crops, no being yoked to a mule behind a plow, no daily tending to the wants of animals, slopping filthy hogs, relieving stupid cows of their accumulation of milk. What white men there were envied you, imitated you. A grown man's life was a boy's life and a boy's life was a pampered pet's. Young Sam Houston was not the first (indeed he was one of the last of the many, for it was so soon to end) to feel the call of that carefree, unconfined, irresponsible existence and to heed its call: to put aside moneygrubbing, social restraints, respectability, cross over his personal Hiwassee and reenter into man's unspoiled, essential state, his original birthright.

Three years Houston's youthful idyll among the Cherokees lasted, three aimless, lotus-eating years before the serpent of discord got into his garden and tempted his susceptible white blood with the apple of ambition. Unsurprising, then, that at the most miserable time of his life, twenty years later, his thoughts should turn to the most blissful time of it. That, toppled from eminence, and from the all-but-certain expectation of far greater eminence, outcast, reviled, he should again seek refuge among those who had welcomed him earlier, whose men were not so demanding and whose women were not so squeamish, who took in a person, a suppliant, a wretch, in the words of that favorite hymn of theirs—second only to "Amazing Grace"—"Just as I am, without one plea."

Oh, what a fall was there! One day, popular governor of Tennessee, newly reelected to a second term in office, likely, almost destined, to become, with the aid of his mentor, Andrew Jackson, President, newly married at thirty-seven to a lovely daughter of one of the state's first families, then, overnight: ruin—stark, utter ruin.

Whatever was the truth of the matter, nobody knew to this day. She refused to reproach him (which was taken to mean that it was something that no woman might sully her lips with), and not even in his own defense, though accused of conduct unspeakable, publicly posted as a cad and a coward, burned in effigy—not even then would Houston offer a word of explanation for their separation. Yet this silence of his, instead of being construed as honorable, chivalrous even, was resented as showing contempt for public opinion and its right to know, and as an ungentlemanly insinuation against his defenseless little wife. (She was not all that defenseless. Her hot-blooded brothers were behind much of the outcry against Houston.)

It was rumored that he had discovered, or that she herself had confessed to him, that she loved another, and that—only eighteen—she had allowed herself to be persuaded by her ambitious family to marry the state's most eligible bachelor against her inclinations. It was rumored that he himself had put it out that he had caught her in his rival's embrace. It was rumored that on their nuptial night his crude frontiersman's way with a woman had frightened and repelled the refined young lady. It was rumored that that old arrow wound sustained at Horseshoe Bend when he was little more than a boy had left him with a lifelong suppurating wound in the region of the groin which the sensitive young bride could not stomach. It was also rumored that it had unmanned him altogether. What was not rumored? It was even rumored that the monster had cynically married and heartlessly sacrificed the young lady to his ambition for empire, and his subsequent career, crowned by his current success and fame, was adduced as proof of it.

Houston had fallen low, and, always immoderate, excessive, theatrical in everything he did, he himself dug his personal pit still deeper. He refunded his wife ("bride" would have been the better word, so short had been her tenure) home to her outraged family, resigned his governorship, renounced his American citizenship, and, disguised by a beard and traveling incognito (and dead drunk, it was said, all the way), rejoined the Cherokees, this time the ones out west (John Jolly was out there now, and he welcomed home his adopted son)—an outcast among outcasts.

There to hide his head in shame and disgrace forevermore? To wallow in the dirt of his downfall? To white Tennessee so it seemed. For soon it was learned that he had become—this man of destiny—a frontier saloonkeeper, drinking most of the profits, gambling away the rest with his patrons, and engaging in rowdy brawls, even knocking his old foster-father to the ground in one drunken debauch, that all traces of civilization had moulted from him to be replaced by the head feathers, and the little else, of savagery, that he had gone native with a vengeance, participating in bestial Indian orgies, and lastly that he had sunk to that state in which none could be more debased: that he had become (it had to be uttered in a whisper, behind the hand) a squaw-man. She with whom he shared the blanket was Diana, daughter of John Rogers, veteran of Horseshoe Bend, and, before that, Ridge's deputy in the bloody dispatch of the traitor Doublehead. That the said Diana was reported to be surpassingly beautiful only deepened the depravity. That she was all of about one-eighth Indian did not lessen the odium of miscegenation.

The People, too, could correspond with one another now, thanks to Sequoyah, and from letters back home of those newly emigrated out there (the concluding message of which was nearly always "stay where you are") emerged a picture of Houston as a man so deep in the sulks, so resentful of those who had rejected him, as to have gone off his head, gone childish, a white man who was now a caricature of all that The People themselves had so painstakingly shed and put behind them. He went around armed with a bow and arrows. He would speak only Cherokee, conversing with white men through an interpreter. His costume was an embroidered hunting shirt, fringed buckskin leggings, beaded moccasins. His long hair was braided in a queue, crowned, when not with feathers, with a turban. As self-appointed Cherokee Ambassador to the Great White Father, he had even appeared in this get-up, all six and a quarter feet of him, in the halls of Congress (where formerly he had represented Tennessee), to the astonishment, not to mention the embarrassment, of none there so much as Ross, Ridge, Agiduda and their delegation, themselves all looking like senators in their swallow-tailed black bombazine frock coats and beaver top hats.

A broken man, a finished man, and stories of him (his platform the dirt-floored barroom of that low grogshop of his, lost in the middle of nowhere) drunkenly declaiming to his audience of drunks that he would yet make his triumphant reappearance on the world's stage, the tastelessness of his having had his portrait painted, on one trip back east, in a Roman toga, standing barefoot amid the ruins of ancient Carthage, as

Caius Marius, the exile who made a comeback, only added to the image of failure that of foolishness.

Now that this has-been, this down-and-outer, this laughingstock had led a handful of backwoodsmen to victory over a disciplined army and drawn upon the map of the world a vast new nation and been acclaimed its President, it was said that the whole thing had been a smoke screen all along, a calculated, incredibly farsighted and devilishly clever charade.

Those who said that Houston had had something in the back of his mind as long ago as seventeen years, when he advised his old friend Diwali to leave The Territory and migrate to Texas, were crediting the man with foresight that amounted to divination. But Houston always had an unrestrained imagination, boundless ambition, and there was before him the historical example of another daring dreamer; he would not have been the first man to let his thoughts wander westward, and Texas was worth keeping an eye on. It was just about the size for the size of him. From the Rio Grande to the Canadian border it stretched, from Louisiana to the Pacific, almost unpopulated, totally ungovernable from a capital a world away of a government only recently emancipated from Spain and still just learning to crawl. To do a friend a good turn by pointing him to this new land of opportunity was to have credit to draw upon, should the need ever arise.

And a powerful friend this one was, chief now of some two thousand, who, since he blazed the trail with his fugitive little band, had emigrated west and joined him. Over the years since his moving to Texas, Houston had seen to it that he had steadily grown in power by sending him Indians from all the dispossessed tribes. These were no longer disposed to fight one another there in territory big enough for them all, and more. There they could bury the tomahawk, smoke the peace pipe. They knew at long last who their common enemy was. They had come to number nearly twenty thousand. All this might

suit the still nebulous designs of that downfallen but determined self-styled Indian, Sam Houston. He had his own reasons for hating whites.

When the time was ripe a provocation had to be found
sufficient in the eyes of the world to make a man give up the
governorship of a state, the almost certain succession to the
presidency of all the states, for a prize greater than these: a
vast country all his own, he its first citizen. What but the
disappointment—cause withheld, no discussion permitted, put
whatever construction you liked upon that silence—of a failed
marriage? It was over poor little Eliza Allen, a pawn in his
plans, that Houston had heartlessly advanced, while intimat-
ing that he himself was the injured party.

But why so elaborate, so indirect a way to the prize he
perceived? According to this script it was because he was not
the first to perceive that prize, there had been that other man,
and his case was cautionary; it was to avoid the mistakes of his
predecessor that Houston had done things in his devious way.
Long before him, Aaron Burr also had studied those vast un-
colored areas on the map and dreamed of an empire in the
west. For his plotting and scheming Burr had been charged
with interference in the internal affairs of a friendly foreign
nation, the same nation whose affairs Houston intended to
interfere in: Mexico. This, under the laws of the United States,
was treason, and for that high crime Burr was arrested and
brought to trial. For lack of evidence, he was acquitted, but
that put an end to Burr's dream.

Now, treason against the United States was a charge that
could be brought only against a citizen of that country. Once
over that hurdle, the moves in Houston's intricate game, including that opening sacrificial pawn, poor little Eliza, all fell
into place. And so Houston renewed and strengthened those
ties with the Cherokees formed when he was a boy on the
banks of the Hiwassee.

It was in alliance with Diwali's army of mixed red warriors, some eighteen hundred strong, that Houston had won his unforeseeable victory at San Jacinto. Not by their fighting alongside him but by their staying out of the fight: that was how they had aided him.

The Mexican authorities had encouraged the emigration of Indians from the United States to Texas. The province was spacious, sparsely settled. These were people disenchanted, to say the least, with Mexico's mighty, and increasingly expansionist-minded, neighbor to the east. They were pastoral, peaceable, unlike the wild Comanches, the Apaches. They were a counterbalance to Austin's Anglos. Not only were they welcomed—now with the growing restiveness of those Anglos, they were promised that, should rebellion break out, and, with their help, be put down, they would be granted indisputable title to the lands they occupied in east Texas. They had every reason to side with the Mexicans. What secured their nonintervention in the war was Houston's old friendship with Diwali—his being a Cherokee himself.

1800! As many as Santa Anna's own troops—but with this difference between them: they were far more warlike because they were far more motivated. Driven there from lands much loved, and having lived there long enough now to love this place, with nowhere else to flee to, they would make this their last stand; what was Texas to those peons impressed into the dictator's ranks? Had the confederated Indians fought alongside the Mexicans that day at San Jacinto, as self-interest suggested they should, the outcome would surely have been reversed. It was their neutrality that made the difference. Houston, too, had promised them title to their land should the rebellion be decided in his side's favor, but in gambling on that the Indians were taking a mighty big risk. The Texans were odds-on losers.

All this Agiduda learned at that meeting of Ross's cabinet. From Texas had come an emissary empowered by Houston and Diwali to offer the Cherokees a home, to urge them to come out en masse to the new country, *their* country, the only one headed by one of theirs. An all-Indian country, outside the reach of the United States. There they could preserve their old ways. They were welcome. They were wanted. They were needed. For no sooner had Santa Anna been released from captivity and repatriated than he broke the pledge which had gained him his freedom and began raising an army to invade and reclaim Texas, and vowing to punish every Texan with summary execution. With their help he could be repulsed. The whole world knew what warriors the Cherokees were!

God knew, by then the Cherokees needed a home to go to! For this was after the government in Washington, in order to get around Ross's stubborn immovability, had taken the simple expedient of deposing him from office and appointing Ridge as The People's negotiator. Yet to this emissary from the white red man for whom time had stood still for the Cherokees since his boyhood, the cabinet members could only listen politely and with straight faces. What an irony! Here was this imitation Indian, Houston, urging them to preserve their way of life when that way of life was long a thing of the past, hardly a memory. Warriors? The Cherokees? Maybe those of them out west, cut off from the encroachment of the whites, the teachings of the missionaries, the blandishments of creature comforts, the things that softened a man, no part of the Cherokees' self-transformation, maybe they still lived in the old tribal way, dancing the Green Corn dance, playing the bloody, the murderous stick-ball game, maybe they were still warriors, but to the ones in the east, now so worldly, so mock-white, these things were quaint and curious, childlike if not childish. Texas, even more remote, was more daunting than

The Territory; what was expected of them that they do to win their place there, fight for it, was the very tactic they had always rejected here.

Said John Ross to Agiduda before the meeting broke up, "David, you look like a man smiling to keep from crying."

Agiduda surveyed Ross from his sandy crown down to his small feet—a survey that took but little time considering the distance to be covered. "I was just trying, John," he said, "to picture you in nothing but a breechclout, a feather in your hair, and war paint on your face."

"And yourself? What about it, David, lad? The unspoiled wilds of Texas, where the buffalo still roam and the alligators enliven your morning dip. Fresh trophies on the old scalp pole. Stewed puppy in the cook pot. You'd take to that life, wouldn't you?"

"Ugh," said Agiduda.

It was not the Indian grunt of assent, it was the white grunt of distaste.

The Ridges, long in favor of going but lingering on in hopes of persuading the others all to go with them, had gone at last. They did not go on foot. They went, for most of the way, by steamboat. Twenty dollars a head was the cost to the government of transporting the volunteer Indians on the open deck, but for the Major and his family stateroom passage was provided at a cost of some three hundred. This too was chalked down, to be remembered.

The Ridges were only being sensible, facing up to reality, and you told yourself that you ought to stop being foolish and follow their example. The day was almost upon you. Yet, like those people who put off making a last will and die intestate because they cannot face death, you made no preparations. How prepare yourself for a life that you had no wish to live, or care how you were transported to the place that you knew as the land of death? The slower the pace you went at the better. In your hopelessness, suffering and the prospect of suffering came to have a perverse appeal for you. You dared your enemies to do their worst for all the world to see and shame. In this there was some small measure of revenge.

And so, some out of fear, some out of faith in their powerful new god, some out of trust in their Tsan Usdi and a last-minute miracle of his, some out of pride, some out of apathy, some dejection, some defiance, some simply out of old age and its listlessness, its indifference to the future, the Cherokees hung on; even as the last day dawned the stockades awaiting them still stood all but empty. And as long as a single one of them held out, Agiduda would hold out with him. As long as a single one was forced to go on foot with nothing but the clothes on his back, nothing to eat but army rations, nothing to sleep under but the blanket he was issued, so he would go. The captain must be the last to leave the sinking ship, and in the lifeboat must share the fare of all.

You waited for them to come to your cell and lead you away. Instead of getting in a late sleep and thus shortening your hours of consciousness, you woke early. You could not sit still. All that you were seeing you were seeing for perhaps the last time, and you found yourself picking up and fondling the familiar objects that surrounded you, and weeping over them. The clock seemed to have broken. It was only a moment ago that you had looked at it, and yet it said now that an hour had passed. One of your precious last few hours, and you had lost it. Better not to look. But of course you looked, and now it was long since, yet the clock said it was only minutes—that much more time to have to get through. As the day passed and nothing happened, you oscillated between a hope that at the eleventh hour you had been given a stay of execution, a reprieve, and the dread that you were being toyed with, that this forlorn hope was your captors' ultimate cruelty: to make you long for release through their coming for you, and even thanking them for putting an end to your harrowing suspense. That night you went to bed certain that tomorrow would be the day that today was to have been, and they would come down upon you all the more ferociously for having been balked in their original plan.

On the following morning the resolution with which you had faced yesterday had to be marshaled afresh. Under cover of darkness hope had stolen back to tease and torment you. Meanwhile there was no knowing what was happening. If anybody knew, he was lying low. The whole world was. It seemed to be holding its breath. No news spread. You could only wait and wonder. And speculate. Tsan Usdi had won from Congress a temporary injunction, a permanent revocation. President Van Buren had dropped dead, been assassinated, impeached. Protest riots in the northern cities had spread into insurrection. The army of troops sent to round up the Indians had mutinied. The British had landed. God's pent-up wrath had been loosed in earthquakes, floods, cyclones. The Cherokees, some at least, maybe many of the young braves, had rebelled against Ross's passive resistance and gone on the warpath.

Surrounded and besieged as you had been for so long, called upon time and again to surrender and go into captivity, your cause written off, a part of you still stubbornly held out, kept its confidence that reinforcements would arrive in the nick of time, the worst would not come to pass. It was inadmissible, unthinkable. It would be like one of those hellfire-and-brimstone millenarian preachers prophesying the end of the world, and the day for it came and went like other days and the world was the same as ever.

But where now were the Creeks and the Choctaws, the Chickasaws and the Seminoles? Where indeed? Where were the Abnakis, the Apalachees, the Biloxis, the Catawbas, the Chickahominees, the Delawares, the Mohicans, the Munsees, the Nanticokes, the Narragansetts, the Natchez, the Pequots, the Penacooks, the Powhatans, the Susquehannas, the Winnebagoes?

Listening for a loud convulsion, you heard the hush that had fallen. The leaves and the blades of grass, the earth underfoot, no longer spoke. The familiar spirits had departed from the Cherokee homeland. You had lived to see and feel the misery foretold of old. Your feet were turned toward the west, never again to turn around.

One thing you must do, painful as the prospect was, by way of preparing for the end, was to pay a last visit to the graves of your kin. It was a long time now since the Fergusons had visited theirs, one reason being that to do so they would have to trespass on their unneighborly neighbor Mr. Blodgett's land, another that they dreaded a reproach from those spirits for abandoning them, leaving them to strangers, a separation which to the ancestor-worshipping Cherokees was the worst wrench of all in this forced removal from their homeland. Now such a pilgrimage could be put off no longer. And so, on one of the last of those last days, Agiduda, Grandmother and Noquisi, pausing on the way to pick wildflowers for offerings, went down to that back section of their former property where, in a grove of ancient oaks, lay the family cemetery containing all the Fergusons who had died in the New World, stretching back in time over a century.

What they found, scattered on the ground, were their skulls and bones, coffin lids and rotted cerements, mounds of more or less freshly dug earth beside each grave, the cavities filled with rainwater. In search of ornaments buried with the dead, Mr. O. J. Blodgett had mined his gold mine.

Their knees buckled and all three sank to the ground amid the flowers that had fallen from their fingers. Agiduda

quickly covered the boy's eyes with his hand and turned his
head aside from the scene—though even as an old man himself, telling the story to his grandson, he could still make vivid
the glimpse he had had of it.

"Now I want to go from here," Agiduda said. "Forever.
At once. We will pack the wagon. Then we will go to the
stockade and give ourselves up."

However, that was not to be. Agiduda was spared the
consequences of his lapse from self-abnegation. No Cherokee
would go west in greater deprivation than he. The bill of sale
for the homeplace produced by its new owner, Mr. O. J.
Blodgett, who appeared early the next morning in the company of the soldiers detailed to capture the Fergusons, stipu-
lated that he had bought the land, the house and all that it
contained. There was Agiduda's signature on the agreement,
forged by someone with access to the genuine article, dated
and witnessed. The cost of that document, with its official rib-
bons and seals, must have been considerable. The Fergusons
knew where the money had come from. Grandmother knew
now where her missing ham had gone, who the fox was that
had stolen her chickens and the rat her stores, who had gathered the eggs and milked the cow before her in the dark of the
morning.

Mr. Blodgett had learned just in time of his neighbor's
race. To Agiduda in parting he said, "Well, Chief, you sure
fooled me. I took you to be a man like me." He said it admir-
ingly and expected it to be taken as a compliment, for fooling
him he felt to be a rare feat, and to be taken for somebody like
himself to be everything any man could want.

"A curse on you," said the old man. "May you be
haunted by the spirits of all my ancestors. May you go unburied for birds to pick your bones."

In token of his contempt Agiduda spat on the ground at
the man's feet. The gesture petrified the boy. For a Cherokee
to do that was unheard of. To Noquisi it signified that his

grandfather had spat out his soul because it had come to taste foul in his mouth in a world where the air must be shared with people such as this one.

They were marched down the lane and around the bend. There the six soldiers mounted their horses that had been left behind in order that the house might be taken by stealth and surprise. Then they were marched down to the main road. There they halted and waited, for what they were not told.

Presently there came down the road a troupe of some forty people with a dozen soldiers riding guard over them. Side by side, four and six abreast they marched, some with walking staffs, some who had readied themselves for this eventuality with packs on their backs, others with small household objects in their hands, a silver spoon, a china cup, a doll—whatever could be snatched up for a keepsake as they were driven from their homes. Mothers carried babies, fathers rode little children on their shoulders, pulled others along by the hand. On army remounts and caisson mules rode old men and women too feeble to keep up on foot, a man with one leg, an idiot girl enjoying her ride and the company of the crowd. Several more mounts, for other handicapped people yet to be rounded up, were in reserve, led on halters by a soldier muleteer. A sick woman was being carried in a litter by two of her three sons in turn while the off-duty one shielded her eyes from the glare with a roofing shingle. Thoroughness was the aim of the army's operation. No Cherokee was to be overlooked, whatever his or her age or condition; from those in the cradle to those with one foot in the grave, all were to be cleared out. The sight of Agiduda drew from them a universal groan. The Fergusons were ordered to fall in and the troupe proceeded down the road.

They had lost—if they had ever possessed it—the stolidity

attributed to them. There was scarcely a dry eye in the crowd. Among them as they marched there was no talk. All were experiencing the same shock and numbness. While they had been driven from their separate homes and might each have had a different story to tell about what he or she had been doing at the moment of the soldiers' surprise appearance, all divergences among them had been canceled by the common fate that had swept them up and hurled them together. They had been reduced to cells of a single body, with a single purpose and destination, like a column of ants on the march. Meanwhile, Indian fortitude and Indian pride imposed silence upon them. It ought also to have forbidden them letting their captors see and enjoy their dispiritedness, but this was too great for them to dissemble. It was to give them an outlet for their desolation that Agiduda sang:

"Naquasdvquo Gatisgani"

The soldiers tensed, rising in their stirrups, twisting about in their saddles, raising their rifles. To quiet their fears that the unintelligible words were a signal to revolt disguised as music, Agiduda quickly, loudly, to the same tune, sang:

"Just as I am, without one plea"

The entire column of marchers took it up, some singing in Cherokee and some in English:

"Tsagigvaqualisgasdodv"
"But that thy blood was shed for me"
"Alesgiyanisgv Tsisa"
"And that thou bid'st me come to thee"

"Wigvlutsi! Wigvlutsi!"
"O, Lamb of God, I come! I come!"

And although the hymn's mournful measure was woefully out of step with the pace they were made by their guards to maintain, they sang it thus in round-song, one tongue answering the other, as they trudged along. The effect was that of a funeral march.

Waiting at every crossroads to join the column were others rounded up in the countryside, in bands large and small, overseen by their mounted guards. Rather than finding strength in numbers, their despair was deepened by these additions to their ranks. It seemed that none of them had eluded the dragnet. They were being eradicated. After a long lifetime as Amos Smith, Noquisi would still remember his feeling of shame—for the defeated and despised learn from their oppressors to despise themselves.

The day was rapidly heating up and the march beginning to take its toll upon the people. All had trekked along the main road for miles and, before that, many of them had trekked for miles more. Now they were weary, hot, dusty, dry, footsore. Children were growing querulous, balky. The old folks were straggling, falling behind.

Upon the soldiers too the march was taking its toll. The pains the people were enduring at their hands irritated them by arousing in them a fellow feeling which they were forbidden to feel. It created disturbing likenesses between Indians and themselves. This warring upon civilians, upon old men, women and children, was a distasteful assignment for men trained to engage other men in armed combat. It shamed them, and shame in combination with power turned them cruel and petty. Impatient to get the business over with, to return to barracks and go off duty, they were annoyed by any laggardness.

In the band of captives waiting at one crossroads was a

lone man who fell in step alongside Noquisi. He was the biggest man the boy had ever seen. No doubt it was his size that first singled him out for the special attentions of one of his captors, a soldier who pestered him with the persistency of a deerfly. A victim so imposing was a provocation. But it was not this alone that irked the soldier. The man's bearing was another goad. Not that he was defiant, sullen; he was anything but that. He was provokingly unprovokable, composed. He seemed to be present in body but elsewhere in spirit. He seemed to be walking in his sleep. This detachment from the scene was what irked the soldier. He wanted the man to experience what he was undergoing, perhaps because what he himself was experiencing was distasteful to him.

The big man was dark-skinned, broad-faced, heavy-featured. His hair was plaited in long greased braids. His buckskin shirt and trousers were frayed and stained. He seemed so out of place as to suggest that he had been found up some remote mountainside or down some distant cove where he had never seen a white man, never heard English spoken. But that was no excuse for not obeying an order so simple it did not need to be spoken: March! And step lively!

The step of none of them was very lively now that their shoes were full of water from fording a creek. The first to arrive at the ford, those at the head of the column, had sat themselves on the bank to take off their shoes and their moccasins, roll up their trousers. It was then that the whips were brought into use. In among the people the soldiers charged, lashing their backs, driving them into the water. "Just as you are!" one shouted derisively, and another added, "Without one plea!"

Once the unspoken inhibition against them had been broken, the whips remained in use. Each soldier was afraid of being thought soft by his comrades and suspected of harboring feelings of sympathy with those animals in human form. They galloped up and down the line wielding their whips and urging the marchers on with the shouts and curses of cattle drivers. "Hi! Hi! Get along there! Hump yourselves, damn you!" Their cruelty fed upon itself; more of the same was the way to dilute and excuse what had gone before. Exposed by his position on the outside of the column, the big man was lashed time and again by the one soldier.

Whenever this happened the man would slowly raise his head and regard his tormentor with a face as blank of expression as that of an ox for the plowman. After a moment there appeared on it a look of mild wonder, as though he were unable to connect so bold an act with the creature that met his gaze. Then, turning to Noquisi, the man gave a little smile. With this smile he seemed to wish to convey two things. First, "He didn't hurt me," and second, "It's what we must expect of them, isn't it, sonny? It's their nature."

For the rest of his long life, whatever his name, Noquisi would repent of his not responding to that smile. It was meant to reassure him, quiet his fears, lend him courage, as was the man's handclasp, proffered when the smile failed of its intention. The boy had not returned the smile, he had rejected the hand. If only he had held on to it! There was nothing personal in this rejection. But to a Cherokee there was no greater dishonor than to receive a blow and not return it, and to the boy the big man, now as impotent as the shorn and blinded Samson, was the embodiment of their people's humiliation and helplessness. He was ashamed of him and ashamed for him.

Thus it was that when they came to the fork in the road where they were commanded to turn, the man, with no hand to guide him, went the wrong way. He had gone some twenty feet when that soldier shot and killed him for attempting to escape. No last words did he have for those who got to him before he died, only the wordless babble of the congenital deafmute.

At first sight of their concentration camp (this but one of twenty-three like it), Agiduda was struck by a sense of having been there before. It looked like one of the old-time Indian camps. They too would have had their tepees as the soldiers had their tents. A corral for the horses. To take refuge in when attacked, they would have had a stockade like this one of logs sharpened to a point on top. They would have chosen just such a tract of treeless, flat prairie land so that the approach of an enemy could be detected from afar. Here, however, it had been done so that any prisoner who succeeded in leaping over the wall could be seen by the sentries long before he reached the distant woods. Now as the column halted at the gates, on one of which was written *TLA* and on the other *YIDAYOJADANVSI,* the bar was lifted, they were swung open, and the people entered the pen that was to be their home for the next twenty days. The packhorse bearing the deaf-mute's body brought up the rear.

Once they were inside, there was a rush for the water barrels with their metal dippers and for the latrines. These needs attended to, they looked around them at the high walls, and relatives and friends fell weeping into one another's arms and sobbing mothers clasped their sobbing children to them. Then some sat while others distended themselves on the ground to rest their aching bodies. Only the young men did not weep. To them, accustomed to the freedom of all outdoors, brothers to the birds, to the wild animals of the woods, being caged inside the compound was a blow to their pride that amounted to a loss of manhood. Wild animals they worshipped, domestic animals, introduced among them by the white man, they despised; now they found themselves penned, collared, their wings clipped. They despised their condition, and would have avoided one another for shame, but that they were confined and there was no place to hide.

Throughout the rest of the day the gates were opened from time to time to admit more parties of captives. Families separated in the roundup were reunited. First they wept with joy at finding one another, then they wept with sorrow at finding one another here.

All, even the frightened children, were drawn for a look at the deaf-mute's body, lying in the shade of the wall where it had been unloaded from the packhorse. A detail of soldiers was sent shortly after it was put there to remove and bury it, but the sergeant in command was prevailed upon to leave it overnight in order that all might mourn for the man. This commenced after they had been fed their rations of salt pork and cornmeal mush: a low, high-pitched wail, much like the distant howling of a pack of wolves.

Among the parties brought in later in the day were some who had known the man. He had lived alone, unmarried, and having lost all his family. When this information became known, the feeling was intensified that, belonging to nobody, he belonged to them all. They were his family. He was mourned through the night as by his blood kin.

In the morning the soldiers came again to remove the body. The sergeant levied two young prisoners to dig the grave. It was the dead man's clan members who protested this barbaric treatment. It was to the Reverend Mackenzie that they appealed. He went to see the commandant.

He went in anger, prepared to hate the man for his cruelty; he returned from his interview despising him for his sense of superiority. He had not known, the commandant said, that these people cared about such niceties. If they wanted the body buried in a coffin, and had somebody in there capable of making one, why, they were welcome as far as he was concerned. He would supply the lumber and the necessary tools.

There was somebody. Every poor Indian farmer was his

own carpenter, but the better-off hired their building done for them, and these two were professionals. So boards were brought in and hammers and nails, saws and tri-squares, and, under the skilled hands of the two of them, a coffin soon took shape. The grave was dug outside the wall. The Reverend Mackenzie officiated while one member of the kinless man's clan, under armed guard, was allowed to represent them all.

That there is strength in numbers is true at times, the very opposite of the truth at other times. Few things in life are more gladdening than a large congregation of relatives, friends and neighbors when the occasion is one to rejoice over, but every additional face at a funeral is one more to grieve with, grieve over. To celebrate a victory, the more the merrier, but in surrender and defeat numbers magnify the loss. The Cherokees were to be removed to the last one, and they were packed inside the concentration camps to await the capture of that last one. The day's catch swelled their universal groan of despair. Though each prolonged their discomfort, they cheered on every one who eluded capture.

Some seventeen thousand were to be rounded up. To do the job seven thousand troops were employed. Of these, three thousand were regular army men, four thousand were volunteers. The regulars did their job out of duty, the volunteers out of zeal. How you got to the stockade, with what, and in what condition on your arrival, depended much upon which of the two it had been your luck to fall into the hands of.

In his orders to his troops, their commander, General Scott, told them that they were to carry out this operation as humanely as possible. There was to be no maltreatment of their captives—not even any abusive language. Special consideration and kindness was to be accorded infants, the elderly, the feeble-minded and women in a "helpless condition." These

orders were generally obeyed by the regulars, generally flouted
by the volunteers.

And so the captives arrived at the camp by ways and in
states as various as the colors of their skins, which ranged
from purest white through all the shades of red to deepest
black. Some came on foot, with nothing to transport but themselves, some on horseback, some in wagons piled with possessions, some with a train of slaves—the captives of captives—
self-propelled possessions—bearing family heirlooms on their
backs. Some were brought in with bruises from gun butts, cuts
from bayonets, welts from whips. In the camp they told one
another their stories, for these belonged now to a common
fund, a collective indictment, like bringing them to the communal New Year bonfire. They had been surrounded and
taken by armed soldiers while seated at table, while milking
the cow, carding wool, nursing the baby. They had been taken
in their privies, while bathing in the creek. Women were taken
while visiting friends, not allowed to rejoin their families, children with playmates separated from their parents. The white
rabble that followed the soldiers were looting their cabins even
as they themselves were driven from the door. They had
looked back to see them in flames. The urge to bear witness, to
have their wrongs on record, overcame reticence, modesty.
Girls told of having been raped by an entire platoon. Husbands, fathers, sons and brothers had watched helplessly while
wives, daughters, mothers and sisters were sodomized.

They were like a shoal of fish caught in a net. Instantly all
privacy was lost. By day they sat on the ground beside one
another, by night they slept there beside one another. Whatever a person did was done in sight of all. In sight, sound,
smell, almost in touch of all. A people fanatical in their clean-
liness, habituated from birth to a daily bath, whatever the
weather, they were disgusted and depressed by the dirtiness
they began at once to feel.

The problem of the latrines arose immediately. A platoon

of soldiers was needed to enforce order because of the distur-
bance caused by their daily emptying. Not in the doing of the
job—once under way it was done with all possible speed so as
to get it over with—but in the drafting of the crew. Some of
the young men had to be whipped into submission. Some had
to be whipped to the point that they were barely able afterwards to do it.

The scheme devised to overcome this unpleasantness by
the corporal in charge of the detail seemed at first to be a
cruelty but was soon seen to be, in fact, a kindness. He com-
piled a list of the eligible men and from it each morning he
read aloud the names of the day's detail. No able-bodied man
was exempted. What seemed originally a wish to degrade and
humiliate them one and all was not what it seemed. When all
were untouchables, none was. When this was understood, the
men cooperated. Stripped to their breechclouts, the crew did
their foul job, accompanied the loaded carts outside, emptied
and scrubbed them, then went, under armed guard, to the
riverbank where they washed themselves with pails of water.
They were not envied, to be sure, but instead of being despised
and shunned, as they had feared, they were appreciated and
respected. The day came when a man whose name had been
mistakenly passed over stood forth and volunteered for the
duty.

The routine of life inside the compound was quickly established; there was little option in it. You staked out a position for yourself on the ground. There you sat. You got up to
go for a drink or go to the latrine and you came back to your
spot and sat. As there was continual shifting about, you might
find that somebody had appropriated your place. Not that it
mattered. Except for near the wall, which you could lean
against, and where there was shade for a while each day, one
spot was the same as another. Even those with places against
the wall abandoned them out of restlessness.

In the night you got up to relieve yourself, stepping over

sleeping bodies on the way, sometimes stepping on them, and afterwards you could not find your way back to your place in the dark. In the depth of night—between the snores—the cries arising out of nightmares—the wailing of wakeful infants— you heard the sound of the sentries' footsteps patrolling the perimeters of the walls. Despite them, a few young men leapt over. Most were caught and brought back at once, some gave themselves up after days of starving in the woods, a few made good their escapes—at least, they were never seen again.

Growing from this inanimation, and from their dejection, a pall of listlessness settled upon them. The sameness of the hours made the days interminable. The sameness of the days made them meaningless; without events to differentiate them one from another they ran together in the mind, confused the memory. There were outbursts of momentary madness caused by the inactivity and the tedium, and the person had to be restrained. The women bore up better; it was the idle men who broke. Stunned, almost stupefied, the women squatted, silent, or else emitting in chorus a low wordless hum of lamentation. The children drew in the dirt. The men gambled with their fingers. They soon lost interest, then sat dozing, hunched like birds roosting along a limb. Some stoked their pipes and smoked without stop. Whiskey was smuggled into the camp and sold to the prisoners by the soldiers; drunks, sprawled on the ground, grunted in their sodden sleep like dogs whimpering in their dreams. Just as did an animal confined in a cage, you stirred, opened your eyes and looked blinkingly around you, saw others in your same condition, and relapsed into torpor. To the old Amos Smith, recollecting his youth, the ordeal that had since come to be known as "The Trail of Tears," terrible as that had been, began as a relief from the mindless stagnation of those months in the concentration camp.

For, months it was. Not for all of them, but for all but a few.

The first contingent of emigrants departed on a day in June that was like a day in August—hottest in living memory. They were of a manageable number—some three hundred-odd. Beef cattle, hogs, chickens to be slaughtered and consumed on the way, and other provisions; wagons, oxen and draught horses, and fodder for them; drinking water to be found for no more than they were would present no insuperable problems. All was orderly. There were sorrowful leave-takings between those going and those forced by illness to stay behind, but even the anguish of separation was tempered by gladness that their loved ones were escaping from the camp.

Before reports could get back on the progress of that first group others set out from the various concentration camps. All wound up stalled together on the east bank of the Tennessee River. This they were to have navigated by steamer and flatboat to the place where they would disembark and proceed overland; now, as army officers experienced in the transportation of people in numbers ought to have been able to foresee, the yearlong drought had lowered the water level so that the river was too shallow to be navigated. The land was parched, a desert. Oxen and horses keeled over in their traces. Before the sun rose to evaporate it, people licked dew from the leaves of trees. Their numbers now were not manageable. They soon exhausted their provisions, their fodder. Afraid of contagion, farmers and storekeepers fled from their procurement agents. For epidemic diseases had broken out among them, including the most dreaded one of all, cholera, and word of this spread like the plague itself. The stifling heat rose daily to new highs.

When word of this state of things got back, the government in Washington charitably acceded to Ross's request that further emigration be postponed until the advent of the cool season. Through the rest of June, therefore, through all of July and August and into September, the Cherokees would stay where they were. Actually it was October before they left.

Meanwhile more prisoners were crammed inside the compound daily as the squads of soldiers combed the countryside in their search-and-seize operation. The condition of these worsened with each batch. Last-ditch holdouts, hiding in the woods, in caves, moving only under cover of darkness, living on roots, on the bark and the sap of trees, forced to search for drinking water, they were brought in too weakened to flee further, or had been forced to give themselves up. Among the crowded masses body lice, nits, ringworm became universal. Inside the stockade, with people bunched together like a bed of maggots, it was as though the rays of the sun had been gathered by a lens and focused upon that spot. Life there became a foretaste of hell.

Dysentery flared like spontaneous combustion, fanned into flames. That there might be latrines for use while others were being cleaned, more were built. The stench of them never lifted. Victims elbowed one another as they squatted over the trench—only to have to return momentarily. They might have been able to laugh in their tormentors' faces as their fingers were lopped off one by one, but dysentery destroyed all defenses by destroying all dignity. They writhed on the ground and groaned like animals in their pain and their punctured pride. Desiccated by loss of body fluid, unable to eat, they grew emaciated and jaundiced.

So numerous did the deaths become that the two coffinmakers worked full-time in the shed they were allowed to erect against a section of the wall, taking advantage of periods when demand was slow to stack up an inventory for busier times to come. They made them in two sizes, adult and child. The sound of their sawing and planing and hammering was daylong. Everybody else being idle, they never wanted for watchers. They were envied for having something to busy themselves with.

Survivors of the dead, if there were any male ones, and their friends, served as pallbearers—members of their clans when there were none. Others, including strangers to the deceased, volunteered to be gravediggers; it was an opportunity to get outside the walls for a little while. Only a little while, because the graves were kept shallow, the diggers' guards being unwilling to stand for long in the heat and glare of the sun. There was much inattentiveness at these graveside services, as the prisoners, waiting for, or waiting out, Noquisi's translation, gazed off longingly at the distant woods. The Reverend Mackenzie officiated.

Between Christianizing the living and interring the dead, administering the communion of the sick and the dying and conducting classes in the catechism, the Reverend Mackenzie and his young acolyte were kept busy. The Reverend Mackenzie had hopes that the boy might get the call to holy orders. He knew much of the prayer book by heart, could have performed the called-for offices without assistance from his elder.

The Reverend Mackenzie had reappeared in the camp on the second day, and he would continue to appear there daily throughout their stay, doing God's work, dispensing what solace he could. There was much in the official line for him to do even before the deaths began. The misery of life inside the stockade and fear of the future converted many of the as-yet unconverted. In all this it was Amos Ferguson who interpreted for him. Thus in his duties at both baptisms and funerals the boy was allowed outside the gates more often even than the gravediggers.

The baptisms were done in the nearby river, the convert marched there and back under armed guard. Their procession made the Reverend Mackenzie think of the Christianized Roman slaves, and he likened the stockade to the Colosseum in which they were martyred. It no longer bothered his conscience to practice baptism by total immersion now that he knew it was not the rite of the Baptist Church but rather the

Cherokee tradition of "going to water." What did bother his conscience was the feeling that in his missionary zeal and out of his longing to give comfort he might have overstepped his commission by allowing simple minds to infer that God had made them promises. He knew that the expectation of deliverance from earthly oppression was not the proper aim in embracing the faith, but he knew it was the aim of many who came to him, and that to preach otherwise to them would be to perplex, discourage and possibly dissuade them. These people were so desperate for a glimmer of hope! Their oppression was so great, their cause so right—perhaps if he could convert them *all,* to the last one, if they were to speak to God with a single, concerted voice, then He would hear and heed. It was as though he himself had said to John Ross, "That petition you took to President Van Buren—let me try it on my Great White Father." Yet he would have dreaded that, as the President had treated Ross, God might refuse to see him. He writes of his sorrowful sense of God's disinterestedness when, while pronouncing his benediction upon a man whose nose he was pinching shut and whom he had just raised from under the water, he saw one of the guards cross himself.

Among the Reverend Mackenzie's camp-inmate converts were a young half-breed couple. The husband's name was *Inali:* Black Fox, the wife's name was *Kanama:* Butterfly. They were from South Carolina, had been caught in the roundup here while on a visit with friends. Kanama was expecting her first child any day now. She was little more than a child herself, but if she was frightened at what lay in store for her she never let it be seen. Those among whom she found herself had much to be frightened of, and they did not have what she had to be glad of.

The older woman, herself a mother, who slept on the ground beside Kanama coached her in what she was to do when her time came, and this woman took it upon herself to make the necessary arrangements. Thus on the morning when

Kanama's water broke, the coffinmakers vacated their shed, which was then curtained with blankets lent by their owners. Taking with her a length of rope, a knife and a piece of string, a pail of water and a scrap of cloth, Kanama went into her labor room. The rope, in this instance suspended from a roof beam instead of the usual tree limb, would be looped under her arms for her to strain against while squatting.

Customarily it would have been some older woman relative of Kanama's, but as she had none of them here, it was her neighbor-sleeper who sat now outside the curtain and chanted the traditional charm. Amos translated it for the Reverend Mackenzie.

Little man, come out! Hurry! A bow and arrows are waiting for you. Hurry! Come out!

Little woman, come out! Hurry! A corn sifter is waiting for you. Hurry! Come out!

It was early morning when Kanama entered the curtained shed. No sound was heard from her until the sun had passed over the compound from one side of it to the other. Long before that time activity had ceased. A hush had fallen that deepened as silence lasted behind the curtain. Sufferers from dysentery too sick to suppress their groans were removed as far as possible from the shed, placed near the latrines for speedy access thereto. Children left off their games, talk stopped, all attended with mounting expectancy. The future father sat with his head on his arms. More and more infrequently, as though growing discouraged, the woman chanted the charm, which appeared to have lost its old-time power. Meanwhile, although the women disapproved, fearing it might invite a curse and bring the child on impaired in some way, or even stillborn, such was the men's love of gambling, greater than ever now because of the boredom of confinement, they made bets on the baby's sex and on just when it would be born. Those gamblers who had picked losing times settled their debts with the winners as the hours passed.

Except for infants and little children, everyone fasted through the day. In this there was nothing traditional—a birth under these circumstances was a novelty to all; the fasting was spontaneous. An hour before time for the serving of the mid-day meal, and again an hour before time for the serving of the evening meal, word was relayed to the commissary that no food was to be prepared. Which of them it was who had taken it upon themselves to issue the order, nobody knew; but all concurred in its appropriateness.

Shortly before sundown there came from behind the curtain a loud, astonished gasp, a deep groan, a long-drawn, quavering cry. It was the moment of birth. Knowing as she did how public her lying-in was, Kanama had endured her pains in silence until then. A moan of support in which all joined answered her. A moment later the baby's first wails were heard. Sighs and grunts of satisfaction sounded.

Minutes passed, then in a weak, tired, but happy voice Kanama announced through the curtain, *"Tseliku."*

"That means 'a bow,' " Amos explained. "It's a boy."

The delivery over, the carpenter's shed reverted at once to its original use, for while all were absorbed in the birth, one of the sufferers from dysentery had died alone and unattended.

As the Reverend Mackenzie tells his diary, he was of two minds during this period. He felt a proud sense of purpose in having this church of his, and he felt a deep sorrow that his church was what it was. He took advantage of every opportunity for ceremonial occasions. To the prisoners they were such a welcome diversion! Yet this very thing bothered him. For the first time he felt a touch of sympathy for those nonconformists who deplored High Church ritual as a distraction from stark spiritual substance. Kanama's baby, however, was such a joyful occasion for all, despite concern over its puniness and what whites might have called its Indian silence and stolidity. It was passed around the compound like a doll, and must have been dandled by every occupant out of infancy, so involved had they been in its birth. This called for "The Churching of Women," with its imagery so appropriate to the setting: *Like as an arrow in the hands of a giant: even so are the young children. Happy is the man that hath his quiver full of them.* And following this, the thanksgiving of the mother after birth: Holy Communion.

Here, confined inside the stockade, for the first time in years they were free to assemble in worship, to partake of communion, and the Reverend Mackenzie celebrated it on every Sabbath, somewhat disturbed in mind always by a suspicion that it was welcomed as an entertainment rather than as the profound mystery and illumination it was, and that some of the communicants had no notion of what it was about, even after it had been interpreted for them by the boy. Yet, said one of the biblical precepts he quoted to them, *The Lord preserveth the simple.* Surely among His limitless abilities, speaking Cherokee was one. Or if not, He could interpret His own word in some sign language understood by His backward children everywhere. It did not bother the Reverend Mackenzie that among them were some who were not members of his own congregation, they having been converted by his predecessors, the Methodist and Moravian missionaries. He did not believe that he was leading them astray from the tenets of their particular faiths—or if he was, that it mattered much now; nor did he believe that their pastors would have refused them dispensations, any more than he would have refused his parishioners under these circumstances. Any version of the gospel was better than none, as in a storm any port. The thought would once have shocked the Reverend Mackenzie to his soul, but it seemed to him now that here denominational differences mattered no more, indeed, they mattered a great deal less, than the differences in complexion of the people whom he saw before him. Indeed, he was learning that denominational differences mattered less anywhere than he had been taught to believe. Surely here, inside these walls, behind those barred gates, with no roof overhead but heaven, was the primitive, universal, ecumenical house of God.

How was it to be explained to people who thought it fitting and proper that they sign their infants' names to petitions that only somebody of the age of discretion could be confirmed, and only by a bishop? Not only the mother but everybody inside these walls was ready to attest that God's servant *Usdi*—Little One—was a true upholder of his and his parents' faith.

At birth the child had been so tiny it looked as though it had hatched from an egg. It had filled out or lengthened little in the time since. It was still as shriveled and shrunken as the oldest inmate of the camp. Solemn-faced and unresponsive, it gazed at you from big, incurious black orbs; wisdom-wearied they appeared. It was as though it had taken one look at its world, at the defeated, despised, dispossessed and despondent people of whom it was one, and given up the fight as lost without entering the lists, had lain down before starting on the long trek west. The concern felt by its mother was felt by all for this child of their captivity, her wants for it endorsed by all. It was uncertain whether Usdi would ever speak for himself.

What his punishment would be for knowingly misusing his priestly office, the Reverend Mackenzie could not even imagine, so great must it be. Nonetheless, he was prepared to bear it upon his conscience and to suffer the consequences. Any guilt and remorse that he might have felt for having confirmed Kanama's Usdi was laid to rest when, aged three weeks and a day, the infant died. The mother blessed her minister; thanks to him she would see her child again in heaven. A synod of bishops could not have made the Reverend Mackenzie repent of his act. Were he to be unfrocked, he would wear a

breechclout without shame in the sight of God, for so he had
seen good men go clad in His sight.

At the funeral service, held inside the compound and attended by all, with the coffin, custom-made by the carpenters
—the work of a morning, little bigger than a loaf of bread—
resting on sawhorses, few eyes were dry, not excepting the
Reverend Mackenzie's own, as he intoned, "Man that is born
of woman . . ." Yet his were moist as much from joy as from
sorrow. It came over him that he had found his people.

The funeral procession, consisting of the young parents,
the Reverend Mackenzie, Amos and their guards, was passed
outside. The father carried the coffin. It was placed in its tiny
hole and covered. When the graveside service was concluded,
Kanama said, and Amos interpreted, "He didn't want to go
west. He wanted to stay here forever." Then the party was
escorted back through the gates, on the one of which was
scrawled *TLA* and on the other *YIDAYOJADANVSI.*

They had languished for months, now they were ordered
to be ready to leave tomorrow morning.

Late that afternoon the prisoners were interrupted at
their frantic wainwrighting, wheelwrighting, horseshoeing,
packing, mending harness, patching moccasins by the specta-
cle of a family brought into the compound. These were the last
holdouts, and they looked the part. They looked as if they had
held out against the first white man ever. The husband was
being led by a rope around his neck, his hands were tied behind him. The wife, babe in arms, was wild with grief. She
wailed the way the old-time Indian women wailed.

They were the purest of purebloods, with the classical, the
quintessential Cherokee color and features, and this automati-
cally conferred upon them a special status. They were the orig-
inals, the Adam and Eve of the tribe. In those like these The

People had seen themselves memorialized as they were before
the coming of the white man; now, in the woman's desolation,
in the infant's homelessness, in the man's defiance and his
defeat, they saw their nation personified.

The officer in command of the detail dismounted. Whip in
hand, he raised his voice and said to the crowd that had gathered round, "This man struck and knocked down a soldier."
He paused for them to be properly awed by that enormity.
Their expressionlessness provoked him. "His punishment is
one hundred lashes."

It was meant as an example to them but it was deflected
from its aim. To a man, the prisoners turned their backs upon
the scene, and their children copied them. Thinking that they
were expressing their contempt for him, the officer laid it on
with the whip all the harder. What they were doing was sparing their brother being seen to undergo this worst of humilia-
tions. Afterwards, they bathed him, symbolically washing
away his shame.

The woman's story, when they were able to get it out of
her, was that she had pleaded with the soldiers to be allowed
to go and find her other child, a four-year-old. He must have
seen the soldiers, been frightened by them, and run to hide. He
would come to her call, she said. But none of them understood
Cherokee. When she refused to leave without her child, one of
them prodded her with his bayonet. It was he whom her husband struck.

She pleaded now for someone to explain things to them
for her.

"Agiduda," she said—although he was not her grandfather—"be my tongue. It is getting dark. The child will be
frightened. He will want his mother. He is hungry. I will find
him there. They must let me go for him. I promise them to
return. They may take me wherever they will, but not without
my child."

He had to tell her that they were all ordered to leave at break of day.

To nobody's very great surprise, the husband was found dead that morning, hanging inside the carpenters' shed on that length of rope by which he had been led in.

That last night in camp the Reverend Mackenzie, with Amos interpreting for him, preached a sermon.

He began by saying that God worked in a mysterious way His wonders to perform. While waiting for this to be translated, he wondered why it was that God worked in so mysterious a way. Was human existence not hard enough without that? Wasn't a little light shed upon life's all too many mysteries what was needed? Wouldn't it have been easier to follow Him if he took us into His confidence and explained His doings?

The Reverend Mackenzie, through the firelight, saw his interpreter attending upon his next observation. He collected his scattered thoughts.

He allowed that at this moment it might seem to some as though God had forgotten, had abandoned to a cruel and undeserved fate, His Cherokee children.

Out of the darkness rose a groan of assent, and when, for the benefit of those whose only language was Cherokee, his words were interpreted by the boy, there rose a seconding groan.

They had, in fact, been chosen, he told them—and waited for grunts of disbelief, disgust, derision. Hearing none, he was pleased but puzzled.

God's chosen people, he said—the Israelites of old, the Cherokees of today—were those whose faith He tested, that they might have the selfless, the pure joy of showing their love for Him. The Reverend Mackenzie believed what he said, yet he wondered what kind of god was that? How could He expect to be loved and worshipped and thanked?

Chosen, he said, to spread His word to their heathen brothers in the west. Into his mind as this was being translated came the picture of some Arkansas Osage listening to the gospel from the mouth of an immigrant Cherokee, and noting his condition, and thinking how he and his had gotten where they were, and saying to himself, "A fine god you've got!"

The grunts he had expected to hear earlier he heard now. Then silence fell, a silence as deep as the darkness from which it emanated. The Reverend Mackenzie could think of nothing more to say. He had failed, had been tongue-tied, ineloquent, unpersuasive; he had failed God: that was what the silence said to the Reverend Mackenzie. What he said to himself was that God had failed him. On his young interpreter's face in the firelight he saw a look of deep disappointment, of barely disguised disgust. The boy looked as though the words he had just had to mouth had rearisen like pap that would not go down. Another opportunity—guidance—His inspiration to do His work, the Reverend Mackenzie prayed for. "Here is your chance," he told Him. But he was not judged worthy to be the vessel of God's word.

It suggested itself that the time had come for the hymn. In the words that the boy had taught him, the Reverend Mackenzie sang:

"Unelanvhi Uwetsi"

Out of the night came:

"Amazing grace, how sweet the sound"

To which the Reverend Mackenzie, accompanied now by half his audience, responded:

"Igaguyvheyi Hnaquotsosv Wiyulose"

And the other half sang back:

"That once was lost but now am found"

To be answered by:

"Igaguyvhonv"

And that by:

"Was blind, but now can see."

Silence fell as the dying notes rose with the sparks from the fire into the darkness.

The Reverend Mackenzie then led his congregation in prayer. He prayed for their strength and courage and good health. He prayed for a speedy journey and for their protection along the way. He prayed that their long years of suffering and disappointed hopes, their patience and faith throughout, be rewarded with a new home in the west of such beauty and bounteousness as to make them forget the one they were leaving—and his words were wormwood and gall in his mouth. What he was thinking was, "If I forget thee, O Zion . . ." Finally he called upon them to go with pure hearts, free from bitterness, forgiving those who trespassed against them, and even as he did so he was saying to himself, "Do as I say, not as I do." For, as he confesses in his diary entry relating the event, he was wishing he had Aaron's rod for a day. Had he had it he would have stretched it over the waters of Georgia and turned them to blood. With it he would have smitten the ground and brought on plagues of frogs, lice, flies, all-devouring locusts, sores and boils upon the people, a murrain on their herds, hailstones and whirlwinds and darkness that might be felt. He was not sure that he would have stopped short of bringing death down upon their firstborn, from that of the governor who sat upon his throne, even unto that of the maidservant behind the mill.

They started on their way westward dejected in spirit and weakened in body by months of bad and insufficient food, inactivity and debilitating illnesses. With the wrongheadedness that has characterized the operations of armies since the first one ever levied, they started at the least favorable time of year. They started then because they could no longer be kept where they were.

Nothing so saddened them as leaving their homeplace, nothing so daunted them as the trip they faced, nothing so appalled them as the place of their destination, but such had been the horrors of camp life that when the gates were thrown open that morning there was a rush to them.

And so the wheels made the first of their million turns and the feet took the first of their million steps toward no promised land, no land of milk and honey, but rather toward the land of darkness, land of death.

The last to exit were barely outside the stockade, to which they had set fire, when "Amazing Grace" was struck up. Down the long caravan of already weary, already disheartened travelers it went, linking them like a joining of hands.

Part Four

By holding out, litigating, stalling, the Cherokees were the last but one of the Five Civilized Tribes to go west. That other one, the Seminoles, were on their way now too.

Thus they went knowing all too well what to expect. Knowing it had been one of the factors swaying them to hold out and resist going. In warning them to avoid a like fate, relatives and friends already out west, those voluntary emigrants, wrote telling them what had happened to the other tribes evicted from their lands and convoyed under government escort. It had been going on for some seven years already, though the experience had taught the overseers nothing, and the money to be made off the operation by profiteers, swindlers and corrupt officials had multiplied their numbers like buzzards flocking to a feast.

First to go were the Choctaws. Pacified for centuries, their boast was that never in their history had they warred upon their white brothers but had welcomed them from the first ones they ever saw. They went without protest, agreeing to the treaty proposed to them offering an exchange of land in The Territory for their homeland, and readying to leave before the ink of their X's was dry.

The Choctaws were dispatched in yearly parties of a couple of thousand head, not in one fell swoop as was the entire Cherokee nation. The Choctaws were a large tribe—over twenty thousand; they had been on the move in these piece-meal installments since 1831, and their remnants still were. For them, emigrating had become an annual rite, almost an inherited characteristic, like the passage of the birds, with the difference that they went north in winter, and none of them returned south. And, not being birds, they lacked wings. The overland trip, on foot, took them all winter long. For it they were issued blankets—one to a family. Natives of southern Mississippi, they hardly knew what winter was. They went shoeless, or at best shod in thin moccasins, many shirtless, and in cotton smocks. It had been the luck of the Choctaws that the seven winters of their expulsion were like the biblical years of leanness in severity.

Of those who got to The Territory to tell their tales, one group spoke of being rescued by a team sent out when they failed to keep a rendezvous and finding them stranded and huddling in a swamp, and their hundred horses—it must have looked like an equestrian statue foundry—standing too deeply in the stiff mud to topple over, though frozen dead for days. Of making camp, and, after dark, the hindmost stragglers limping in to report leaving behind on the trail the bodies of relatives unburied at the roadside, dead of exhaustion, exposure, hunger and of the diseases that struck and raced through them as through a single body. Yet so destitute was the condition of those left behind, their homes and farms taken from them, that, knowing all this, they still flocked to leave for the north each winter like misdirected birds.

The Creeks of Alabama had farther to travel than the Choctaws, and the going was inch by inch. Survivors told of making five miles, and often less, in a long day because of having to stop half a dozen times to warm the children at fires. Their comfort was short-lived, and their wailing soon re-sumed, for they were returned to lie on the frozen tents cover-ing the wagon beds. Infants were carried by mothers and fa-thers taking turns like the parents of incubating eggs to share

the warmth of their bodies. They trudged for days at a time in
snow up to their calves, crying in pain with every step, their
unattended tears freezing to their cheeks.

There being no time in such pressing cold to bury the
dead, the bodies were barely covered over with brush. The
living learned not to look back. While they were still in sight,
the buzzards that blackened the skies overhead were already
settling to their work, and just as often they were driven from
their prize by the ever-present packs of wolves which, at night,
serenaded their future fare with hungry howls.

Born businessmen, the Chickasaws held out for, and got,
a good price for their choice lands in Mississippi and Tennessee, and saw to it that payment was in cash, not in another of
those promises of tribal annuities every one of which had been
defaulted upon. A proud, regal, overbearing people, longtime
exacters of tribute from other tribes, breeders of fine horses,
and of daughters renowned for their beauty, they were the elite
of the Indian world. When they went west it was at a favorable
time of year, and they went not as prisoners overseen by government guards, not fed on government handouts. The Chickasaws went west at their own pace, they paid their own way.
They paid through their high-held, hawkish noses the piratical
prices for furthering them along the route which their style of
travel and their air of superiority invited, and the high and
mighty Chickasaws, as susceptible to the white man's deadly
epidemic diseases as their humblest red brothers, arrived in
The Territory as debilitated, as decimated in numbers, as poor,
and as broken-spirited, as the lowliest of the low.

Only one of the tribes, the Seminoles of Florida, had
fought. Vastly outnumbered, disadvantageously armed, poorly
provisioned, they had fought the United States Army for
twelve years. Seminole women had fought alongside their men,
and just as fiercely, murdering their infant children so as not to
be hampered by them nor given away by their cries. They
might be fighting yet but for an act of deceit and treachery in

violation of the fundamental rule of civilized warfare. Invited, under a flag of truce, to a conference on peace proposals, their chief, the resourceful and inspiring young field commander, Osceola, was seized and put in prison, where he soon died, as hostage for the surrender of his followers.

Of the forty thousand of the four tribes deported so far, some ten thousand had perished on the way.

That first day they traveled through territory familiar to them. Here they had lived and worked and courted, had visited relatives and friends, had explored as children, had hunted and fished and trapped, gone nut-gathering, berry-picking. The very houses, or their ashes, that some of them had been driven from, had been born in, they passed. Of these some were now occupied by white squatters. From them the occupants came out to watch the Cherokees' exodus, some to pelt them with stones and hoot them on their way. Even so, it was land with associations that urged them to linger, not leave. Their steps lagged that day. At the end of it they had accomplished less than ten of the hundreds and hundreds of miles that stretched before them.

That first day's march gave a bitter foretaste of all that were to come. With its end came the heart-sickening realization that it was only the first—the first of how many? It was not long; after months of inactive confinement, they must be toughened gradually. Even so, it was wearying, particularly to those who were leaving the most behind, not the most in material possessions but the most in time spent and memories accumulated, like Agiduda and Grandmother. In camp that evening the boy went to fetch water for them. There at the wagon he met the Mackenzies.

"But, man," said Agiduda, "you don't have to do this. You are not one of us."

"I am if you will have me," said the Reverend Mackenzie. "I'm certainly not one of *them*. I got the call to go. I hope to be useful."

Thereupon Agiduda adopted them both into his clan. The boy said to them, "Please, sir, please, ma'am, from now on call me Noquisi. But only when there's nobody but ourselves to hear."

Later that evening Agiduda said, "Saints, my child, are all fools, bless them. Now don't go telling him I called him that. 'Saint' I mean. The 'fool' part he wouldn't object to."

They were not linked by collars and chains but it was as though they were. In the morning when the starter's bugle blew and those in the lead took the first forward step, the lurch was felt all along the line.

This was after they had been issued their daily ration of salt pork and cornmeal from the commissary wagons and allowed time to cook them.

Fire was obtained from wagons in which they were kept burning day and night in pots and pans. Some of these were true *tusti* bowls, replicas of the one in which *Diyunisi,* the Water Beetle, first fetched fire, preserved from olden times and handed down in the family, the holiest of household vessels, snatched up to be taken with them when they were seized in the roundup. Along the route the children were the tenders of the fires. They minded their duty with the seriousness of little priests and priestesses, knowing well that the fires were sacred, that The People's continuation depended upon them, that their very name, *Tsalagi,* or Cherokee, as the whites called them, meant "the fire-bringers." They gathered sticks from the roadside, then scampered to catch up with the train. In the night, while the children slept, the adults took turns feeding the fires. Being the blessing of all, they were the care of all.

Even to those for whom the old tribal customs had lost their religious significance, these symbolic fires were now a common bond. One at least must still be burning when they reached their distant destination. In the village council houses to be built there the fires would be kindled with fire from the old country, and would burn until ceremoniously extinguished at their first *Ah tawh hung nah* in exile. That would mark the end of the old life and the commencement of the new. In the meantime they ate their meals cooked over fires kindled in common, one big family.

Ultimately the search-and-seizure operation, the roundup of the Cherokees, although thorough, allowing few to escape, had been so haphazard that now on the march were people in all stages of dispossession, of preparedness. Depending upon whether the U.S. Army, by far the more lenient, or the more disinterested, of the two, or the Georgia State Militia had been their captors, depending upon the humaneness of the officer in charge of the squad, some prisoners indeed came with nothing but the clothes on their backs while others came in buckboards, in oxcarts, in wagons drawn by teams of their former plow horses containing everything they owned. Some had a train of slaves to bear on their backs their owners' worldly goods. Some rode saddle horses, with colts accompanying dams, some were followed by faithful dogs. The work animals had grazed outside the stockade during the detention time, the dogs fed on scraps from the soldiers' mess. They could be heard whimpering as their owners spoke to them through the tall pointed pailings.

For the very old, the very young, the weak, of body and of mind, for nursing mothers and for women big with child, for the lame, the blind, places were provided in army wagons. They would have been better off walking, if only they could have, so rough was the ride on the uneven road—where there was a road. Children took turns riding in the wagons, resting their legs for an hour, then yielding their places to others like them and trotting alongside.

Light would be just breaking when the day began with the bugler's sounding of reveille. In those early days on the road progress must be made in the relative cool of the morning. The heat of midday slowed, often stopped them altogether, prostrating even the fittest. They rose, stiff and sore, from their bedding grounds, hastily cooked and ate their breakfast rations, and readied themselves for the starter's bugle. The sound of getting under way, overtopping the first creak of the wagon wheels and the rumble of their beds, was a groan of reluctance uttered in a single concerted voice.

They enjoyed one regular day's rest a week. In their rigid observance of the Sabbath, the Reverend Mackenzie took satisfaction, but it was a mixed satisfaction. Pagans and Christians both, the former as adamant as the latter, refused to move a step on Sunday. The others spent the day in communion with the Great Spirit; for the converted the Reverend Mackenzie conducted Holy Communion. The rite only. He preached them no homily. He felt that to these brave and hard-pressed people he had nothing to say. They needed no exhortation. God's holy words, not his. He had become acutely conscious of the color of his skin—though among his flock were many as fair as he. All the more reason for holding his tongue. They saw that he was voluntarily enduring their hardships. Did that not do a bit to expiate for his race? Or did they merely think that he was a paleface fool to endure on his own what they were condemned to endure? Did they perhaps censure him for making his little wife accompany him on this comfortless mission? These self-questions he enunciates in his diary.

The bandanas masking their lower faces as they marched made them look like an army of bandits. The dirt road, following months of unbroken drought and searing summer heat, was powdery. The water wagons with their tin dippers to drink from were spaced at intervals along the line; still they choked and were blinded by the dust raised by hundreds of marching feet, the hooves of the horses and the oxen, the wheels of the wagons. It was like groping their way through the smoke of a fire, and the coughing and hawking were incessant. Hard as it was to break the old taboo, they were forced repeatedly to do it and spit out their souls upon the ground, to be trodden upon by those at their heels.

They were out of reach now of the state militiamen. Those convoying them were soldiers carrying out orders, not zealots. There were no whips nor prods, no shouts nor curses. On the contrary, their guards were as considerate of their welfare as circumstances allowed.

Still, there was a long, long way to go, and they must take advantage of the weather. This heat was bad, but the coming cold, already overdue, would be worse. For their own good a pace must be kept up.

As the fittest and the less fit and the least fit and the unfit were sorted out and separated, the column straggled like an old animal whose hindquarters are failing it. And now that sense of their being yoked together ran not from the lead to the rear but from the rear to the lead. All were restrained by the pace of the slowest, the very young and the very old, and those with one or another of these on their backs, like Aeneas or else like St. Christopher, and when one of their number faltered, all felt the check, as though they were chained together.

They tried to keep up their spirits by talking as they trudged along. They soon found that they had nothing to say. Memories of home were a subject to avoid, their recent detention in the camp an experience to suppress, their present existence no occasion for conversation, the country they were passing through nothing for them to remark upon but merely something to put behind them, and of their destination they felt only dread. They were not travelers seeing the sights. They were more like workhorses with blinders plowing an endless row. Yet to do nothing but plod daily like dumb animals was to fear becoming one, forgetting how to speak, losing your mind. They marched to the slow measures of "Amazing Grace" and "Just As I Am." Over and over again in their two tongues they told themselves that they were wretches who had been saved, were lost but now were found, were blind but now could see—that they were coming at the bidding of the Lamb of God.

Meanwhile, as they strained toward their remote goal, how many of them, Noquisi wondered, knew of the prophecy made by the wise men of the tribe—so far remarkably fulfilled —that even there they would find no resting place, but would be driven all the way to the western waters?

He felt the isolation and the oppression of being young and being the bearer of a burdensome truth, one affecting them all, that his trusting elders did not know.

Noquisi—or as he was soon known to them, Tad—short for Tadpole—another of the many names his eventful early life would confer upon him before he settled down to Amos Smith —was not the only one to serve as the soldiers' interpreter whenever one was required, whenever something untoward occurred, an accident, a breakdown, a person's sudden collapse, but he was the one most often sought out. He was nimble in both tongues, he was bright, and he was small. To his added weight no horse objected. He could be lifted with one hand and swung up to ride behind the saddle and quickly transported to the scene.

It was while riding behind him, holding on around his waist, and hearing him mutter to himself, that Noquisi got to know something of Captain Donovan, the caravan's commandant. It was from the Captain's grumbling and cursing that he got an inkling of the muddleheadedness of those who had projected this operation, the bureaucrats far from the scene in Washington, and even further from a sense of reality, of their blithe confidence that all factors would comply with their paper plans, that hundreds of people of all ages and conditions could be led as one, and that he, Captain William Donovan, to whom the experience was as novel as that of Moses in the wilderness, would know exactly how to solve any unexpected hitch that might arise as though he had a field manual.

To many Captain Donovan was an unfeeling man who viewed his job as that of a cattle driver determined to deliver to market the greatest number of head he could. He was determined to do just that, but he was not unfeeling. Noquisi, with a hand on the man's heart, had a knowledge of its beats, and its skipping of beats.

Riding thus post-saddle, Noquisi heard the Captain always answer the question, one asked more and more frequently as time went by, "Where are we, please, Captain, sir?" with a gruff, "We're here. On the right road. Follow me and we'll get to where we're going." Sometimes the boy did not bother relaying the question when it was spoken in Cherokee but responded to it on his own with the Captain's stock reply.

"They wouldn't know if you told them," the Captain muttered, which was true. But, employing his growing Cherokee gift of being able to read a person's thoughts, Noquisi knew that the man feared the opposite of what he said: he wanted no knowledge of where they were—which was to say where they were not—to spread among them. They were making such slow and difficult progress, Captain Donovan feared that should they learn how far behind schedule they were—or have their suspicions and fears of it officially confirmed— should they realize how far they had yet to go, they would be swept by despair, would give up en masse, would sit down daunted and dispirited beyond coaxing or goading, and refuse to move on. His field map, which he was often seen to spread and study, he consulted as guardedly as he might the weak hand with which he was bluffing at poker, and always poker-faced. Even his troops, all of them strangers here, were kept in uncertainty as to their whereabouts lest they be demoralized by the knowledge.

One day a man fell out and sat himself down beside the road. This was something that happened all the time. A person rested for a while, then caught up again. But this man sat on as the marchers passed him by, until the column had left him behind. They slowed and slowed and at last came to a halt from that sense that they were linked together and that when one of them faltered, all faltered. A soldier spotted the laggard and reported him to Captain Donovan, who picked up Noquisi on his way, set him behind him on his horse and galloped back to the scene.

"He says he cannot go any farther, sir," the boy translated. "He says this is a good day to die."

"Tell him a place will be found in one of the wagons for him to rest up over the next few days."

"Sir, he says it is not his body that is worn out. It is his spirit."

"One case of that," said the Captain, looking ahead at the arrested line of his charges, "and it will spread quicker than measles." Surrender was unthinkable to the soldier that he was through and through, desertion under fire punishable by disgrace from the ranks and summary execution.

"Ask him who he is to give up while old women and little children push on? Is he a Cherokee or isn't he? Ask him that."

"His answer, sir, is, yes, he is a Cherokee. That is his trouble."

"We're in this all together. One for all and all for one. A chain is only as strong as its weakest link. Tell him that."

"He says tell you that you are a good and brave man and he wishes you a long and happy life, but as for him, he will die here."

"That he will, and damned quick, too, if he doesn't get to

his feet and start moving," said the Captain, drawing his pistol. "I will make him an example to all by shooting him dead on the spot and leaving his carcass for the wolves."

Another day Noquisi was picked up by Captain Donovan and ridden to the dispensary wagon to help the doctor deal with a refractory patient. This was a man with a carbuncle at the base of his neck, grown huge from neglect owing to his fear of the doctor, now grown fearful enough to overcome that fear, but not enough to induce him to submit to what he gathered from the sight of the surgical instruments to be the treatment for it. As much as anything, he was resisting the first step in the procedure, the cutting off of his braids. Having it explained to him in his own language sobered him into submission. The whiskey he was given had the same effect through the opposite means.

To the doctor's amazement, the boy began by asking to be shown what the medical problem was, as though he—all four and three-quarters feet of him—were a colleague called in for consultation on the case. Now he said, "I have told him, sir, exactly what you are going to do, and why, and have warned him that with that thing so near his brain, he runs the risk of death if it is not done."

"But I haven't told you any of that, boy," said the doctor.

"My father is a doctor," he said. "Your patient is ready. You may proceed."

It was an operation that he had watched his father perform. Thus when Dr. Warren finished with his scalpel and turned to reach for his curette, it was ready and waiting. As he probed, extirpating the roots of the growth, the boy, taking turns at it with him, sponged the area. When the final cleaning swabs were needed, there they were. When the time came for it, there was the bottle of permanganate. And when the cavity was ready to be packed and dressed, there were the bandages, one folded into a pad and the other unrolled to bind it.

Equally as impressive as the boy's competence was his composure. In his lack of any squeamishness when the incision was made, his indifference to the sight of the blood and the pus, his acceptance of the patient's unavoidable pain, he was a seasoned professional. He was engrossed in the work at hand, and he was offended at being patronized by the doctor's compliments afterwards upon his part in it. Having seen it done by a graduate of King's College, he had been about to offer *him,* whose training consisted of the standard two years apprenticeship with a country-town practitioner, *his* compliments. As for himself, he had assisted in surgery far more complicated than this.

Thereafter the boy had another job in addition to that of interpreter, and another name to go with it: "Doc."

Serving as Dr. Warren's assistant when needed not only relieved the monotony of the march for the boy, it was a recovery of the self that had been taken from him. He was doing again what he had done with his father. He regained a sense of purpose and usefulness. He enjoyed making himself helpful to people in pain, and the satisfaction of their praise and thanks. He welcomed the responsibility. He familiarized himself so thoroughly with the inventory of the dispensary that he was able to fetch whatever the doctor required.

They had been on the road for just under a month and were somewhere in Tennessee when something happened one day up at the head of the line to stall the march. The question —what was it?—was relayed. The answer was a long time in getting back to those as far in the rear as the Fergusons. At the side of the road had been found the graves of a family of Cherokees, father, mother and daughter, casualties of an earlier emigration. It was what all had been dreading and none dared speak of.

When his turn came to pass the spot, Noquisi saw that the family's name, burned, along with their familiar names and that of their clan in Sequoyah's alphabet, into the wooden crosses marking their graves, was Grant. He dared not speculate on what it might have been that had wiped out a family at a stroke. Grant: he could recall knowing no one of that name, yet it was one that seemed to have a significance for him.

Three days later, and just twenty miles farther along the way from the site of the first ones, two more Cherokee graves were found at the side of the road. The victims here had been unrelated.

Then a week later came Beesville, where the message relayed rearward from the head of the march coursed through the column like a shudder down a person's spine.

Beesville? Yes, said the owner of the Cherokee Trail Motor Lodge and Trading Post, whose overnight guest I, Amos Smith IV, had been, he knew the place. It was about a hundred miles up the road. Why?

I was his only guest, and, being otherwise unoccupied, after frying my bacon and eggs and dishing them up, he had seated himself, uninvited, at my table. Looking at the showcases around the walls while waiting for my breakfast, I had been reflecting upon the revolution in Indian trade goods. Nowadays it was they who sold trinkets to the whites: Navaho earrings, Cherokee beaded belts, Cheyenne feathered warbonnets, tom-toms of no known tribal design.

There was something in Beesville I wanted to see. Was there a decent place to put up there?

"Tex," said my host (he had seen my auto license plate), "there ain't *nothing* to see in Beesville. Blink as you pass through and you'll miss it. No, sir, there ain't no decent place to put up at, nor even an indecent one—reason being there's no reason why anybody in his right mind would want to stay overnight there. This here is a one-horse town, but at least it's got both ends of the horse."

But there was something to see in Beesville, or its environs, and I had a map to it. It was a hand-drawn map on U.S. Army stationery, stained, faded and creased, giving the location I sought to the minute of latitude and longitude, for it designated the site of something that had happened long before Beesville was there as a reference point. It was one of three such maps I had, handed down through four generations of us Smiths.

Although the road was a good one, those were one hundred and more miles of sheer mountain climbing. It was a hot day and three times my laboring car overheated and had to be rested. But notwithstanding these stops, plus one for a leisurely lunch and another for a service-station rest room (thinking the while of doing what I was doing in public view, when the urge was not to be denied and there was not so much as a bush to hide behind, telling yourself that it was only human, when that was what it was not, it was animal: a memory of humiliation and shame that had lasted my namesake into his deep old age), I still made it to Beesville by midafternoon. I tried to imagine what it had been like to do it on foot and in the cold of one of the worst winters ever before or in all the many years since.

Their party of just under a thousand was now following several days behind another one the size of theirs. In the personal possessions they found abandoned and scattered all along it there was evidence that the road had been wearisome enough for the earlier travelers; for those who came after, it was the worse for their passage. In dry weather all those feet, hooves, wheels churned it into a choking dust, in wet weather into a quagmire—at times they struggled on the sticky road like flies on a strip of flypaper—and when sunny or frosty weather followed wet, into hardened furrows like plowed land. Bare feet and feet shod only in thin-soled moccasins were bruised and torn. It was hardest on those in the rear, the ones least able to keep up. They had to breathe the dust and slosh in the mud and stumble in the ruts of all those ahead of them.

It was as though the rain had been accumulating all through the months-long drought, for when it came it seemed that a dam had burst. In the beginning the emigrants permitted themselves the luxury of finding some stretches temporarily impassable, some weather unsuitable for travel, and camped to wait things out. The change that now came was one that made travel not easier, but harder, and yet imperative, for just as the drought was broken by torrents, so the long heat wave was broken by cold that corresponded in its severity. Now that road conditions were truly impossible and the weather worse than unfit, they must push on or perish. Ironically, they must hope for the cold to worsen. The freezing of the roadbed would ease travel.

As the sodden and shivering emigrant train toiled through the mire up one steep slope after another, the roadside crosses appeared with the frequency of mileage markers—with the difference that, unlike mileage markers, these spoke not of your getting nearer to your goal but of the lengthening odds against your ever reaching it. Meanwhile, Noquisi had his own reason for approaching each new one with dread. Though he had never known them, he had remembered who the Grants were.

They were an old mixed-blood family of considerable substance in their part of Georgia. They had been steadfast holdouts, supporters of Ross, opponents of Ridge. That the Grants had changed course, had decided that the cause was lost and

the time had come to leave, had carried weight with Abel
Ferguson. Such a big, such an unpopular, even heretical step it
was that he contemplated taking, he argued with himself as to
its rightness up to the end. The Grants' going had been a
factor in swaying him. They would be in the same wagon train.

Of his identification of the Grants as members of his parents' party of emigrants, Noquisi said nothing to his grandparents. They had enough to worry them as it was.

But for him, Beesville, though no less of a shock—rather
more—came not with the shock of complete surprise.

A century and a half later, just as the motel owner had
said, there was nothing in Beesville to see. The site that I,
Noquisi's descendant, located was a bare plot of ground indis-
tinguishable from its surroundings. There was no monument,
no marker, no memory. The earth in its gyrations, the frosts,
the rains, the snows, the winds of all those years had long ago
tumbled down the wooden cross and plaque and leveled the
shallow mound, hastily heaped up over a shallow pit hastily
dug, by people hard-pressed and anxious to get away from this
place of pestilence. But the meticulousness of Captain Donovan's map left no doubt that I stood on or near the spot where
my great-grandfather, as a boy, had stood and read, among the
names of the fourteen buried in the mass grave, that of Anne
Ferguson, his mother.

There was no time for him to mourn. That was an indul-
gence that would have to wait. The train was already in motion under a steady cold rain, and keeping up with it demanded all one's strength of will. There was no time and there
was no allowance. He had his duty the same as everyone to the
spirit of the group. They were in this all together, one for all
and all for one. He must not be the weak link in the chain.
Most of the journey must be made knowing what he now

knew, and he must act as though he did not know it. With apologies to his mother's spirit and solemn promises to remember her later, when this was over, Noquisi resolutely put her out of mind. Familiarity with death had toughened him, and that was as well, for he now had adult responsibilities. Nor must he live constantly in dread of having to ask Captain Donovan, somewhere farther along the trail, to draw him a second map. His father had never broken the news of his wife's death to the family back home. Had that been to spare them? He had never written anything. Had that been to spare himself? Or had he never been given the chance? Of this also the boy must forbid himself to think. Because from now on his grandparents would often be entering his mind and reading his thoughts, and they must find him courageous, resolute. They would have need to draw upon all his courage, and more, for, despite his resolutions, that was not much. Grandmother, as he soon found, was already in need of borrowing some.

The door to Grandmother's mind stood open as had that of her home to company. Now, as the Fergusons, restricted to her pace, slipped daily rearward in the march, Noquisi found in it two things: a determination to push on to the last footstep she had in her, and a conviction, enforced by this discovery of her daughter-in-law's death, that she would not make it to the end of the trail. Ahead, at the side of the road down which her thoughts plodded, loomed a cross. Far off and small when first seen, it grew steadily larger. It neared even as her progress toward it on foot shortened by the day, as though she and it were both on the move, narrowing the distance that separated them. She faltered more and more frequently, but that marker in her mind now served as her incentive to rise and carry on. It stood awaiting her like a lover, arms outspread for the welcoming embrace. She joined in now with a fervor all her own to the words of the hymn, "O, Lamb of God, I come! I come!" This combination of frailty and spirit was an inspiration to those beside her, they marching reluctantly as before to their resting place, she now longingly to hers.

Now the train was being followed at a distance by a lone wagon. Its soldier-driver, a different one each day, made no attempt to catch up with the column: on the contrary, whenever there was any slowing of the main body, he slowed. When the day's march ended and camp was made for the night, this wagon was not drawn up to join the rest but stayed back in its isolation. It was so far behind as to be almost out of sight, but it was almost never out of anyone's mind. Only Dr. Warren went near it and he went several times a day. Otherwise not even the family members of its invisible occupant approached it. Though this wagon kept its place, stopping when all stopped, it followed when all moved on again as surely as a ball and chain. Its occupant was a young man with smallpox. The fear of one and all was deepened by their tribal sense. The blood that flowed in one flowed in everyone. They were the same in their susceptibilities.

On the fifth morning of his patient's quarantine Dr. Warren sought and found the Reverend Mackenzie before the day's march began. Noquisi saw the doctor give the Mackenzies that quick examination which he had seen his father give people whose appearance worried him. The one was as unsuited to this ordeal as the other. Outdoors work, manual labor from early youth, life as subsistence farmers had conditioned most of the Cherokees; not the Mackenzies. A bit of flower gardening was the extent of her work out of doors, and that was more than his. University studies and then composing and delivering sermons were what he had exerted himself on. They had their faith and dedication to draw upon, but while the spirit was willing the flesh was weak. Yet no one had even suggested that they take seats in a wagon, knowing they would refuse.

The doctor was about to make his morning visit to the

patient in quarantine and he asked the Reverend Mackenzie to accompany him.

"I don't know what we will find," he said. "When I left him last night he was sinking. I've done all I know to do. It's out of my hands now. The time has come for you to do your part. Prayer might help. It can't hurt, can it?"

The patient was one of the Reverend Mackenzie's converts.

"I'll come too," said Noquisi. "He won't know what you're saying without me." What he was thinking was that without him to interpret God would not know what the man was saying with perhaps his last words.

The white doctor's medicine was not working and the sick man's family had taken matters into their own hands. While they squatted around a fire heating stones, the exorcist they had engaged was inside the wagon with the patient. The trials in the camp and on the road, and now the appearance among them of this dread disease, were turning The People back to their old ways and beliefs. They were moulting the civilization they had acquired with such effort. These here were mumbling prayers in Cherokee and in English—both broken, Noquisi noted. The Cherokee prayers were not addressed to God but to various pagan gods. They were Christians but they were also half-breeds, and in this dire circumstance they called upon both their resources as they employed their two hands at a task. One needed all the help one could get. "Thou shalt have no god before me": to this they had subscribed. But it was not "before." It was like a chief and his subchiefs. In case the headman was occupied with weightier matters than yours, you might get a hearing among the lesser ones. This was an attitude of mind that Noquisi understood because he shared it.

The patient was wrapped in his blanket with hot stones inside to sweat the evil spirits out of him. They were tenacious ones and the exorcist was obliged to use strong language on them and to menace them with shakes of his rattle. He paused in his work just long enough to assure his colleagues—or his competitors—through Noquisi that he had immunized himself by eating buzzard meat. As was well known, buzzards were immune to disease. Their foul odor kept evil spirits away.

The exorcist finished his operation and grunted with satisfaction at the result, or at the prospect of the result that might soon be expected. It was a look of some superiority that he bestowed upon Dr. Warren, whom he had been called in to relieve of the case, when he climbed down from the wagon. The Reverend Mackenzie, followed by Noquisi and the doctor, climbed in. The doctor signified by a look that the matter was indeed out of his hands now.

Even had there been time for it, the Reverend Mackenzie could see nothing to be gained by going through the Order for the Visitation of the Sick. His missal stayed in his pocket. What would it mean to this semisavage dying on the barrens of Kentucky to hear of the Holy Ghost, virgin birth, Pontius Pilate? Nor would he cheapen the solemnity of the moment with false assurances of recovery. In the little time he had he absolved the man and prepared him with a few words about the better life that would soon be his and the promise that he would be joined in eternity by his loved ones.

The man had reserved the strength for his last duty, to make peace with his fate. He said, "This is a good day to die."

"*Ai!*" Noquisi wailed, and the family outside responded. It was a Cherokee farewell to the man, to let him know that he was mourned by those he was leaving behind. And though they were separated from the column, the boy heard the cry run its length like the calls of a flight of geese.

The dead man's four survivors took it upon themselves voluntarily to march in the rear of the column and to camp alone at night. They segregated themselves so as to spare the rest fear of contagion from their nearness. They did it also out of shame at one of theirs having been the harbinger of trouble.

The detached wagon was rejoined with the others.

But it had been a fuse lighted at the end of the train. The spark had leapt the gap and spread through the line with the speed of fire.

Their oneness, the loss of their individuality, caught up as they were in the common plight, was nowhere more evident than in this: illness, when it struck, was instantly epidemic. Hard-driven, unrested, poorly fed, huddled together, exposed to harsh elements, inadequately clothed, all sharing the same conditions, as bound to one another as the pages of a book, they succumbed as one.

Still they pushed on, those unable to keep pace lying in wagon beds head to toe, to save space, like fish packed in crates. The outcries of the delirious sounded above the creaking of the wheels. Some survived to tell of riding in length-long contact with bodies hot and thrashing with fever, then burning out and growing cold and stiff. To escape this, people kept marching until they collapsed in their tracks.

The cold winds whipped up and they fell like the leaves from trees. For protection against its bite and its chafing, Agiduda took grease from the axletrees and coated the family's faces. Wagons were emptied of goods to make room for the invalids. At night they were emptied of their dead. Another inspection of them was made first thing in the morning. Before the day's march got under way the burials were conducted. The Reverend Mackenzie read the service from his prayer book. For Noquisi the text was unnecessary. He had served as its interpreter so many times he now knew it by heart in both English and Cherokee.

Word of the contagion they carried ran ahead of them, and at the edges of towns and settlements they were met by armed bands who forced them to detour around. These men, determined by fear, stood their ground against mounted troops of the United States Army.

The Reverend Mackenzie tells of married couples being buried together and their orphaned children being adopted at the graveside, motherless infants put to other breasts. And the trek was resumed.

Noquisi—old Amos Smith I—would remember all his long life long this reversal in the normal order of things: how the grown-ups cried more than the children did. The ones cried because they could not restrain themselves, the others did not because the sight of their elders crying like little children struck dry-eyed terror to their souls.

Your tears at first were spontaneous, intermittent, personal. These were trivial tears, sentimental tears. The mindless marching in one set direction left your thoughts free to wander. They wandered toward what you knew. You remembered a favorite nook in the house where at a certain hour of the day the light fell with a special glow; a flowery path; the mouse you had trained to eat from your hand; the pleasure of sunny summer afternoons with you stretched out in the shade on the bank of the brook; the coming on of evening and the homeward lowing of the herd; you remembered wrapping the comforting darkness around you as you tucked yourself into bed at night. Then you were ashamed for your weakness in giving way to your feelings while others with as much to regret as you trod staunchly on.

The notches cut nightly by Agiduda in his walking staff amounted to two months' worth, and still they had farther to go than they had come. All this while a tithe was mounting of tears for the common weal. One dismal day they overflowed the font. Reduced to a single purpose and a single fate, the people cried with a single heart. In this, as in so many things, they acted tribally, with a blood bond that amounted to mass mental telepathy. Once one of them cried for all, then all of them cried together. They looked up from their endlessly plodding feet at the indifferent heavens and heard the ceaseless grate and creak of the wagon wheels, they felt the sting of the sleet that hissed in their faces, and through them one and all swept the sense that they had been abandoned by God and their fellowman, that nature herself had set her hand against them. They were in truth the Chosen People—chosen to be the scapegoat of the human race, sent into the wilderness to atone for all its sins. They were marching to perdition, and the groan they gave seemed to rise out of the earth, up from the horizonless plains of Hell.

The longing now to reach the place you dreaded to reach, and there rest, the rearward pull of the place you had left behind, the ache in your every cell of the long weary miles you had marched, that of the many still before you, made one of your feet push you forward and the other one hold you back. You were pulled on as though by a halter, held back by the tug of homesickness as though you strained against a tether. And knowing that their feelings were reproductions of your own, you felt not just for yourself but for all those trudging alongside you.

A thousand people cried as one, yet it was not just for the hardships they were enduring that they cried. For physical stoicism they had no equal. It was not for their tired, cold, aching, ill and hungry bodies, it was for their lost homeland that they cried, and the farther they got from it the greater was the pain. To them it was like an elastic cord to which they were attached: the farther it was stretched, the stronger its pull.

The beef cattle purchased wherever available along the route, their doleful bellows accompanying the groans of the people, though they were a welcome rare relief from the sameness of salt pork, proved to be almost more trouble than they

were worth. In the night they strayed off, wandered into
woods and swamps, and precious marching time, more and
more precious in the ever-worsening weather, was lost in finding and herding them back. They stopped to graze wherever,
in this recently drought-parched and now frost-blackened
land, they found something to graze on, and had to be driven
by force. They ate poison ivy, sickened, and delayed the
march. To water them, all must halt while they were taken
aside to the source—when, after a search, a source was found.
Yet they were too valuable to be abandoned, and not just because they had been bought at a profiteer's price, but because
they were mobile food, nonperishable, rations for who knew
what emergency might arise. For days at a time the caravan
was stalled while quartermaster corpsmen scouted, in a countryside of subsistence farming where fodder barely enough for
the family cow was as much as most men raised, for grain and
hay for them. Fed as they were fed, watered as they were
watered, driven as they were driven, these starvelings made at
best lean, tough and tasteless eating.

But it would have been welcome now. It would have been
devoured raw. Under these conditions the hides, the horns and
the hooves would have been eaten. The last of their number
had been slaughtered far back down the trail.

For three days now they had marched on empty stom-
achs, and on almost empty ones for another two days before.
This after Captain Donovan had called a halt, drawn the train
together, ordered shot and butchered six head of the draft
oxen, roasted them and rationed the meat. The portions were
small, soon consumed, did little more than whet the appetite,
but more than six he dared not sacrifice even to this exigency;
they would be needed to haul supplies—when they ever got
more—and the more and more people unable to walk, for the
rest of the journey. Without their animals at the tongue to
draw them, the oxcarts left behind had the look of carcasses.
What little they had left to eat went to the children and the

nursing mothers, the pregnant women. Delays, one on top of another, had caused them to consume before time the provisions allotted for this stretch of the route. Axletrees had broken; replacing one took at least a day. One group took a wrong turn in rain and fog, went miles before the mistake was realized and had to retrace their steps.

Those were some of the minor delays.

They had spent the better part of a week with every able-bodied man felling trees and driving piles in the construction of a forty-foot bridge. To ferry them across another river, too broad to span, too deep to ford, they had built a raft. They had widened a stretch of road five miles long where, in this little-traveled country, there was nothing but a narrow overgrown trail. They had hacked their way through a canebrake. To moccasined feet, even to the pads of hooves, the stubble was a veritable bed of nails. And these obstacles were minor compared to the swamp.

That the road continued beyond the spot where it disappeared from sight was evidenced in the fact that the clearing between the trees ran on. But the roadbed was lost, drowned by the recent rains. There was no knowing how extensive the swamp was. It did not appear on Captain Donovan's field map because it had not previously existed. There was no detouring around it. This was the only road in that part of the world.

The swamp could only be traversed in two stages because the wagon teams would have to be doubled to get through the mud. Even so, those who were able were soon obliged to wade in icy water waist-deep to save weight. Loads were lightened of wagons mired up to their hubs by jettisoning hundred-pound barrels of meal, meat, molasses. Men slithered and floundered in the mud pushing on spokes and tailgates. The crossing took three days and two nights. The first group camped on the far side while the animals were returned for the rest. The second detachment too emerged with as much of their provisions sacrificed to save weight.

Here they were now still a good two days away from the depot where the next food was stored in wait for them. Driven by hunger to move faster, weakened by it they slowed. Just as they yearned now to reach the place they dreaded, so they hoped for no interruption in the mind-numbing monotony of the march. Monotony meant progress.

Paradoxically, this worst of the woes they had encountered silenced their crying, dried their tears. They were drawing upon a tribal second wind, a reserve of fortitude. Or—so it seemed to the boy—they were afraid now to cry. Afraid that all spirit would desert them and they would drop by the wayside and give up the ghost as one.

To Captain Donovan this stoical silence was more worrisome than wails. To him it portended trouble. Emotion given vent was easier to manipulate than emotion bottled up. Wounds opened and permitted to drain were healthier than wounds closed over to fester. These people had been tested to the outermost limit of their patience, and he wondered what form their outbreak of impatience would take. As he drove them daily onward he wondered what rebellion was fermenting in their minds. The Indian mind was a mystery to this native of New Hampshire. The very endurance and docility they had so far shown was potentially explosive.

He felt they had reason to hate every white man without exception, especially those nearest to hand, the representatives of the government which had dispossessed them and set them on this deadly exodus. They showed it in their faces. Initially their expressions had been ones of unrelieved sorrow and dejection; now they flashed frequently with resentment and rage. What they were enduring, coming on top of their detention-camp experiences, and the never-ending heartache for the loss of their homeland, was generating uncontainable hatred. When and on whom would they take it out? This had worried the Captain all along, but now that they were starving he feared something more. He worried at night, after camp was made and darkness fell upon these supperless and sullen people in his charge.

"You've spent time among them," he said to the Reverend Mackenzie. "Tell me—I'm thinking now of some of those real dark-skinned ones—you don't reckon that if they get hungry enough they might turn cannibal, do you? Not against one another, you understand." It was for his men's safety that he feared.

The Reverend Mackenzie assured him that he had nothing of that sort to worry about.

At sundown that wintry late-autumn evening, approaching a large farm, they saw something that stopped them in their tracks. It was the very familiarity of the sight, formerly, that made it now such a wonder. It was a field glowing with pumpkins on the vine as thick as hailstones. Nuggets of gold of that size and in those numbers could not have amazed them more, nor stirred greater longing.

The well-to-do farmer, along with his wife, having heard from a distance the approach of the procession, had come out on the road to watch. He gazed appalled at this stream of wretches in their rags.

Captain Donovan dismounted and saluted the couple.

"Sir," he said, "these here are Cherokees on their way west. We've been held up on the road by one thing and another. They've had little or nothing to eat for several days and still have miles to go before they get their next meal. Will you sell your crop of pumpkins?"

The farmer looked inquiringly at his wife, and, satisfied with the answer he read in her face, emphatically shook his head. "No, sir, Captain," he said. "I couldn't do that. Not and live with myself afterwards. There but for the grace of God go I. They're welcome to them every one, poor souls."

They flocked onto the field. The pumpkins were sliced and, frosty as they were, eaten raw, down to the shell. And promptly produced cramps and pandemic diarrhea.

The prosperous pumpkin grower, though more lavish in his generosity than most because he could afford to be, was representative of the treatment they received along the road once they were out of their homeland. In this there was sorrow, not solace. Another farmer turned them in upon a field of turnips he had not gotten around to harvesting. They gnawed them salted with their tears. Seldom did a landowner deny them permission to camp on his property. Hearing their approach, people came to watch, and often pressed bits of money on them. As they slowly wound through the thoroughfares of towns, a herd of human cattle on the march, storekeepers and housewives stood looking on from their doorways. Many, including men, wept at the sight. Noquisi would never forget seeing a man sit down and remove his shoes and hand them to a barefoot Indian, and another put his coat on the back of a woman wearing nothing but a summer dress of cotton cloth, originally thin, now little more than gauze. This sorrow caused by the sight of their suffering saddened them further for themselves, and often they wailed their way through the town. Captain Donovan had more to fear from these sympathetic bystanders than he did from his charges. He was subjected many times to their hoots and catcalls. He was pelted with stones. Once quite a large crowd blocked the road. "Good people," said the Captain, "I am trying to shepherd these poor souls to their new home, and they are tired and anxious to get there and rest. I ask you, please, to stand aside and let us proceed. Thank you." Yet, as Agiduda said, "They feel for us, and I am grateful. But where were they when we needed them?"

Three—not two—days after the pumpkins, famished, almost faint, they arrived at the food depot. Cornmeal, it weevily and with abundant evidence of rats, and beans, they worm-riddled, were distributed. The barrels of salt pork and bully beef were broken open. From each and every one the odor was the same. It was not their many delays on the road that had caused the meat to spoil. It had been improperly

cured, if cured at all. Its condition was such as to indicate that
it had been bad already when sold and put in place.

To prevent people from eating it anyway, and poisoning
themselves, Captain Donovan ordered the ramshackle store-
house put to the torch. Around it he posted armed guards,
otherwise the smell of roasting meat might have maddened
some of them into risking the flames. The sickening smell of it
charring subsequently drove them out of range.

"That low-down son of a bitch," said the Captain of the
sutler who had purveyed the provisions. It was an epithet that
Noquisi had heard before and in the course of a long life would
hear many times more, but never before or after with the force
of an original expression coined for the occasion.

Grandmother would have walked herself to death had the
boy not complained occasionally of being tired and needing a
rest. Agiduda understood this to be the pretense it was; Noquisi had entered his mind and read his thoughts. So the family slipped steadily a little farther behind in the march. It was
as though each day added to their years as they found themselves among the aged, those still ambulant and deathly afraid
of the infirmary wagons, down toward the tail of the column.
Darkness would be closing in and the line of campfires aglow
as they reached the rearmost one.

They were huddled around the fire at the end of another
day that had actually been short because of its difficulty and
for that reason seemed long. Grandmother, dazed with fatigue,
sat gazing dully into the flames, forgetful of the bite of tasteless
food unswallowed in her mouth. Without her knowing it, and
without himself knowing that the boy was reading his
thoughts, Agiduda was studying her.

Now he was remembering his courtship, the story of
which Noquisi knew, for it was a piece of family lore he was

now old enough to know, and a lesson in how times had changed. Agiduda was trying to forget where he was and cheer himself. He was thinking, "Your people, my dear, the Camerons, were no more Indian than mine but were one of those that we say are more Indian than the Indians, the purebloods. Never in all his life did your father—nor his before him—set foot inside a church, nor permit his womenfolks to do so, though in appearance he might have passed for a deacon. Church was one of the things the first Cameron had come here from overseas to get away from. He lived in a big stone house, but its observances were those of the wigwam.

"Your father was a stickler for the Cherokee laws of hospitality. He had been the beneficiary of them and he would have been disgraced for life ever to have failed to observe them. No stranger could stop at his door without being invited to a meal. In hopes of much more than just a meal, many did stop. Fortunately, your home was not so far from neighbors as to oblige him to offer every man a bed. Many were sent on their way toward evening with never so much as a glimpse of you, if they failed to pass your father's test. He was, naturally, proud of you, and eager to spread your fame and that of his house, but you were too fine a prize to be awarded to every Tom, Dick and Harry.

"Us young bucks were always swapping word of old-fashioned fathers like yours. Not only did we know of those like him, with desirable daughters, we knew also of those strict observers of the old customs who, unfortunately, had ugly daughters, and we were careful not to get caught in their vicinity at the approach of night, for to refuse the offer of hospitality, and all that it entailed, was as much of an insult as to be refused it—rather more. Besides, for a single man, a polite proposal on the morning after was the expected thing. The more of these a daughter turned down, the prouder the father —as he would formerly have been of his son's prowess as exhibited in his growing collection of scalps. Those girls with few

trophies, or none until now, were prone to overlook the polite
formality and accept.

"Needless to say, no shame attached to the practice—
before the spread of the missionaries. For a lone stranger, far
from the comforts of home, to be given a daughter of the house
to share the blanket for the night was a part of the hospitality
of the frontier home, however humble or grand, along with the
food and the shelter. She was pleased to be gracious, flattered
to be desired, basked in the praise lavished on her the next
morning, was proud of her father's pride in her and in himself.
Every young woman, if she was at all attractive, did it, and
every young man—including suitors—knew they did it; none
would have wanted one whom nobody else wanted. Long sanc-
tioned, enjoyed by all, it was a custom not easily stamped out.

"When I stopped at your house that day forty and more
years ago now, I asked directions of your father, pretending
not to know whose place it was, nor ever to have heard of the
daughter of the house. I had, of course. There was not a young
buck in Georgia who had not, for you were the talk of the
land. I had heard about you from a friend of mine.

" 'Go!' said this friend. 'Go! It is three days ride from
here, but worth doing it on your hands and knees. If you're
lucky enough to be invited, you will have the night of your life.
You might even be luckier, though many have tried and none
has succeeded. When I proposed marriage the morning after, I
meant it! Like all the others before me, I was refused. Why
should she be tied down to one man when she can have them
all?'

"Having timed my arrival for sundown, I doubt that I
fooled your father with my asking for directions. Playing in
the yard were the handsome little boy and the lovely little girl
from the overnight unions with the fine young men chosen as
partners for you by your father, your gifts to him and your
mother to brighten their old age. I had come hoping for noth-

ing more than a night of pleasure; seeing them, I thought, I would like a woman to make me some just like those.

"I was invited in and given refreshment. As we talked I heard the whisper of a light-footed moccasin on the floor of the next room and I felt myself being observed. I wondered, is she hoping, I hope, that I will be asked to stay?

"As your father and I talked the twilight deepened into dusk. Still there was no invitation for the night. I drained my drink and said that I must go.

" 'Go if you must,' said your father. 'I would be honored to have you stay. My home is your home, and all that is in it.' Then he called you in.

"You appeared in all your youth and beauty, and your many lovers were like jewels in your crown.

"After our meal I said that following my long day's ride —actually I had spent the day in the neighborhood resting up in preparation—I would excuse myself for bed early. You lighted the way. We slept little that night.

"When you said yes to my proposal the next morning I felt I had in my headdress the feathers of all those before me who had tried for the prize and lost.

"I settled your purchase price with your father. It was high, and that filled me with pride of possession. It saddened your father to lose his home's greatest attraction.

" '_Ai!_ The fine young men will come no more,' he said.

"Your hair is gray now, and thin. It was auburn then, long and thick as the tail of my horse, and watching you unbraid it to fall was all that was needed, if anything more was, to put me in the state you welcomed."

She had led a life of ease all those many years. Nothing had prepared her for this ordeal. Yet she endured it uncomplainingly. A little, frail, old woman, she was stronger than the soldiers. They rode, she walked.

He appeared to be in a trance as he rose and went toward her—almost reverential. She looked up at him wonderingly, still lost in her daze, near sleep in her tiredness. He could not at once find the words he wanted, and during that moment of tongue-tiedness there passed over her face a look that seemed to anticipate some new trouble, maybe a criticism—she who did not know what criticism from him was, but who now felt herself to be a burden and deserving of complaints.

"You, my soul, are the bravest of the brave," he said to her at last.

She burst into tears. Two sorts of tears, as Abel had said of his: one sort from one eye and another sort from the other. She appreciated the praise, but brave was not what she wanted to be, and praise for her bravery was to rob her of what little she had, was to remind her of her unsuitability for this grueling experience. She longed for her lost life of ease, and was ashamed of her longing, here in the midst of her companions who had never known anything but a life of hardship, and she did not know that she did indeed suffer more than they because she had theretofore suffered less. She felt herself woefully inadequate to be anybody's soul, and her tears flowed.

They had been on the road for over two months. Ahead of them, at this rate, stretched as many more. Their pace continued at about the same. For although all were weary and none was strong, attrition had winnowed out the very weakest and left them behind, victims fallen by the wayside. A caterpillar (and in its heaving and toiling, its pauses and resumptions, the column undulated like a caterpillar) achieved more, comparing the size of their goals. They averaged, over a week, some five miles a day. That might mean ten one day, none the next. They were slow getting going after the starter's bugle blew in the morning, not only because they were tired from the day—the many days—before, and the restless night spent on the hard cold ground, but because they were loath to move on.

But the stiff and aching bodies were unbent and stretched and the sore and swollen feet made to step, the animals were yoked and harnessed and the wheels made to turn—they too groaned—girls and boys saddled and shouldered themselves with little brothers and sisters, some recently orphaned and adopted into the family, and it was another day like another lash on that man's bare back there in camp, except that his lashes ended with the hundredth and nobody knew how many days they were sentenced to. People avoided looking one another in the face for fear of spreading their discouragement, or of contracting others'.

Yet, having eaten their meager and monotonous breakfast, they drew from some common store the courage to get going. It was around noon usually that memories of happier times, brought on, as the feet plodded forward, by the mind's wandering backward, triggered the tears.

Those able to walk at all walked for as long as they were able. They yielded to entreaties by the soldiers or by their neighbors in the column to take places in the wagons only when they were unable to move a step farther, and then they did so with two emotions; fear that they had reached the end, and shame that they had failed. The best way to persuade them was not to pity them but to chide them. "You are holding things up. For the sake of all, rest in the wagon for a day or so. Then you can walk again."

The sense grew daily that they were on a treadmill, like so many squirrels in cages, not only not reaching their journey's end, not even getting nearer to it, but actually, as their pace slowed throughout the day, falling back, as though as they moved the earth moved beneath their feet, outran them. Had they not passed this settlement, this farm, this hill once already—more than once? The country being sparsely settled, there were few signposts, markers, county or even state lines by which to gauge their progress, check their whereabouts.

"Sir, where *are* we?" the boy asked a soldier riding by.

He hardly expected an answer. He would not have known if he were told. It was not a question. It was a cry. He just wanted to be told that they were *somewhere*.

"Your guess is as good as mine, son," the soldier replied. "All I know is we're headed in the right direction."

Along with the sense that you were getting nowhere, standing still, treading in place, was an equally strong sense of having left yourself somewhere far behind. Of the things you used to do, the routine things and the unexpected things that arose daily, you did none now. All you did was walk. Meals, even sleep, were nothing more than refueling stops. You were not you. You were not a person. You were an animal being herded.

Possessions became burdens, growths, sores. And not just those borne on backs but those in wheeled conveyances as well. Mired in mud, slowed or stalled by underfed and over-worked oxen and mules, many were abandoned. Those with nothing to their names to have to carry were the best off. The Reverend Mackenzie writes that never before had he so fully appreciated the adage that it was hard for a rich man to get to heaven.

And a heaven their destination now seemed to be, as bliss-ful, as unattainable. By the end of the day that land of dark-ness, land of death had become the land of heart's desire.

In camp at night they had nothing to say to one another. Not just because of fatigue but because, except for their being a few miles farther along the road, it was another day like all the rest, alike now even in their accidents and alarms, and as for death, it was their pied piper. They would have buried, or have left unburied, another half dozen or so. They swallowed their meal and sat for a while staring into the fitful fire before falling asleep.

To sleep sitting was better than to sleep lying. Less of the body came in contact with the ground that way.

The snow that came out of a black sky in midmorning one December day was the first ever seen by many of the children, even some of those almost out of childhood. None of the parents had ever seen it in this quantity. For them it had been a rare delicacy, to be gathered, sweetened with honey and eaten. This now was nature in a mood unknown to them.

The snow came a-slant, borne on a driving north wind, striking full in their faces. Blinded by it, they lost sight of all but those nearest them, feared getting separated and lost. Unused as they were to such weather, they would have shivered if booted and dressed in woolens and furs. They wrapped themselves in their blankets.

Bit by bit as the snow deepened, their footfalls, the crunch of the wagon wheels, grew muffled, and this silence, the spectral trees, the whitened landscape made them feel that they had left this world and entered another one, had become the ghosts of themselves. These were the approaches to that land of death in which they must try to make a new life. They mourned for the one they had lost, and their wails were blown back in their mouths.

The pace of the march slowed steadily, ran down like an unwound clock, finally in late afternoon stopped dead. In a spot without shelter they made camp.

When the Fergusons straggled in that evening the boy fetched water from the wagon and put it to heat on the fire. He unlaced his grandmother's moccasins and unwound the rags that wrapped her calves. Her feet, blue with cold, were a mass of blisters, fresh and old, all rubbed raw. While they soaked the boy rubbed them. They puckered and swelled in the warm water.

He tucked her into her blanket, bathed his grandfather's feet, then put him to bed. Their sleeping bodies sought each other's warmth. To get into his place between them the boy had to squeeze.

Sometime later in the night he woke to see his grandfather huddled beside the fire. He had put his blanket over the two of them.

Now the ambulance wagons, in which the occupants were pitched about on the rutted roads and the pathless prairies like seasick passengers on waves, could no longer hold all those too enfeebled to march. Death, though working overtime, did not cull them out fast enough. They toppled and fell like dominoes by the roadside. Soldiers, giving up their mounts, hoisted them into the saddle and walked, leading by the bridle reins. Those in the rear of the procession, the old, the slow, the sick, were brought down as is the weakest of a herd by a beast of prey. Stalking them was cholera. Dr. Warren and his young assistant dispensed calomel.

Of the buzzards hovering high overhead like kites there seemed at times to be one for each and every marcher. They took their places as did the people on command from the conductor in the morning and there they hung daylong, moving at the people's pace, and when that slowed, dropping expectantly a notch lower in the sky. By night they settled to roost in trees nearby, in such numbers that by morning their droppings had whitened the trunks. There was no stopping the mind from thinking of what those droppings were composed of.

For now the weather was often too cold, the ground frozen too hard, the necessity to keep moving too urgent, and the number of dead too great to bury them all, or sometimes any of them all. They were left covered with brush—to Cherokees the ultimate desecration.

Robbed of the opportunity to observe their customs, even the most hallowed, their tribal tie was unraveling. They were becoming brutalized. If they ever reached their goal (and the saying "If we ever get there we'll all be dead" had ceased being funny), and established a new life, how purge themselves of their dishonor and shame, essential to making a fresh start?

The tribal tie was being frayed in another way as well. It had kept them in step, it had kept them in chorus, but now as the party progressed through lengthy stretches of unsettled and thus inviting country, as they got farther from the home they could not return to, yet were still far from the destination they feared, people dropped out of the march to seek their private fortunes. They were not officially missed, not pursued. From the outset all had refused to be mustered. No roll was called. Heads were not counted. Captain Donovan relied upon their bond to one another to keep them together.

That bond was strong, but it was being tested as never before, and even it was not unbreakable. And so you might awake one morning to find that the person, or the family, alongside whom you had marched these many miles, with whom you had shared the fire, had made off in the night. It was a measure of their misery that these desertions were not condemned but accepted and forgiven. In the tribe they found their individuality and their collective identity, and they pitied the defector and feared for him, as a driven herd might mourn for a maverick lost and left behind on the trail. Yet each was a decimation of their numbers and a discouragement to the general spirit. What would become of the lone stray? But then, what was to become of them all?

Debilitated and dispirited as they were, Captain Donovan drove them onward. Riding up and down the straggling column, he urged, "Push on, folks! Don't waste your strength in tears."

They pushed on, but still they cried.

They were being pursued by a pack of diseases, and when cholera, the leader of the pack, had taken its toll it was followed by typhus. Though to keep going was all but impossible, to stop was impossible. They desperately needed rest and recuperation, but there was no resting place, no shelter.

Meanwhile, with the seasonal shortening of the days, as night fell earlier, as the sun rose later, as they steadily weakened, as the need for fires made them stop early so that wood sufficient for the long night could be scavenged, their progress slowed daily. This slowness made it more imperative that they push on if any of them were to reach their still distant destination.

The thing most demoralizing was the incidence of children's deaths—a Herod's hand laid upon their newborn. Each and every dead child was mourned by all as a common loss, a threat to their continuation. The seed of the nation was planted in holes by the roadside, never to bear. Day after day, step after weary step, they plodded on, but to what? Not just to exile, but to extinction? They knew well that entire tribes had been extinguished. And even as they grieved over this decimation of their young, many were determined to bring no more of their kind into a world so hostile to them, to pass on the curse they were under. So they told the Reverend Mackenzie, appealing to him to explain what they had done to bring down upon them the wrath of God. He replied with "Suffer the little children to come unto me, for of such is the kingdom of heaven," and with "Those whom He loved He chastened and scourged."

The Reverend Mackenzie was embarrassed to think now of his fatuity in supposing that he might be an inspiration to these people; it was they who were the inspiration to him. He was awed by their courage, their patience, their singleness of purpose and solidarity one with another.

Heroes, martyrs, saints, he would call them in his diary. He tells of marching amid a constant chorus of wails and groans from a people as devoid of hope for deliverance as the damned in Hell. Then among them first a single voice, then others, then all would hymn their thanks to God for His

Amazing Grace. There was a note of query and almost a note of reproach in the Reverend Mackenzie's observation "Lord, you never had more devoted servants than these."

Suffering seemed to stiffen them, adversity to spur them. The Reverend Mackenzie tells of burying the young wife of a man whose father he had buried just days earlier, and of the man's then shouldering his bedroll and marching on with a step no less determined than before—if anything, rather more so.

He believed that he was witnessing a mass miracle, one being reenacted daily, a demonstration of the unflagging faith and trust that God in His greatness was able to inspire. It compared to the martyrs unflinchingly facing the lions in the Roman arena, to an entire nation of Jobs, never doubting, though tested without precedent or parallel. These were truly the Chosen People, wandering in the wilderness. The Reverend Mackenzie's question was, Did He who had chosen them know what they were enduring? No place on earth was godforsaken he knew, but there were times, especially at night, with the cold winds and the hungry wolves intermittently howling and the horde of vultures roosting in the nearby trees, their dreadful droppings audible, when it was hard to sense His presence here.

Yet the unconverted were as courageous, as persevering, as helpful to their companions in misery as the members of his congregation. Endurance and patience were not confined to those of the faith. The Reverend Mackenzie's creed underwent another change for the worse. He offered not God nor his bishop nor his diary any apology for his deviation from doctrine. At mass gravesites, unmarked for lack of time, he gave Christian burial to all, converted and pagan, shriven and sinner alike. The gospel had not been rejected by these souls, it had never reached them, in part because of the language barrier, in greater part because of the interdiction by the government of Georgia. Were they to be made to suffer, after all their earthly woes, the fires of hell in eternity because of their deprivation, their ignorance, their innocence? They were like those Cherokee children whose parents had signed their names to that petition to Washington against removal: they would have signed it if they could. That petition had been rejected by the one to whom it was addressed, but he was a man—and a hardhearted one. The Reverend Mackenzie's petition was to God. A jealous god, to be sure, so self-described, but a merciful one, a forgiving one. Works, not faith, were the path to salvation, and these souls had worked! The path they had traveled was straight and narrow! They would never reach its end in The Territory. They must find a resting place, one more hospitable than this bleak one which, in its frozen state, often refused to receive even their mortal remains.

To heaven's gate they would wend their way instinctively as to their cote, as sure of shelter as lambs. There they would meet their master and would thank Him for deliverance from their fellowman. He was jealous but He was not petty. He would not insist on inspecting them each and all to see that they bore His brand. A flock without a shepherd, then and there they would be purified like a sheep sent through the sheep-dip and passed through the gates into the fold.

"At least, Lord," he ended his prayer, "make a place for them in that purlieu of yours, limbo. After what they have been through, to them it will seem like heaven."

To his young friend and acolyte the Reverend Mackenzie spoke so many times of his people's patience that at last the boy grew annoyed with him for his simplicity. He was still one of *them*. He was still white, after all. Not only for the tongue but for the Indian mentality he needed an interpreter. Even an adopted Cherokee ought to have been better at thought-reading. In any and every mind of all those around him he would have found burning the same bowl of sacred fire, all kindled at the same source. What now impelled them, and to which each new woe was an added goad, was not meek acceptance, not blind faith, not hope of reward in some life to come; it was wrath. Enlightened by a boy, the Reverend Mackenzie learned that the lure now drawing them toward their promised land was the exaction there of revenge Old Testamental in its stark severity. The Cherokees were on the warpath.

"This is a good day to die."

Some Cherokees lived to say that more times than one but for most it was said just once in a lifetime. It was held in reserve until that day declared itself indisputably. Knowing this, those hearing it did not gainsay it. It was said in submission, to placate death so that one's spirit might rest peacefully, not forever contend against its fate. Best that it be said where one was born and had lived and would have kindred spirits close by, but wherever it was said would be one's resting place; peace must be made with it, acceptance. When living relations came to commune they would find tranquility.

Long since gone now is the grave at the roadside, indicated by the second of Captain Donovan's three maps, on the spot where Sarah Ferguson, wife of David, said those words, and where she was buried together with a boy of ten who had died within the hour along with her. This was done at the bereaved mother's suggestion and with the bereaved husband's concurrence. In this alien and lonely place, remote from kith and kin, woman and child would forevermore have each other for company.

It was a time for tears, but the time was short, just as the grave was shallow. Here where people, benumbed by hardship, had ceased to be persons and been dehumanized, death had lost its sting, and the loss was felt as the ultimate deprivation.

The old man and the boy marched no faster now that

they were no longer held back by the old woman. The pull of still another place, a part of themselves, tugged at their steps.

After the allowance of a few days privacy, Noquisi revisited his grandfather's mind. As though on tiptoe, having timidly knocked and gotten no answer, he peered inside. He drew back from what he found and quietly beat his retreat.

To make sure he had not just happened in on a passing thought, he returned several times over the succeeding days. Always it was the same, still and silent, dominated by one image: that of his wife's grave. For the boy's sake, his body marched on, but his spirit had stayed behind with hers, and there it would always remain.

The time came when they could go no farther. Too many were too sick. They made camp and settled in. A hospital camp it was.

Captain Donovan armed able-bodied men and sent them to hunt game for fresh meat. He combed the countryside and at large farms commandeered livestock and stores. He paid for them, but he commandeered them, and he named his price—a fair price. He sent wagons to towns within a radius of fifty miles with orders to come back loaded. "Buy whatever you can find. We need everything." If the town was one big enough to support a chemist, he sent a shopping list of Dr. Warren's needs. It was seldom fully filled, although—or perhaps because —the remedies he prescribed were of the commonest. Captain Donovan bought out whole dry-goods stores and issued the cloth for as far as it went. An ironically gaudy assortment of tents and tepees it made, in stripes, dots and flowers, like a gypsy encampment. He shocked all, yet won their practical endorsement, by forbidding the dead to be buried wrapped in their blankets. He would have stripped them of their clothes, he told the Reverend Mackenzie, but, fearing that such a barbarity might provoke an uprising, he stopped short of that. The blankets were redistributed among the living, who, in their dire necessity, overrode their superstitious objections and slept in them.

The doctor and his assistant went their rounds from tent to tent, both those of the emigrants and those of the sick soldiers. More than one disease was loose among them but the most prevalent and the deadliest were cholera and typhus. They bundled their patients in blankets with heated stones inside to sweat the poison from their systems—the same remedy as the exorcist's but with a different explanation for it—a white man's explanation—a similarity not lost upon the boy. They dispensed calomel.

Then the doctor came down sick. The boy nursed him. He felt himself responsible for the health of the one responsible for the health of all. On him the calomel had no effect. Or rather, it had its effect: it hastened, if it did not cause, the man's death, as on a distant day—a man well past middle age by then and long since known by another name—Noquisi would learn from his reading. (He maintained a lifelong interest in medicine, owing to his brief juvenile career at it, and in secret loving memory of his real father, the doctor.)

"Ai!" he cried, holding his finger on the doctor's pulseless wrist. Back from out of the darkness, echoes of his own, from all over the camp, came the wail, *"Ai!"* Roused to join in the chorus was the pack of wolves encamped nearby.

Said the Captain after the funeral, "Looks like you're our doctor now, son."

"I'm not off to a very good start," he said, looking at the grave of his first patient. "But I reckon I'm about as near to one as we've got—Lord help me and help us all! I'll do my best, sir."

"Spoken like a trooper," said the Captain.

He had the feeling that to Captain Donovan his youth and inexperience were not disqualifications. It hardly mattered who their doctor was, so little was any able to help them. The post was mainly ceremonial. He himself thought that too. He would do what little he could, but his main worth, he suspected, would be to give dying people the comfort of thinking that somebody was busying himself trying to do something for them. Many would expect of him just what they would expect of a witch doctor whom they called upon in extremity despite knowing that profession's record of failure and because at least they did no harm. He was saved from feeling like an imposter by his own modest estimate of his worth, and sustained by the sense that he was of some worth at least.

Actually, he would tell his grandson all those years later, disclaiming the boy's admiration for his taking on, at age fifteen, the job of doctor to some seven hundred people (that was what they were down to) there was not all that much to know about the profession back then. To be sure, it was a lot more than he knew; still it was pitifully little in sum. In fact, he was already more of a doctor than many of his more backward patients had ever consulted. They believed that medicine was white man's magic, and he did nothing to discourage them from believing that he, the son of a doctor, had inherited it.

And so indeed he had. His father had always explained to him what the symptoms were that had led to his diagnosis and what the treatment prescribed for the illness was. If the demands upon his attention were too pressing at the time, then he described the anatomy of an injury and the procedure for dealing with it afterwards on their way home. The uses of the herbs they gathered and grew were known to the boy by heart. He was a walking pharmacopoeia.

True, his apprenticeship with his father had been short, his experience limited, but to make up for what he did not know he now had the book.

The late Dr. Warren's formal education had been supplemented by study of the one volume comprising his medical library. It was entitled *The Doctor's Vade-Mecum*. It was some three hundred pages long. It contained the whole art and science of medicine, human and veterinarian. That it had been closely read was evidenced by its thoroughly thumbed condition, and that it had been consulted often in haste and anxiety at times of emergency—especially its index—by the drug stains and the bloody fingerprints on its pages. It became the boy doctor's bible.

He had not yet reached the chapter on fractures when a child who had fallen out of a wagon was brought to him with a broken arm. However, he had once watched his father set a similar break and listened to his explanation. He knew he would need splints, bandages, the flannel ones used also to bind the fetlocks of horses, and a sling.

As he had seen done for children with teething pains, he made a cloth sugar-tit, soaked it with whiskey, and gave it to the child to suck. On second thought he gave the unhappy father a shot of the whiskey too. Then, both to nerve himself to inflict the pain he must, and to seem more of a man, he took a shot of it himself. When he gave the arm the first wrench the little girl passed out. The father, unable to watch, withdrew. He was then able to work on an unconscious patient and without an anxious observer.

"That was as good as your father could have done," said Agiduda, just before the boy threw up.

But though the old man was proud of his grandson, he feared for his safety in exposing himself to contagion. For soon there were a dozen tents segregated from the rest, with people in them suffering from a variety of communicable diseases, if the boy was right in his diagnoses.

"I must do what I can, Agiduda," he said. "I am my father's son. He would do it if he was here." As he said that he wondered where his father was, whether he was alive. "He would expect me to do what I can. I'm better suited than anybody else we've got, though not by much, I admit. But I'm learning fast."

He made his rounds carrying Dr. Warren's black bag morning and evening, in between times reading the book, often in search of clues to cases he had just examined, and having his grandfather, text in hand, quiz him. Often he would identify a set of symptoms accurately, and name the specific prescribed for treatment, only to have to say of the latter, "But there isn't any more of that. It's been all used up." Or that he never had had any.

One of the tents contained half a dozen children with whooping cough. Their convulsions racked them, bent them double, turned them blue in the face. They had every appearance of suffocating, of drowning on their phlegm. They sweated profusely. They ruptured vessels and bled at the nose. He dosed them with ipecac and sulphur, belladonna, a sweetened elixir of dilute nitric acid, as recommended by the book. Their mothers nursed them—their older sisters in the mothers' absence.

Having had the disease as a child, as he learned from her family, and being now immune to it, a young woman was placed in this tent to recuperate from her latest fit of the falling sickness. She had frothed at the mouth, had convulsed violently. Her tongue had had to be held by hand to keep her from swallowing it and choking. She lay in a comatose sleep for two days. Awake, she lay in a daze, corpselike, staring, too weak when spoken to to answer, deaf to the whooping and wailing going on around her, regaining her shattered strength. Possible causes of the falling sickness, according to the book, were "fright, distress of mind, passion, worms, and many more." He had seen dogs with worms slathering at the mouth, contorting, running in circles and biting their tails. He gave his patient the vermifuge wormwood. Before she could be discharged from the tent she had another fit, as severe as the first.

That sick people worsened and died before their time despite doctors' help he knew, and now from the book he learned why. He learned it over and over. For so many maladies there was no cure nor even any treatment. For all its leather binding, its Philadelphia imprint, its woodcuts, its learned tone, there were times when his book was no more help than the witch doctor's rattle.

One morning on his rounds he reached the tent in which were two women and a girl whom he was treating for pneumonia. The evening before he had thought that all were improving. Now he thought that all were asleep—that deep sleep they fell into after long bouts of fevered sleeplessness. To check her temperature he felt the girl's forehead. He drew his hand back as though it had been burned—what it had been was chilled. Both the women also were dead. There came over him then, and would come over him afresh later while serving in his other capacity as the Reverend Mackenzie's graveside interpreter, a desolating sense of his inadequacy, a crushing sense of responsibility too big for him, a frightening sense of the imperfection of mankind's means in its war against disease and death.

After the funeral Captain Donovan said to the boy, "I know it must be discouraging, Cap, but don't let it get you down. You did your best and nobody could have done better. You went by the book. You must have seen your father lose patients too. When this is all over with and you rejoin him, you'll have nothing to be ashamed of."

You did not have to be a Cherokee to thought-read.

"Cap" was short for "Captain," the boy's latest acquired name. It derived from the old tunic, its tails descending to his knees, its cuffs turned back, one of his own that Captain Donovan had given him.

"What is the rest of life to be for someone who has already seen what that one has seen?" said the Reverend Mackenzie. What he did not say, but what he wrote, was his fear that the boy's day-to-day involvement with death and the unfairness of his competition with it might so disillusion and dishearten him as to turn him doubtful of the verities, even cynical. He knew how great that temptation was.

The two of them, boy doctor and minister, were often teamed at sickbeds, the one striving with his meager means to save lives, and then when he had failed, the other taking over from him and striving to save souls. This made theirs something of an uneasy partnership—or so at least the Reverend Mackenzie suspected. He felt his presence to be a discouragement to the boy, a forecast from the start that his efforts were expected to fail. The boy was alone, he himself had the mightiest of allies, God and His ally death. He confides to his diary his feeling of having become almost a demon, an ogre, of the sight of him at their bedsides terrifying these already frightened people, reducing them to hopelessness, and thus perhaps undoing whatever good the boy might be doing them. He wondered whether he might not actually have hastened the end of some of them, a black-clad messenger of despair with that book in hand containing, in a tongue which to many of them was a dark mystery in itself, a collection of spells, almost of invocations to death. Life everlasting was what he offered, but it could be attained only by losing this one, the one that even people in these straits clung to so tenaciously. He felt sometimes as though he was God's recruitment officer in His insatiable levy of souls, and that not Captain Donovan, leading the way to life in The Territory, but he, leading the way to the afterlife, was the marshal of the march.

Yet, he notes hopefully, reversing the adage "In the midst of death we are in life."

In giving birth, Cherokee women normally did it without help. Midwifery as a profession was hardly known among them. Sometimes an older woman, herself a mother, stood by in attendance, but most often it was done as Kanama had done it with her Usdi in the detention camp, by themselves. It was regarded as no big matter. Usually the mother was back at her work the same day. There had been several births on the march. So seldom was a doctor called in that only twice had Noquisi assisted his father at a delivery. So when he was sent for in this case he feared that things were not going well. When the messenger asked the Reverend Mackenzie to come, too, his fears increased.

But the messenger was young, perhaps overly alarmed, and at least he had seen it done twice, both difficult times, and that was twice more than any other man in the camp.

"You are the son of your father," said Agiduda. "May his hand guide yours. I will be praying for you."

"Thank you. Pray also for the woman and the child."

"That is for our clansman, Reverend Mac. My prayers will be for you."

As Noquisi drove them to the scene in the dispensary wagon, the Reverend Mackenzie refreshed the boy's memory by reading to him from the book.

" 'An examination with the finger is to be made to learn the presentation, that is, to learn which part of the child comes first into the mouth of the womb. If the head present, the labor will probably go on without the need of medical aid. But in all labors there is a liability to dangers from unforeseen accidents, which renders the attendance of an intelligent physician highly prudential.'

" 'If the breech present, do not pull down the feet; let the child come double; it will make more room for the head. If the feet present, let there be no pulling on them to hasten the birth of the breech.'

" 'After the feet and breech have fully cleared the external orifice, the delivery may be judiciously hastened for the purpose of preventing the death of the child from pressure on the umbilical cord before the head is brought to the air and the act of breathing thus permitted. For after the pulsations of the cord cease, the child must either breathe or die.' "

Like Kanama, this young woman had gone into seclusion when her time came and had suspended herself in squatting position by a rope from an overhead limb. Her husband waited within hearing. He waited and waited, listening to her cries—finally to her silence. Ashamed of her inability to do this common thing, not wanting to create a fuss nor to alarm anybody on her account, assuring herself that all would soon be well, that such contractions as she was experiencing could not possibly go on much longer without producing their result, answering her husband's calls that everything was all right, she had allowed her labor to grow so protracted that when finally he sought help she had to be cut down, half conscious, and brought by litter to a tent.

Outside the tent a woman chanted the spell, "Little man, come out! Hurry! Little woman, come out! Hurry!" The lying-in, with its mounting threat of danger, had drawn an anxious crowd, among them a woman with her newborn in her arms.

"You," said the boy to her. "Come with me." Here was firsthand experience at his side.

The patient, little more than a girl in years, lay wrapped in a blanket. After sending the husband—who was not much older than himself—outside, Noquisi unwrapped her. She was young, but just as he himself was now a man—a role for which suddenly he felt himself unready—so she was fully a woman. He had thought about women's unclothed bodies during the inactivity of the detention camp and the mindless monotony of the march. The instinct was insistent enough to be felt even at those untimely times. He had thought about it when looking at the anatomical plates in Dr. Warren's book. This one in its distortion and pain, brought on by the act of pleasure he had imagined, was not what he had in mind. What he was seeing now reproached him for his idle thoughts, or rather for his thoughtlessness of the consequences for the woman. It made him feel beholden for being male.

"When this is over," said the Reverend Mackenzie, "she will be a mother, something you and I can never know. Then it will all have been worth it. She will be proud of what she has been through."

It was another instance of the power of a white man to thought-read.

As the boy was making his examination the Reverend Mackenzie was reading the section of the book pertaining to breech delivery. He was not reading aloud but to himself.

"What do you feel?" he now asked.

"I think it must be the head."

To himself the Reverend Mackenzie said, "I hope you're right!"

"I'm pretty sure it's the head."

Again the Reverend Mackenzie said to himself, "I hope and pray you're right!" For of breech delivery what the book said was, "In this type of presentation the child's life is in great danger."

The examination stimulated a contraction. The woman gave a groan as the child's black hairy head began emerging slowly, like that of a turtle from its shell.

As the Reverend Mackenzie watched amazed, the boy poked his finger in the child's mouth. With all the professional offhandedness he could summon, he said, "Helps them get started breathing."

Then with that same finger hooked in the child's mouth, he drew the head out fully. Then he grasped it in both hands and pulled on it. You could pull quite hard so long as you pulled straight. A twist could break the neck. But though he pulled as hard as he dared, the shoulders remained wedged. He was getting no help from the mother. Her strength was spent.

He could never have brought himself to do what he did

next without having seen it done. Saying, "You can't help without hurting"—oft-spoken words of his father's to him—he gave the woman's abdomen a blow of his fist. The child issued forth. The mother's screams subsided into sobs.

The boy pinched the cord shut. "You do this to keep the baby's blood from draining back into the mother," he said, repeating his father's words to him. The sense was strong upon him that his father was looking over his shoulder, his hands guiding his own. He felt confident, competent, in command. All was going as it should go. With his free hand he lifted the child by its heels and slapped its back. With its first breath it uttered its first cry.

Crying in protest against their narrow passage and the inhospitality of their new element was the first thing all infants did, of every race and rank, the Reverend Mackenzie comments in his account, but this one, he adds, was born to do more cying than most.

The Reverend Mackenzie resumed his reading. He read silently. He felt himself to be a prompter. It was as though he were following with the script a performance he was watching. Now no prompting from him was needed, all was going according to the script. With the other woman pinching the cord for him, the boy was wiping the mucus from the child's eyes, its nose and its mouth. Now he laid it down, tied the two strings and snipped the cord between them.

"It's a girl," he said. The others could see for themselves that it was. It was not to them but to himself that he spoke. His self-wonder was enhanced by its being not one of the same sex as himself but one the opposite of him that he had brought forth. Now that it was all over and the fruit of it crying lustily, his part in the transaction made him feel as though he were the prime mover, as though the child were his creation.

"A girl," he said again. And with that he cut the cord joining him and her. It made her real, not a doll, and a being especially to be pitied. Latest born of Eve's daughters, she must one day undergo the same pain that had produced her.

He turned his attention to the mother. All was not over, as he knew. There was more to come. What he did not know, until the Reverend Mackenzie read it to him, was that it must come "promptly," and that if it did not it must be "expedited."

" 'If the afterbirth be not promptly expelled it must be expedited by the application of judicious pressure on the abdomen in the region of the womb.' "

Wondering just how much was "judicious," the boy pressed, and it was expelled, though he had to tug to free it.

He had once helped his father, now with the Reverend Mackenzie helping him he raised the woman and bandaged her with cloth soaked in cold water to contract the womb and stanch the bleeding. Within minutes the bandage was soaked. He changed it and within minutes the second one was soaked.

"Did you bleed like that?" he asked the other woman, who was now holding both babies.

"I bled," she replied. "But not like that."

"What does the book say?" he asked.

The Reverend Mackenzie was at that moment reading about hemorrhage. "It says the most common cause is failure to expel all of the afterbirth."

"What does it say to do about it?"

"It says to insert your hand. This will stimulate the womb to contract and it will be expelled."

This he did, but nothing more was expelled, and the bleeding continued as before.

It continued for an hour and through three more changes of bandage. The other woman placed her baby on the dying mother's breast. She did not accept it. Her face grew paler by the moment, her breath was labored, and the pupils of her eyes dilated.

All this while the Reverend Mackenzie was silently pray-

ing. Never before had he pleaded so fervently. He was praying
not for the woman's soul but for her life. As he admits, it was
as much for the boy's sake and his own as for hers. He feared
that he might fail this test of his faith and that the boy might
lose all faith in himself, in life. He should be confessing her,
absolving her in what time she had left and preparing her to
meet her maker. By delaying he was imperiling her immortal
soul. But he could not bring himself to terrify her dying moments. Let her drift off thinking that it was into her rest after
her travail. A spirit of challenge had been aroused in him by
this taking of one so young and blameless in the act of birthing
a soul for God. Let Him turn her away from the gates of His
kingdom if He would because in this outpost of misery on His
earth the formalities had gone unobserved.

"She is in heaven at this moment," he said when the end
came. "If anybody is."

The boy's look alarmed him.

"Don't blame yourself," he said. "You did all that anybody could. Your father could not have done more."

This time the Reverend Mackenzie misread his thoughts.
He was undergoing the final stage of his own painful passage
into the big world. In this woman's death he was experiencing
also that of another, she, too, a mother, in a place behind them
on this tearful trail.

Dismaying to the Reverend Mackenzie was the number of
deathbed reversions. Not conversions—though there were
those too. Reversions. Outright repudiations of faith. From the
lips of people soon to face His everlasting judgment he heard
God cursed. He heard His existence doubted—denied—de-
rided. He was asked scornfully by one man, "Did he who
made Old Hickory make me?" His answer, prompted by the
man's complexion, was, "Out of clay of two different colors."

Meanwhile he prayed, "Forgive them, Lord, for they know not what they do. Simple souls, Lord. Childish minds. Consider how sorely they have been tried."

But this extenuation on the grounds of their simplicity received a shock when a civilized man, an educated man— none other than his friend and fellow-clansman David Ferguson—said with a fatalism that left him wordless, "Last night I got a glimpse of heaven. Just a glimpse. I saw it through the gates. It didn't look like I picture The Territory. It looked to me like Georgia—or like Georgia used to look to me. I was told by the old gentleman standing guard that this was not the place for the likes of me. I turned and went my way. I knew it to be my way because in the dirt were the prints of many moccasins."

Came the night when the Reverend Mackenzie kept bedside vigil with his own patient. A black night it was. The light of the fire was not enough to read by. But for the present occasion he did not need his book. Two of its orders, that for the sick and that for the dead, he had come to know by heart, so many times had he had to repeat them. They had become compositions playable without the scores. In this performance of the one called for now, however, he foresaw some difficult passages.

The opening was already troublesome.

Peace be to this house, and to all that dwell in it

There was no house, there was only the thinnest of cloth tents to shelter from the cold the sick young woman who had dutifully followed him here to do God's work. She lay on the ground. He must be grateful that instead of just one blanket to wrap her in she had three, including his. The third had belonged to somebody now dead.

Remember not, Lord, our iniquities

Iniquities? His Nell? He verily believed that in her incorruptible purity she would have resisted the inveiglements of the original Serpent.

And the iniquities of our forefathers

He knew hers back to her great-grandparents. Iniquities! More virtuous souls could nowhere be found. To confess their sins, they would have had to commit the first one by inventing some. How many generations must bear the dusty guilt of their progenitors? That the sins of the fathers be not visited upon the children was belied by every prayer in the book. In Adam's fall we sinned all. The forgiveness of a grudging god must be sought forever after. Repent. Repent. Repent.

In the darkness of the night that surrounded him in this lost and lonely place he felt the lurking presence of Satan, tempting him to question and rebel.

In terror of himself, he skipped the next words of the service to get to:

Our Father, which art in heaven, Hallowed be Thy Name. Thy kingdom come. Thy will be done, in earth as it is in heaven. Give us this day our daily bread. And forgive us our trespasses. As we forgive them that trespass against us. And lead us not into temptation. But deliver us from evil. Amen.

Whether after that he recited the text as prescribed, he could not, in his fright, be sure. Perhaps by rote.

He next found himself at this passage:

Dearly beloved, know this, that Almighty God is the Lord of life and death, and of all things to them pertaining, as youth, strength, health, age, weakness and sickness. Wherefore, whatsoever your sickness is, know you certainly, that it is God's visitation. And for what cause soever this sickness is sent unto you; whether it be to try your patience for the example of others, and that your faith may be found in the day of the Lord laudable, glorious and honorable, to the increase of glory and endless felicity; or else it be sent unto you to correct and amend in you whatever doth offend the eyes of your heavenly father.

Take therefore in good part the chastisement of the Lord, for whom the Lord loveth he chasteneth and scourgeth—

Satan had stepped into the circle of firelight. He could not be seen but his face was prefigured in his voice. Both were sorrow-laden. His words were, "Poor pitiful fools! Poor, long-suffering, misguided fools, to worship and give thanks to a cruel and capricious god."

Fortifying himself with, "The letter killeth, the spirit giveth life," the Reverend Mackenzie discontinued the text. The deity addressed by it, the one who for his glorification tested beyond endurance the weak, imperfect vessels of his own creation, who exacted tribute by scourging, not a healer but the very god of affliction, every sickness a visitation from him: that was not the god he served. That was some implacable stone idol left over from early man, cringing and quaking in superstitious dread. That was Satan's god.

To his he prayed, "Dear Lord. Just and merciful God. Hear me in my hour of need. Lead me not into the slough of despond. Expose me not to the temptation of despair."

Out of the darkness came the piercing long-drawn *Ai!* that announced another Cherokee death.

Shaken, shivering, he continued. "Thy servant Nell is sick. Spare her. Take her not unto Thee at this time, Lord, I beseech Thee. Leave her to me yet for a while. Man that is born of woman hath but a short while to live. Let her live her short while. The joys of motherhood she does not know, nor I, Lord, the joy of fathering a soul for Thee. Heaven is populated by her kind. Thy world here below hath need in it of those like her. A virtuous woman, who can find? For her price is above rubies. She will be with Thee in eternity; let her now be Thy beacon shining in the darkness for those who have strayed from the straight and narrow path and lost their way."

With a fearful hand, warmed at the fire, he felt her forehead. It was chilled by a cold from within.

"My God, my God, why hast Thou forsaken me?" he cried, fully expecting to be struck dumb for his audacity in appropriating those words from their source. Out of the night there thundered no voice of anger or reproof.

He felt choked by the clerical collar that his wife had kept clean for him, both unfit to wear it and resentful of it, and he ripped it off. Without it he felt naked, alone and afraid. He was not himself—no longer knew who he was.

At her burial he was too sullen, despondent and defiant to perform the funeral service. He could not in conscience plead for God's mercy upon her soul. It had no need of any plea. As unspotted as it had come from His hand, just so was it returned.

It was noted and remarked upon that the minister's wife had been put into the alien earth without ceremony. To his embarrassment, it was those who had left the faith who were the most sympathetic toward him, and the saddest. It further dispirited them as the final evidence of their abandonment, one and all. His still-faithful flock solaced him, saying, those whom the Lord loved he chastened and scourged. Coming back to him now, those words of his own to them were like his gorge rising. Most still affirmed in song that they were lost but now were found, were blind but now could see; but many showed in little acts of kindness and consideration their pity for him as the ill-rewarded servant of a thankless and hard-hearted master. He felt it was for God, not him, to explain His ways, if He chose, to such unassailably primitive minds.

At length the plague ran its course and lifted. The survivors rose from their sickbeds pale, thin and shaky, struck their colorful tents and resumed their trek.

At this point in his tale to his grandson in Texas old Amos Smith I was given a sign that his time to conclude it was growing short. The words "This is a good day to die," beginning distantly, rapidly relayed nearer, sounded in his mind like tom-toms.

Remaining to be related was the final chapter that would bring the story back to the spot on the banks of Red River where his recital had commenced.

The vision vouchsafed to Agiduda of a heaven closed to the likes of him had been prophetic. On a morning not long afterwards, at the site of the third of Captain Donovan's three maps, he could not be awakened for all Noquisi's shaking.

A shallow grave was dug for him by the side of the road and a few stones heaped on it. There was not time to dig deeper, gather more. They must push on. One of the pots of sacred fire was placed on the mound in deference to his age and his standing in the tribe, to burn itself out after they were gone.

The Reverend Mackenzie prepared to orate. He had grown very weary of his oration. He could do it word-perfect without the book.

This time he was not allowed to speak. Noquisi stopped him.

"I am my own man now," he said. Then, in English, but in the only way to say in Cherokee that a person is mistaken, he said, "Sir, you lie."

Knowing this usage, the Reverend Mackenzie did not bridle. He did blush, however.

The boy looked around him, at the dismal day, at the endless road both behind and before them, at the huddled and shivering mourners, wan and wasted, at himself in his rags, so unready for this role of man thrust upon him.

"Your god is not his god," he said. "Nor mine. Nor theirs. Ours was taken from us and yours won't have us." And once again he looked around him, tabulating the misery of their lot.

Their difference did not divide the two friends. Rather it strengthened their bond, on one side at least. The man would be enthralled by the boy's staunch and unwavering disbelief, elevated by the example of his resoluteness, alone and unsupported by trust in any power outside his own small self.

"Out of the mouths of babes," the Reverend Mackenzie writes years later. He contrasts his conversion there on the road to Arkansas with Saul's on the road to Damascus. He could never afterward justify the ways of God to man. It was not that what he had seen and experienced on that trail of tears had made him lose his belief in God's existence. His heresy went deeper than that. Gone from him forever was his faith in God's goodness. He would survive the long march, in time would take a Cherokee second wife and would spend the rest of his life ministering to his adopted people in The Territory, blessing them in God's name into and out of this world, revealing only in one of the last of his letters, this to a fellow seminarian, that the words of his which his flock wanted to hear, and which he mounted the pulpit, like a scaffold, every Sabbath to tell them, were words in which he himself had long ago lost all belief. This life of imposture and deception he defends on the ground that having seen the suffering he had seen he was not only justified but in duty bound to tell whatever harmless little lies might alleviate any more.

Part Five

Like Sam Houston not long before him, Noquisi was a Texan as soon as he crossed Red River, and to himself he called himself one: *Nvdagini*. The Cherokee prophets of old were wrong: here, at the end of a trail bordered with roses, white streaked with red like himself, he had found his resting place. Perhaps he had even found a foster-grandfather, a substitute for the one he had lost.

Everything about Texas appealed to the boy. Its very name meant, in the language of one of its native tribes, "the friendly country." To one who in a short life had already encountered as much unfriendliness as he had encountered, that phrase sounded like "Rainbow's End," "The Happy Hunting Grounds," "Land of Heart's Desire."

Of the place's many attractions, the paramount one was that it was not a part nor a protectorate of the United States. He had seen what guarantees by the United States of protection for him and his kind were worth. This was another country, one too young for the old animosities, vast, still sparsely settled, still unspoiled, largely unexplored. Though it almost staggered the mind in trying to comprehend this, it was a country won—with the help of his red brothers—by one of their own. One without a drop of the blood in him, a Cherokee by choice. Awaiting Noquisi here were not just his own people but those of many tribes, all living together in harmony, uni-

fied at last, not divided, by their red blood. Among these Texas
Cherokees were none of the differences inflaming the others. A
week on horseback he and his father had spent following that
trail of roses, and the distance and the time added to the sense
of having put all that division and strife behind him and finding here peace and friendship and a new beginning.

The sight of Chief Bowl, a man of almost as many names
as Noquisi—The Bowl, Diwali, Colonel Bowles, Chief Bowles
—was a comfort in itself. In him, every Indian had a grandfather—or a great-grandfather. His very age was an inspiration
and a joy. It denoted peace, security and that most precious of
rights, privacy, the opportunity to live one's personal life and
not be just another of history's hapless pawns. He had attained
that age: you could hope that you might. He had attained it
here, away from America, away from the hostility toward and
among your kind, back there.

They had been taken to him immediately upon their arrival. Now, as Dr. Ferguson told their story, with assistance
from the boy when his Cherokee failed him, the old man listened in silence and with his eyes shut. The huffs he emitted as
the account took its turns seemed not to evince his surprise but
rather the contrary. It was as though he had heard it all already, or as though it was all just as he had foreseen. It seemed
to the boy impossible to tell a man his age anything new to
him.

As the refugees straggled in, Dr. Ferguson visited the re-
ception camps in search of his son and his parents. Finding the
one was easy, because in his role as doctor-interpreter, always
on the scene of whatever went wrong, tending the sick, continually galloping up and down the column behind one or another of their mounted escorts, Captain Donovan's second

tongue, he had come to be the best-known person on the march.

When father and son met, the boy allowed his being alone to speak for itself. As he observed the effect of this, a new conception of his father came to him. Seldom until then had he thought of him as somebody's child, always as somebody's father. In his childish self-centeredness he had not really thought of him as somebody's husband. Older and wiser now, knowing that one could be a child without being a *child,* he recognized his father's right to his private grief, and that for even him to attempt to mollify it would be meddlesome.

After a short while he said, "You don't need to tell me about my mother. I found the grave."

Then there was nothing the orphaned widower could say to solace the orphan. Together in their losses, each must cope with his special own, respect the other's. There was an exchange of roles between father and son. Bereavement had for the time made a man of the boy and a boy of the man.

The doctor regained his presence to find himself under study by a number of people ranged at some little distance from him. They were in tatters, wasted and gaunt. The unnatural jaws denoted to his trained eye gums swollen by scurvy, pigmentless patches on the backs of their hands a condition he recognized but for which medicine had no name (his Dust Bowl era descendant, Amos IV, would know it as pellagra), and the bloated bellies of the thin-limbed, owl-eyed children malnutrition brought on by their months-long diet restricted to salt pork and cornmeal and molasses. On approaching nearer to offer his professional services, he saw that one man was missing the tip joints of all his fingers. Frostbite. In lieu of a surgeon, nature herself had amputated the affected parts, sloughed them off, and the decay had been prevented from spreading farther up the limbs by the very cold that had caused it.

At the doctor's approach they shrank from him as one,

shrank not in fear but in hostility. Just as he feared, they identified him with those who had brought upon them the ordeal they had endured. Rather than blaming John Ross for encouraging them to hold out until things came to such a pass, they blamed those who had sold them out, and for those who had tried to warn them, and had been proved right in their predictions, there was no forgiveness.

The doctor sensed a reproach, silent as a volley of arrows and just as piercing, in their stony stares. Not a word was spoken. Their condition was expressive of itself; let it accuse him. For his personal loss, for his having only just learned of it, no special pity. Though his was their common lot, it did not make him one of them. His father had been one of their headsmen, much respected; his death, and that of his wife, known to all, the loss felt by all, yet that gained the son none of their sympathy. His father had been a holdout, he a sellout. The Indian talent for bearing a grudge Abel Ferguson knew in his veins.

In one long exchange of looks all these understandings transpired.

Yet, paradoxically, as he would later tell his son, never had he felt himself to be more one of them than in that moment when he stood rejected by them. Outcast by his own, he felt an odd pride in their obduracy. What a people! Who but they would refuse the desperately needed services of the only doctor they had?

The reckoning was quick in coming. Its thoroughness, its brutality was meant as a lesson to last Cherokees forever. On a morning just eight days ago John Ridge was dragged from bed and hustled outdoors. While his wife looked on, he was stabbed twenty-five times, once for each member of the posse. Then his throat was slit. His body was tossed high into the air, then stamped on, in file, by all twenty-five. Meanwhile his cousin Elias Boudinot was being hacked to death on the site of the house he was building for himself and his new wife (the first one had died in childbirth on the eve of their departure from Georgia), and his father, old Major—the framer of the law against the sale of tribal land, and its one previous enforcer—gunned down from ambush.

Others, less prominent, identified with the Ridge party, were also killed on that day. Abel Ferguson knew now that he could not rely upon his value to them as their doctor to protect him from this prairie fire of vengeance. The boy had been told by his grandfather of The Bowl. To him they had fled. With his skills he hoped he might make himself useful. Here he hoped he had found a home, peace, brotherhood, a new life.

The old chief's comment upon what he had heard was one that permanently impressed itself upon the boy, both by the unexpectedness of his having picked up the expression on which it was a twist, and, in the light of subsequent events, its appositeness to his own situation. He said, "They who take the pen shall perish by the sword." He said it almost as though pleased. At his age there was satisfaction in having the world confirm you in your disenchantment with it.

He said, spreading his arms to include everything in view, "You are welcome. What is mine is yours." Although he said it, they felt, with something less than wholeheartedness.

The confederation was separated by their different languages into several tribal villages. In the principal one, this of the Cherokees, The Bowl's was the biggest house, not just because he was Chief but also because his family was, or had been before the many children whom he, and others, had begotten upon his three wives grew up and left home, a big one. The three wives were all with him yet but that still left plenty of room, and his home was their home for as long as it was his. Time was when he would have been honored to lend them each one of his wives, but they must excuse him, for he feared that even the youngest of them was too old now to be found attractive by younger men.

Dr. Abel protested that he was not to give it a thought, and the red- but straight-faced Noquisi held up a palm to signify that for his part no apology was needed.

The Chief remembered the Ferguson family from the old country, and they would have been welcomed out of respect, even just out of frontier hospitality, but, having heard the boy speak both Cherokee and English, he invited them also out of curiosity and admiration.

The curiosity and the admiration were mutual, as was the pleasure of their hearing each other speak. The nucleus of The Bowl's band had left the old country before Cherokees in any numbers had begun to learn English, and they had later come to a country where the official language was Spanish. The dialect he spoke was Noquisi's own, liquid and musical as a brook, but more so in its nearness to the source, for this was the pure-blooded, hundred-proof speech he and his band had taken west with them two generations ago and preserved in isolation, uncorrupted. It tasted on the palate and tongue like a fine old liqueur, mellow but with a kick to it. The old man had been called the Moses of his people; to the boy it seemed rather as though he were listening to Adam bestowing upon the things of the world their names. The aged patriarch looked elemental, a living anachronism. He had at least as much white blood in him as red, probably more, yet to the boy he seemed their people's prototype, their progenitor, straight from his Creator's hand, immune against mortality and apt to last to Adam's age—almost to have reached it. He had lived as a savage. He had been a warrior, a killer of men. He had drawn the bow and seen the arrow pierce human flesh. He had swung the tomahawk. He had wielded the scalping knife. Now, though he still stood as straight as a gun barrel and his stride was upright and brisk, his sandy hair was streaked with white and his weatherworn and suntanned face was as wrinkled as the rind of an Osage orange, the fruit of the tree of the ark. His eyes were gray with age, it seemed, as though they had once been a darker shade but had been bleached by time, had faded from all his close and wary observation of life. In the Indian fashion, he kept them shut for lengthy periods when he was speaking and when he was listening—they opened, suddenly or slowly, for emphasis, of his words or of yours, and this suddenness or slowness, combined with their paleness, made them unfailingly startling.

"Theirs for as long as it was his"—in reference to the Chief's home—turned out to be something other than the formality that the Fergusons, nodding politely, had taken it for.

"It is bad news that you have brought me," he said. "I am sorry to say that I have got bad news for you too."

It was only yesterday that he had been visited by the commissioners of Houston's successor, President Lamar. They brought him a letter from their chief saying that the Indians would never be permitted to establish a permanent and independent jurisdiction within the country, that their claim to their territory would never be recognized.

The Fergusons felt as though they were back in Georgia. Well they might. Lamar was a Georgian, had been personal secretary to Governor Troup when the lands of the Creeks within that state were taken from them.

In his inaugural address as President of Texas, Lamar had declared his intention of ridding the country of Indians. Should they be driven out, they would travel up that same Cherokee Trace which the Fergusons had just come down, and would join those whom they reported to be now in open and bloody conflict, perhaps on the verge of civil war, the destruction of the tribe.

The Texans offered the Indians twenty-five thousand dollars for their homes and their standing crops and all the improvements made over twenty years time to the land, some thirty by fifty miles in extent. That worked out to about three dollars per household. The Chief had succeeded in putting them off for the time being, saying that he must confer with his subchiefs. Meanwhile, he had a plan of his own.

The Chief excused himself and went inside the house. He returned carrying a tin box. From this box he drew a sheaf of papers. Noquisi read over his father's shoulder. It was the treaty, dated some three months before the battle of San Jacinto, between the Indian Confederacy and the provisional government of the Republic of Texas, reaffirming the Indian claim to the land granted them by Mexico. This was the receipt for their neutrality in the revolution. It bore the signatures of a dozen Texans, headed by Sam Houston's, and the marks of half a dozen Indians, headed by The Bowl's.

Lamar claimed that the treaty, ratified by a government that was only provisional and had not been elected by the people, was not worth the paper it was written on. Houston maintained its validity. Without it, he said, there would be no Republic of Texas, and he and his co-signers would all be dead at the hands of Santa Anna.

Houston was out of office now, forbidden by the constitution to succeed himself, and the Chief had to admit that among Texans he was almost alone in his friendliness toward Indians, but he was still the most powerful man in the country, revered as its George Washington: its victorious revolutionary commander, its first President. He was the Chief's longtime personal friend; he had once given him one of his daughters overnight. Lamar had been Houston's Vice President, and in that time Houston had learned to despise him—to despise him all the more, perhaps, for having himself been the making of the man, for not having seen through him from the start. The wretch had grown in his own shadow, like poison ivy underneath an oak. The two were at odds on every issue, and most of all on the Indian question.

Now, even as they talked, a runner, a white man married to a Cherokee, one who could pass unchallenged, unnoticed by the Texans, was on his way to Nacogdoches, Houston's home —a distance of a day. This runner, Grandgent by name, was a man whom nothing could stop, or even long delay. He would deliver his message before the sun went down. When Kalunah heard what that snake Lamar was up to behind his back, he would come at once to his old friend Diwali's aid. He would address the Texas Senate. He would remind them of their debt to the Indians and insist upon their duty to honor the treaty. It was to be hoped that he might prevail. The expulsion order would be revoked. They could go on living peacefully in their home of twenty years. There would be no bloodshed. No widows. No fatherless children.

Meanwhile the drums had relayed the news throughout the territory, and that same afternoon of the Fergusons' arrival the subchiefs assembled in council. Some rode on saddles, some on blankets. Behind many rode a boy or a girl, the man's interpreter, for it was the children who were quick to learn a second language. Proud, not to say vain, men, in their prime, they bore themselves like finalists in a contest.

The Bowl's homesite had been chosen for the gathering because of the deep, cool, ever-flowing spring just behind it, and on this hot and dusty day all went there on arrival for a drink from the gourd dipper and to water their horses at the trough. Several chieftains arrived together. They passed the dipper among them. Before drinking, they deliberately ceremoniously spat on the ground. It was an attestation of their trust in one another, their putting their lives in their brothers' keeping. Nothing like it had Noquisi ever seen before. It made him feel that he had found the good place, the safe place, the friendly place—only to be threatened with the imminent loss of it.

Having unsaddled and hobbled or tethered his horse, each man spread his saddle blanket on the ground and seated himself on it, in token of a friendly powwow. Like the numerals of a dial, they disposed themselves around the Old Chief, with him at twelve o'clock. Awaiting them were large steaming crocks of stewed meat and cornmeal mush, served by the three wives. From his pouch each man produced his spoon, some of metal, some of wood, some of bone, some of horn. With it he fed himself and his child interpreter. After eating, many packed and puffed on pipes. In their colorful costumes, such a contrast to the Cherokees with their white man's clothes made from bolt goods bought from itinerant peddlers, they made the boy feel that at last he was seeing *Indians,* and he thrilled with pride and savagery. Here was his racial heritage surviving and asserting itself.

The Bowl was the Chief of the Confederacy but he was the elected Chief, and while his word carried the most weight, it was the will of the majority that he must abide by and carry out. Although the Cherokees were by far the most numerous of the various tribes, they had but one voice in the council, the same as the rest. Quick work was made of the Texans' offer. The vote to reject it was unanimous. The chieftains were then given time to speak. In each case it went more or less like this:

"I am the voice of the Kickapoos. There are no greater warriors than we. When we frown the sky darkens. When we stamp our feet in anger the earth trembles. When we shake our fists the sun hides its face in fear. We strike like the lightning. We shed blood like the rain. At the sound of our war whoop the palefaces turn and run for their lives." And so on.

All present knew that not one of them, except for the old man, and he for the last time before they were born, had ever been in battle, had ever uttered a war whoop. But they were men now prepared to die defending their homes, and they were working themselves and one another up.

Throughout all this rant the old Chief sat and dozed— shut eyes as one listened signified rapt attentiveness—grunting from time to time as though in approval of the speakers' declamations. The more steam let off into the air the better. The pot on the fire would not boil over with the lid lifted. If a boy like

Noquisi could think it, must not the old man also be thinking, "If you are so invincible against the palefaces then what are you doing here?"

The Caddo and the Choctaw chieftains sat discreetly silent. It was a long time since the Caddoes had been known as warriors; their pottery was the envy of all other tribes. As for the Choctaws, their proudest claim was that they had never warred upon the white man. Thus of them too one might have asked what they were doing here.

The old Chief dozed and nodded and grunted, knowing all the while that he had his messenger on the way to Houston, perhaps by now closeted with him. When the others were finished and his turn came to orate, he said simply, "The Cherokees' record speaks for itself."

The decision on whether or not to stand and fight was put to the vote, Diwali presiding.

"We are many and time is short," he said. "I ask you to be brief. Now, what do our brothers, the Shawnees, say?"

The man in the long blue tunic, tight-fitting blue trousers gartered below the knees, wearing a red turban crowned with five fluffy black plumes, a red sash and a bandolier, his cheeks painted vermilion and with silver pendants the size of dollars hanging from his ears, said, "We Shawnees say to fight."

"What do our brothers, the Coushattas, say?"

"The Coushattas say fight," said the man with the silver ornament in his nose.

"What do our brothers, the Delawares, say?"

The man in the knee-length cape said, "Fight."

"What do our brothers, the Caddoes, say?"

"To fight," said the man in the smock and the broad-brimmed sombrero.

"What do our brothers, the Choctaws, say?"

"The Choctaws say to fight." This drew grunts of surprise and approval. Even the Choctaws!

"What do our brothers, the Tamocuttakes, say?"

"Fight!"

"What do our brothers, the Kickapoos, say?"

The man encased in the skin-tight suit of white deerskin as though he had been born in it said, "The Kickapoos say fight, and win!"

"What do our brothers, the Alabamas, say?"

"Fight."

"What do our brothers, the Quapaws, say?"

"We Quapaws vote to fight."

"What do our brothers, the Utangous, say?"

"Fight!"

"What do our brothers, the Yowanis, say?"

"Fight!"

"What do our brothers, the Biloxis, say?"

"Fight!"

"What do our brothers, the Chickasaws, say?"

"Fight!"

"What do we Cherokees say? We say, don't fight."

This settled, a battle commander was elected.

"The Shawnees?"

"Diwali."

"The Coushattas?"

"Diwali."

"The Delawares?"

"Diwali."

"The Caddoes?"

"Diwali."

"The Choctaws?"

"Diwali."

"The Tamocuttakes?"

"Diwali."

"The Kickapoos?"

"Diwali."

"The Alabamas?"

"Diwali."

"The Quapaws?"

"Diwali."

"The Utangous?"

"Diwali."

"The Yowanis?"

"Diwali."

"The Biloxis?"

"Diwali."

"The Chickasaws?"

"Diwali."

"The Cherokees?"

The old man kept them waiting upon his answer for some moments, though there was little doubt what it would be.

"We Cherokees cast our vote with our brothers for Diwali," he said.

This piece of diplomacy was something other than what it appeared to be: a politic bid for unanimity and the graceful acceptance of an unsought honor, although it was allowed by all to pass for that. It was tacitly understood as his acknowledgment of the code binding both him and them. Had he refused the election, even on the seemingly unarguable ground of his age, he would have been summarily executed, and while he had so little time left to forfeit that this was a matter almost of indifference to him, such a death would have dishonored his tribe. Actually, a plea to be excused on account of his age would have been the least admissible; his age was his qualification for the post. Years were experience, wisdom, survival through cunning and guile, and the attainment of them a mark of the special favor of the gods, a favor extended to those who exalted and followed you. Respect for you was respect for them, and was rewarded accordingly. Battles were won by the combination of age and youth. Age was the bow, youth the arrows.

As honored houseguests of the Chief, the Fergusons, father and son, were present at his next meeting with President Lamar's commissioner, General Rusk. (The boy would live to see the time, long after the disappearance of the last Indian, when this area would be a part of Cherokee County, one of its streams Bowl Creek, with nobody to tell how it got its name, and a nearby town, Rusk.) The day was hot enough to suggest that hell had just received a fresh consignment of souls. Except for a breechclout, The Bowl on this occasion was naked. His wrinkled skin and gnarled veins made him look like an ancient tree, its bark entwined with clinging vines.

"Colonel Bowles," said General Rusk, "your presence here can no longer be tolerated. You have stolen our livestock. You have burned our houses. You have attacked and killed our people."

The Chief had heard all this before. He had heard it ad nauseam. The last charge referred to the massacre the year before of a family of settlers named Killough. Sixteen of them there were, three generations, blood kin and in-laws: not one was spared. The details were gruesome. Unfortunately for the Cherokees, it had happened inside their territory. The whole country was enraged and clamoring for the expulsion of the Indians. Which tribe had done it was not known, thus all stood accused—were judged guilty.

"It was the Comanches," said the Chief. He had no proof of that, but the Comanches were always blamed for everything, and most often deservedly. They would have been blamed by the Texans for this atrocity had they not been nomads with no land to seize.

But this was a distinction which to most whites meant little or nothing. Indians were Indians, and any difference between one tribe and another was like that between the copperhead and the diamondback rattlesnakes. This time the Coman-ches, next time the Cherokees.

"This land," said the Chief, spreading his arms wide, "is ours. It was deeded to us by the Mexicans twenty years ago. I myself travelled to the capital city and negotiated the treaty."

"This is not Mexico now."

Ignoring the interruption, the Chief continued, "And the one with the Republic of Texas confirming our rights."

Meanwhile Noquisi was doing what his Cherokee blood empowered him to do: thought-reading. Having entered the Chief's mind, he found him thinking that the hatred of some-body for you because of your difference from him was intensi-fied by all the many inadmissible but undeniable resemblances that you bore to him. You, too, stood upright, had two eyes, were tailless, could utter speech, or some sort of sounds that to you passed for speech. That did not make you like him, but it made you too much like him.

Inside the Commissioner's mind Noquisi found a refine-ment upon his distaste for the likes of himself. He was a mon-grel, but just barely one. He might have concealed his Indian blood and passed for white; to be inferior by choice was to be a creature beneath contempt.

"That treaty was never ratified by our government," said Rusk. "It is worthless. So is all this palaver."

With that last remark the Chief agreed, and, indeed, he was hardly attending. Going through this routine was like wild animals in their ritualized disputing over a mating territory. He was thinking of Grandgent's protracted absence and of the mounting pressure upon him by his young men to stand and fight.

For his own life he cared next to nothing; he had lived it —had outlived it; but for the rest the loss would be cata-strophic. If they fought, and shed one drop of their enemies' blood, and were defeated, those of them who survived would be treated like vermin to be exterminated.

At the next conference the weather was even hotter than
before. Again the chief wore nothing but a breechclout. Yet
Noquisi sensed (or else he interpreted it thus in hindsight long
years later, in relating the incident to his grandson) that the
old man's reason for this was not the heat. He had bared
himself to the skin to remind his uninvited guests that,
stripped of their coverings, all men, red and white, were alike,
and with his aged body to demonstrate that all faced the same
end. It was both a gesture of pride and a plea for elementary
humanity. In his nakedness he was both regal and as common
as clay.

This time the Commissioner came with an ultimatum. He
produced an intercepted letter from the Mexicans reminding
the Chief that he was a colonel in their army and inviting him
to join in a plot to overthrow the government of Texas. The
Indians were promised their disputed land forevermore if they
rose up in a counterrevolution. The Chief protested that he
had never so much as received the letter, and that the Mexicans, or anybody else, could write him without it implicating
him. But that such a proposal could even be made was all the
evidence Rusk needed to prove that he was amenable to it.
With the Texans demanding that he go, he would have been a
fool not to be amenable.

They must begin preparations for their removal at once.
They would be compensated for their properties and provisioned for the journey. They would be escorted by troops. The
locks, with their hammers, would be removed from their rifles,
rendering them harmless, and deposited with the Texans, to be
restored to them at the international border.

Drawing himself up still straighter, the Chief declared
that they would never go under escort. It would made them
look like prisoners. They were a free people. As for surrender-

ing their gunlocks, his men would suspect that, once disarmed, they and their families would be slaughtered. They would never consent to it.

"Those are our conditions," said Rusk. "You have three days time to assemble your people for removal."

"They will assemble, but not for removal," said the Chief. He sighed sorrowfully. "There will be much bloodshed. Many widows. Many fatherless children."

For his part, the threat was hollow, meant not to precipitate a confrontation but to delay and perhaps avoid one. He still hoped that Grandgent's message had been or soon would be delivered and that Houston would yet intercede. This was a gamble, intended to give Rusk pause and make him ponder his willingness to go that far. It might instead provoke him to attack. To do that he might have to send for authorization to Lamar, or he might have his contingency orders in his pocket even now. How much if any time he had gained the Chief did not know. Little at best. Meanwhile, a man of eighty-four must pretend to be frightened by the Texans' threats to kill him if he fought and the unspoken threats of his own people to kill him if he did not.

Had all gone well, Grandgent ought to have been back by this time. The distance was not more than forty miles each way. The weather was dry. And the man was one who could cover ground like a chaparral. But he was not back, and the Chief thought he knew why. He had made some allowance for this from the outset. Whenever he himself went to call on Kalunah he always took the precaution of bringing along his tepee and a dog for the cook pot. Once he had camped in Kalunah's yard for three days waiting for him to drink his fill, then sleep it off and sober up. Not that the cares of office had kept tightly corked the former President's jug; he seemed confident of being able to run the country part-time; and there was nothing in his performance to complain of—dead drunk, Sam Houston was a better man than Mirabeau Buonaparte Lamar cold sober—but now that he was free of those cares he was rumored to be drinking harder than ever. To think that this was the case now did not trouble the Chief. On the contrary, Kalunah would come to in a bilious temper, and he would take it out on the detestable Lamar.

During these days of negotiations with the Texans a change was noticeable in the old Chief. He appeared more and more detached, remote. Those pale, depthless eyes of his seemed to see beyond the visible horizons. His spirit had gone ahead of him to scout out the well-traveled path that went in one direction only, and he was attending upon its call.

Meanwhile, he was busily preparing for the battle he hoped never to have to fight. Gatunwali, his second in command, as opposed to war as he was and just as doubtful about its outcome, was out in the countryside alerting the headsmen of the tribes. They knew where and at what signal to join forces. They knew the battlefield. They knew from which quarter to expect attack. They knew where to take cover if forced to, and where then to regroup. Those who lacked them were supplied with guns and ammunition.

Not even Kalunah could go on the binge for this long. Grandgent had found him away from home and had either set off to find him or was waiting for his return. That had to be the explanation for the passage of such an amount of time.

The day before the one set for the battle, the warriors of the many tribes were summoned by drums from their scattered villages to the command post. That evening, hot as it was, they gathered around a blazing bonfire for a performance of the long-disused going-to-war ceremony.

The near-naked old Chief seated himself idol-wise inside the circle of light, shut his wrinkled eyelids and invoked the attendance of the ancient gods. *"Hayi! Yu! Sge!"* Then in a low singsong, his voice crackling like the blaze, he chanted the traditional spell:

"Nagwa usinuliyu Atasu Gigagei hinisalatagina. Usinuli dudata unanugatsidasti nigesuna. Dudanat elawiniyu atassu digunagei degulskwitahisesti . . ."

There he stopped. He uttered a few exploratory words, shook his head and gave up. It was plain to see that there was more to it, and that he had long ago forgotten the rest.

Then for the edification of the young men, to incite in them the martial spirit of their fierce forefathers, half a dozen of the old ones staged a war dance. In former times all the warriors would have participated, but those now of fighting age were seeing the ceremony for the first time. The dancers were naked except for breechclouts; they had breasts as slack as old women's; the muscles of their arms sagged; their scrawny shanks were knotted with sinews. They had shaved their heads, leaving only a topknot in which to tie feathers, as had been the custom when their enemies were other Indians, for to be scalped defiled the body and made it unfit for burial. Their faces were painted vermilion all over while one eye was circled with white and the other with black. Brandishing red and black clubs, they stooped and rose and shuffled and stamped around the war pole, for which an ancient, moth-eaten human scalp had actually been produced—somebody's heirloom and curio. After about five minutes the dancers came to a halt, uttered four whoops and the performance was over.

Then to his untrained and inexperienced army the old Chief gave a lesson in the Indian art of battle.

As was always the case, alas, he said, they were less well armed than the enemy. Thus they must draw his fire. They must make targets of themselves.

This was translated into twenty tongues.

"Single out one of them as you single out a goose in a flock. Shoot at them all and you hit none. Concentrate upon your man. Make him think that you are to be the death of him, that his is the scalp you crave to add to your collection. Make yourself his target. Stand still while he takes aim. Tease him, taunt him, so that when he fires he fires too soon, from too great a distance, shakes with fear of missing, and misses. Then while he is reloading or running in retreat, rush him."

He awaited a grunt of understanding, approval. He was answered by the silence of dismay. Let the enemy try to kill you? Stand still while he takes aim? Make *targets* of themselves?

Any man caught slipping through the Texans' lines trying to reach the Cherokees now must be one of them; if he was white, then he was a renegade from his race, to be dealt with as his degenerate kind deserved. So it was after dark, on the eve of the battle, when Grandgent, The Bowl's messenger to Houston, finally got back, ten days after setting off on his mission.

It was as the Chief had surmised. Lamar had timed his move with care. In Nacogdoches, Grandgent was told that Houston had recently left for Tennessee. However, he would be stopping over for several days in the vicinity of Jackson, Mississippi. So Grandgent set out across Louisiana. In Mississippi he missed his man by two days. He would have gone after him to Tennessee except that he could never have gotten back in time to influence events here.

"So, Chief, are we going to fight?"

The old man nodded sorrowfully. "You have been heroic," he said. "If you had found him, you might have been the savior of your people."

It was the least he could say to a man who had run some five hundred and fifty miles. He would later that night tell the boy that he was by no means sure of what he said. It was to be wondered whether even Houston could have prevailed against his fellow Texans' hatred of Indians. Had he said, "If my red brothers go then I go," they might have said, even to him, "Go." The Chief had tried the only thing he could, had hoped it might work, but had felt all along that the odds were against it. His own rejected counsel to his people against their fighting had made him wonder how much influence any leader, even a Houston, had over his people in an unpopular cause. Looking back on it from his long perspective, it seemed to him, for whom, when he was young, war was a calling, a joy, a necessity, that opposing war was the most unpopular thing a leader could do—unless perhaps it was to defend a minority race. Houston was revered by the Texans, but his feeling for Indians was a blemish upon him and had to be overlooked. "Houston's pets," they were scornfully called, and this reason was given for it: his taste for their women. And for that this reason was given: with them he could do things he would never dare propose to any white woman—an incompatibility which for some explained the failure of his first marriage.

The Chief would not sleep that night. For years he had slept little anyway, but tonight he wanted to talk. He was pleased to have as his listener one who might outlast him by many years and give long life to his words. Between the man and the boy there was this mutual attraction: both longed to reach across the void of time, the one by grasping the distant future, the other the distant past. That night, while readying himself for battle, the old man talked as only a man could talk who knew that this night was his last.

By candlelight he laid out the tricornered hat, the red sash and the bright, shiny red silk vest given to him by that flamboyant dresser, his friend Kalunah-Houston. In these he was going to make a most conspicuous target. He tested the soundness of his saddle girth, his stirrup straps, his bridle reins. He drew the old charges from his brace of long-laid-aside but well-kept pistols, snapped the hammers, oiled them, loaded them afresh and returned them to their holsters. He filled his powder horn and his bullet pouch, cut patches. With his horny thumb he traced the edge of his bowie knife, found it dull, honed it on a stone, then he whetted the edge of the long sword given to him by Houston to commemorate their signing of the treaty between them. The one thing reminded him of the other, and, although he was unable to read the words, he took the paper from its box and looked at it for a long time, grunting in affirmation of its validity, and sighing as he put it away.

He had been called the Moses of his people. He knew the story of this Chief Moses. How, long ago and in another world, Moses had led his oppressed people out of a land called Egypt ruled by a tyrant named Pharaoh across a red sea and into a wilderness before reaching the land promised to them. Twelve tribes they had been, all living together in peace and brotherhood. The fitness of the comparison to himself drew from the old man a satisfied grunt. It was as though he were conferring upon his predecessor a pat of approval.

He had been the Moses of more tribes than those of the Israelites, red refugees from America come to join him in the Mexican province of Texas. With Houston's help, and under the altered circumstances, he had succeeded in doing what the great Tecumseh had tried earlier and failed to do. From Tennessee by way of Louisiana came the Coushattas. From Delaware, Pennsylvania and New Jersey, with a stop for a generation in Indiana before being driven farther west, came the Delawares. Driven from Wisconsin, the Kickapoos had settled in Illinois, only to be driven from there. The Quapaws came from Missouri. The Caddoes were native Texans, and the Tamocuttakes and the Utangous had been here for so long they had forgotten where they were from. The Alabamas had left behind them in their homeland nothing but their name. The Choctaws, the Yowanis and the Biloxis came from Mississippi. The Shawnees, Tecumseh's tribe, had sided with the

British in the last war, and had been driven by the victors from their home in Tennessee. The Cherokees had helped the Americans win that war, yet they were here now too.

But though he had brought his people across Red River and through the wilderness to this land of milk and honey, even here his Pharaoh, Mirabeau Buonaparte Lamar, had pursued him. Now, instead of fleeing further, he was going to stand and fight, and on the eve of the battle a vision had come to him. In the course of nature, it was time for him to die— long past time; it was not dying that he regretted so much— although he did regret it; what he regretted more was that he would have liked as his last act on earth to lead his people, all the tribes, back across Red River to their promised land. That was no land of milk and honey, as he knew from having lived there, but it was promised to them, and this was now taken from them. Their presence there might have tipped the balance toward peace among the feuding Cherokees.

That vision vouchsafed to him of his own end had freed his spirit from his body and enabled it to venture into the future which he would not live to share. He had thought that here he had escaped from that Egypt of his called America. Instead he had seen it advance steadily throughout his long life until even here it had caught up with him. The first waves of that white flood, felling the forests, breaking the land, exterminating the game in its path, had reached even here. He saw in his vision that the way he had lived his free and unfenced life could never again be done. There were too many people and not enough room. The whites littered like possums. There was fast approaching a time when even in a place as vast as Texas the Indian would occupy an impermissible amount of space. Through scribes, he had communicated with Chief John Ross, and he understood, not in all its details but in essence, something of the new age and of The People's efforts to adapt themselves to it. The lands of milk and honey were the ones the whole world wanted, but a man could learn to love any spot on earth as long as it was his, and his to leave to his. Give the Indians a land of briers and nettles, and then maybe they might be left alone at last.

His old—or rather, his young—friend Kalunah had revolutionized their world, yet the country he had created was not the refuge for his dispossessed red brothers that he had envisaged, rather it was the latest in a long series of lands for grab beckoning to the outcasts of Europe and to adventurers from the states. Those now coming here in wave upon wave did not share Houston's affection for Indians; they were the same ones, even the very generation, who had driven them from their homes in the east. Texas was now another America. Houston may have dreamed of an empire, a blend of white and red, like the roses of the Trace, but the Americans who had followed him down that very road were those whose grandfathers had thrown off one king and those Europeans escaping from theirs. They established a republic. They made Houston their President. They limited his term in office to two years. Upon the expiration of that term they replaced him with the man of his own creation—there that day on the battlefield of San Jacinto. He brought with him from his native Georgia his hatred of all Indians, Cherokees in particular.

The young braves chose to fight. Perhaps some even believed they would win. Others were doubtful about the outcome; it was just that after being driven so far there came a time to make a stand. Among them were not more than a handful who had ever fought, but they were determined to fight now, and he, a man of eighty-four, whose last engagement with an enemy had been before their grandfathers were born, was to lead them in battle.

Truth was, he had thought at the time when he was asked to remain neutral in the war against the Mexicans that Houston overvalued his neutrality. Kalunah was living in another of his youthful memories, that of the Cherokees as ferocious warriors. They had been, but they were no more. They had last

fought with Jackson, alongside young Houston—much good
had it done them!—but that was long ago; men were now
fathers who were infants then. He had accepted Houston's
gratitude and his gifts, and his copy of their treaty, and had
felt that he was cheating the man—certainly that the man was
cheating himself. His followers, the Indians, were brave
enough, no doubt, but they had become farmers, cattlemen,
sheepherders, family men—in all but color, white men; inexperienced as they were in war, their very valor would cost them
their lives. They had lived in peace. Now they were to do
battle with the soldiers who just three years ago, outnumbered
three to one, had slaughtered Santa Anna's Mexicans. And to
lead them they had chosen their oldest man—the Indian veneration of age, their belief that every additional year conferred
that much more wisdom. How untrue that was nobody knew
better than he. He had seen more than most men but most of
what he had seen had been more of the same. They had chosen
him because he was the wisest of them all. In his wisdom he
had counseled them against fighting, and they had chosen him
to lead them in the fight.

While the Chief prepared that night for tomorrow's battle, Dr. Ferguson, with Noquisi's help, prepared for it too. He
also had blades to sharpen: those of his scalpels. He filed the
points of his surgical needles, dampened catgut for sutures to
make it supple. With the saw he used for amputations he cut
lath into strips for splints. While he packed his saddlebags
with whiskey, laudanum, forceps, tourniquets, cauterizing iron
—supplies the packhorse had ported down from The Territory
—Noquisi rolled bandages. Father and son together would be
the campaign's medical corps.

Now it was time for the boy to go to bed.

"Agiduda?" said Noquisi.

"Sgilisi?" said the Chief.

"We are going to lose, aren't we?"

"It is in God's hands."

"Ai!" said Noquisi to himself. "We are going to lose."

Next morning the old Chief found that many of those who had been so hot for blood had made their private peace and stolen away in the night. He was not much surprised. Nothing could surprise him much anymore. He was wryly amused. They had elected him, unanimously, against his will, to lead them, and then had deserted him. Now instead of the fifteen to eighteen hundred he had reckoned on, he estimated that he could field maybe half that number. That would still make his force about equal to the enemy's, according to his scouts' reports, but being less well-armed, they needed superior numbers.

Dressed and painted for battle, with dyed feathers in their hair, slit-eyed, hawk-nosed, the warriors of the different tribes looked like an aviary of rare and colorful birds of prey in full plumage. The shaven heads of the Kickapoos, painted red, were like the bald domes of vultures; the contours of their jaws were striped white. The Caddoes, from whose ears hung pendants that stretched the lobes, and from some of whose noses hung silver plates that had to be lifted aside for every bite they ate, blackened their faces all over. The Delawares looked as though their chins were smeared with their enemies' blood. Down to their mouths the faces of the Yowanis were solid red, their jaws were vertically striped with white. The Shawnees painted round red spots on their cheeks and chins. Many had stripped down to breechclouts and had greased their bodies to make them slippery to hold in hand-to-hand combat. In the heat of this hottest day in even the old Chief's memory, all glistened with sweat.

They bore long guns, mostly old flintlock rifles but some

few more modern percussion-cap-and-ball rifles, and many carried pistols, with powder horns and beaded pouches, for bullets and wads, slung from shoulder straps. Some carried bows and, on their backs, quivers of arrows. Few were mounted, most were on foot. These forest-dwelling eastern Indians had no tradition as cavalrymen.

The Chief rode a sorrel horse with four white-stockinged feet and a white patch on its forehead that looked like war paint. The old man sat as erect as though he were cast in bronze. His varnished black hat shone, his red vest blazed, his long sword glinted. Tied to the pommel of his saddle was the tin box containing his treaty with the Texans. Perhaps he thought of it as his last will and testament, and hoped that when it was found on him and read it would gain his followers their rightful heritage, after all.

Out of the woods on the far side of the battlefield, a quarter of a mile away, the Texans issued like birds from their roosts. They, too, were mainly foot soldiers. In their lead rode their mounted officers. They dubbed themselves "Rangers" since their defeat of the Mexicans three years earlier, and while at San Jacinto they may have been an undisciplined assortment of erstwhile civilians, following that victory they had shaped themselves into a formidable fighting force, self-confident, proud, with a strong sense of esprit de corps.

Their officers were now within range to be identified. The old Chief was flattered by their ranks and reputations. They took him seriously. There was Vice-President Burnet, Secretary of War Johnson, Adjutant General McLeod, General Rusk, the fast-rising Colonel Burleson—all their big men except the biggest one of all, the one who had ridden to his eminence on horseback: Mirabeau Buonaparte Lamar. Although ridding the country of Indians was his top priority, and this was the occasion he had created to do so, he was noticeable by his absence today. No doubt he was occupied with weightier affairs of state. Or perhaps he had been taken with the inspiration for another of those poems of his which so tickled Houston by their unintended humor.

Noquisi, watching from the woods in which he and his father had set up their field hospital, and on the margin of which the Indian forces were ranged, was surprised to see how formal a thing a battle was, at least as the curtain rose. The opposing sides might have been dancers at a ball advancing to square off with their partners and waiting for the music to strike up. They approached, both waiting for the other to fire first. It was as though the two players of the game of checkers were disposing their pieces on the board and deliberating their opening moves.

The beginning and the end of the battle were all that Noquisi was able to relate to his grandson having seen, because from the first the Indian casualties were so heavy that he and his father were too busy attending them to look up from their work. The old Chief chose his moment when the Texans were fully exposed on the prairie to open fire, then rush them. Like a volley of arrows he loosed his warriors. The boy heard the crackle of gunfire and the screams of the wounded. He saw men reel and fall, saw others spin around and double over in pain, clutch at themselves, at their arms and their legs and their midriffs, saw the shock and stunned surprise of flesh struck and invaded by bullets. On the bare bodies of those of his side he saw blood burst forth like messy, misapplied war paint in inappropriate places. Then the ones who could do so began limping and staggering to the field hospital in the gulch below the line of fire just inside the woods.

After that the boy heard the gunfire in bursts and the silence while weapons were reloaded for another round. Mainly what he heard as he sponged wounds while they were probed for bullets and dirt, and passed the gut and the silk thread for suturing them and the saber cuts was, "Tourniquet. Scissors. Forceps." Finally the gunfire grew sporadic, like the fading thunder of a passing storm. The patient on whom they were working died from loss of blood. Father and son peered over the bank of their gulch.

Long after his warriors had fled for cover, the old Chief fought on. When he gave the command to retreat he was almost alone on the field, engaging the enemy single-handedly. Of the hundred and more dead and dying, no more than half a dozen were Texans. His own men lay like spent arrows that had missed their mark.

Now by drawing their fire while his few remaining men made good their retreat, he was commanding his enemies. He was playing with them, playing upon them, playing to them. Every bullet aimed at him missed one of his men. It was to his enemies that his life mattered; to him it meant nothing. His battle now was not with Texans; they were merely the henchmen of his mortal enemy. He would lose this contest; all men did; there was no indignity in it. He would have in his defeat the triumph of dictating the terms of his surrender.

Already bleeding from several wounds, his horse now received a fatal one. In its fall the Chief was thrown, thereby losing his hat and sword, but clutching the box containing the treaty with Houston. One of the few Indians remaining on the field dashed in and snatched it from him like the next runner in a relay race being passed the torch. The Chief rose, took a few steps, then fell, shot in the back. He lifted himself and sat facing his foes.

"This is a good day to die!" he cried.

Two Rangers came running. The first one to reach him, disregarding the other's shout not to shoot, put the muzzle of his pistol to the old man's forehead and fired. At point-blank range, the shot could hardly be heard.

Other Rangers on the run reached the spot while the body still sat upright. One of them toppled it face down with his foot, and with his bowie knife slit in half the red silk vest. Then while he skinned and sliced the corpse's back in strips the width of harness straps, another one, lifting the head by its hair, circumscribed the scalp with a cut and peeled it from the skull.

By the time Amos Smith I told his grandson about it, sixty-odd years later, the biggest battle ever fought on Texas soil was forgotten.

The Texans withdrew to the shade of the woods on the opposite side of the battlefield, taking with them on horseback their wounded and their few dead. Once they were out of gunshot range, a party of Indians, stripped to the skin to show that they concealed no weapons on them, ventured onto the field. They were not fired upon. The Fergusons, father and son, worked on the wounded they brought in, most of whom, injured beyond help, died on their hands. The dead were left where they lay on the field. To the survivors' grief must be added the shame of leaving them unburied. There were too many of them, and there was not time. The Texans' victory was so conclusive they had not bothered to follow up on it by pursuing their enemies in retreat, but in the morning they would return to confirm that what they had won was not just a battle but a war, and that the Indians, to the last and least one, were on the road, fleeing the country.

From village to village, from farm to farm, word of the outcome of the battle was relayed, and all day long the women and children and the old men streamed in to join the defeated warriors. All through the night they chanted their dirge of defeat. At daybreak they scattered in coveys like birds flushed from cover.

There was not safety but rather danger in numbers now. Alerted by hoofbeats, shouts, gunshots, the band would scatter, every man for himself, then later regroup like a covey of quail finding one another again, often by imitating the whistle of the quail. As water seeks its own level, so the Cherokees sought their trail of roses. Some strayed so far from it as to be long unable to get back, others had been too closely pursued to dare to move. Afraid to build fires for fear of giving away their whereabouts even when they had anything to cook, afraid for the same reason to shoot game, they went without eating for days.

Their route was all too familiar. They had blazed it, cleared it, decorated it, for twenty years had traveled it to visit relatives and friends in The Territory. They might have found their way by smell alone, and sometimes at night, along stretches near settlements to be avoided, they did.

They were entering Sulphur River Bottom now. The Rangers called off their pursuit when they were satisfied that they had achieved their objective. They had not done so quite as thoroughly as they supposed. Some of the fugitives dropped out of their bands to settle in those vast bottomlands. Mostly members of the lesser tribes those were, never numerous or now decimated in numbers, with few of their own kind to welcome them in The Territory. In time, after the old hostilities had faded from memory, and after intermarriage between them and the loggers, the trappers, the market hunters, the farmers on the edges of the woods had lightened skins and mongrelized features, they ventured out from their lairs as foxes do after the dogs have been called off. Even two generations later, Amos Smith would see faces on the streets of the county town of Clarksville that gave him a start of recognition, and sometimes his look was fleetingly returned, as two people of a banned belief or an outlawed taste might identify each other in passing and, although disposed to mutual self-disclosure, to alliance against the world that had branded and ostracized them, hesitate, out of conditioning and cowardice and fear of being mistaken about each other, and hasten on their separate ways. Inaccessible, counted in no census, in Amos Smith IV's time, in a county dry by local option, these people would be moonshiners long after the repeal of national prohibition, and as dangerous to approach in their dens as a nest of water moccasins.

By the time the Fergusons' band reached Red River, ten days after the battle of the Neches, it was down to a dozen men. Of that dozen, seven were already halfway across the river, out of rifle range, when the party of hunters appeared out of the woods. Still stripping themselves for the swim were the last five, including the Fergusons. Seeing the hunters, they broke and ran. What stopped Noquisi at the water's edge was the explosion of the shots. There he stood waiting to be shot. Offshore, where his father's body was sinking from sight, the red water swirled a darker red, like paint when it is stirred.

"All right, young'un. You're safe now," he heard a man's voice call.

It was his stopping at the water's edge at the last moment and not diving in along with the rest that saved him—saved Captain Donovan's maps in his pocket too. Had he done so, not even his size would have saved him. Indian children were fair game. It was his pale skin, his blue eyes, his freckled face and a frontier folklore of captive white children that told his story at a glance.

We reach our resting places, if we ever do, we restless Americans, by roundabout routes sometimes, and so, too, do some of us come by our lasting names.

"What's your name, boy?" asked the leader of the hunting party that had rescued him, powder smoke still drifting from the muzzles of their rifles.

"Amos, sir."

"Amos what?"

The boy shook his head and tears started from his eyes. To the hunter it was evident that his family name, that of those of his kin slaughtered, perhaps tortured to death before his eyes, was too painful to pronounce.

"You'll take mine, son," said the hunter. A boy already reared to working age was a prize on the frontier; besides, the hunter was a kindhearted man—he just, like everybody else, hated redskins—and would prove a good foster father to the boy.

As it was an old Indian custom for a man's killer to adopt his orphaned children and bring them up, to the boy this seemed fitting. Tired of running, tired of being Indian, and having nobody of his own in all the world now, he was grateful for a home, a settled life.

And that is how I, Amos IV, of the clan of Smiths, author of this book, got my name there on the bank of that red river which gives its name to my home county in the northeast corner of Texas where the trail of Cherokee roses begins and ends.